Holly Jolly Summer

Holly Jolly Summer

TIFFANY STEWART

FARRAR STRAUS GIROUX | NEW YORK

Farrar Straus Giroux Books for Young Readers
An imprint of Macmillan Publishing Group, LLC
175 Fifth Avenue, New York, NY 10010

Printed in the United States of America
Designed by Christina Dacanay
First edition, 2018

1 3 5 7 9 10 8 6 4 2

fiercereads.com

Library of Congress Cataloging-in-Publication Data

Names: Stewart, Tiffany, author.
Title: Holly jolly summer / Tiffany Stewart.
Description: First edition. | New York : Farrar Straus Giroux, 2018. |
Summary: In Christmas, Kentucky, fifteen-year-old Darby Peacher stumbles her way into a job at the town's run-down holiday-themed amusement park, Holly Jolly Land, but her summer quickly goes from merry to miserable when the boy of Christmas present is absent, the boy of Christmas past is her supervisor, and the town seems to be losing its cheer as it strives to become more commercial.
Identifiers: LCCN 2017042499 | ISBN 9780374305758 (hardcover)
Subjects: | CYAC: Dating (social customs)—Fiction. | Summer employment—Fiction. | City and town life—Fiction. | Christmas—Fiction.
Classification: LCC PZ7.1.S7463 Ho 2018 | DDC [Fic]—dc23
LC record available at https://lccn.loc.gov/2017042499

HOLLY FOR ERIC,

who has an evergreen soul,

steadfast and true.

JOLLY FOR SAMUEL,

who has overflowing joy in his heart.

SUMMER FOR ERICA,

who has all the sunshine in her smile.

ACKNOWLEDGMENTS

In memory of my grandmothers, Vista and Virginia, who kept Christmas in their hearts year-round.

Angie Chen asked me to write a book about a ramshackle amusement park, and *Holly Jolly Summer* was born. Thank you for asking me to turn your wonderful idea into a story. I am blessed beyond measure to work with Wesley Adams, who found the heart of the story and drew it out. Thank you for the love and effort you put into this project, and thanks to everyone at Farrar Straus Giroux.

A writer is nothing without her critique group, and I am proud to call the Marauders mine: Lyle Harvey, Kathy Keyes, and Vicky Morris, I love you all!

My parents have always encouraged me to chase my dreams. Mom told me daily I could do anything I set my mind to; Dad nodded in agreement. Thank you for being my first supporters and my biggest cheerleaders. I am so blessed to be your daughter. This book is because of you.

To Jesus, the author of my salvation, thank you for loving me. *To God be the glory, great things He has done, so loved He the world that He gave us His Son, who yielded His life our redemption to win, and opened the life-gate that all may go in. Praise the Lord! May the earth hear His voice.*

Holly Jolly Summer

One

IT WAS A BLUE-SKY KIND OF MORNING, WHEN the breeze begs you to come outside before the humidity sets in and makes everything sticky around the edges. I'd been lying out at Holiday Beach since nine, desperate to get a jump on my summer tan for once. I'd slathered SPF fifty on my nose and shoulders but went for number eight everywhere else. It was a long shot; if you looked up my name online, it would say, *Darby Peacher, fifteen, never been kissed. Synonym:* pasty. Still, I was determined to get some color on my legs so I didn't look like a sundress-bedecked Q-tip this season.

I'd been on my back for half an hour, so I flipped over to my front, checked my phone, and ran my hands through the stark white sand. I wondered if the sand down in Florida was really this fine. I'd never seen a real beach; being landlocked in Kentucky, we only had the man-made kind. It was a great imitation as far as

I could tell. We even had a few potted palm trees, blooming with silver and red glass ornaments, where the beach met the grass, to give the place a tropical feel.

Holiday Beach was really just a strip of sand at the edge of a zero-entry wading pool, next to the greenway and the town playground. Everyone hung out here all summer, but only little kids and their moms were out this early. The toddlers shrieked and poured water from buckets onto one another's heads while the moms sat grouped together in the shallowest part of the pool, splashing water onto their knees while they talked. I knew Fran and her son, Tony, and recognized a few other ladies from town, but no one else was around. Another benefit of sunbathing before noon. No one important would see my pasty legs.

Unless . . . No, he wouldn't be out yet. I checked my phone again. No texts.

An older man in a UK ball cap strolled by on the walking trail. He saw me and smiled. "Morning, Darby."

"Hi, Mr. Oates!" I called.

"Ready for tonight?"

"Yes, sir, we're ready."

"Looking forward to it." He passed with a wave.

I checked my phone again. Was it even on? Yep.

Maybe he was waiting for me to text him. But what had Penny warned me before she left for riding camp? *Never be the one to start the conversation; don't break the seal.*

"Easier said than done," I muttered.

I rested my cheeks on my hands and closed my eyes. The breeze was warmer than it had been at eight, but it still felt fantastic when it blew across my back.

"Hello, Darby!"

I looked up. A woman was running along the trail, checking her pulse.

"Hey, Dr. Hoey! Are you coming tonight?"

"Wouldn't miss it. Use sunscreen!" she called over her shoulder as she jogged past.

"Yes, ma'am, I am!"

I wiggled around in the sand to make more of an indention under my stomach.

Maybe he was still asleep. After all, it was almost one a.m. when I'd sent the last text, asking if he'd ever seen a blue moon. He had never responded, probably because he had fallen asleep. I stayed up until nearly two, waiting, just in case. I sensed he was *this* close to asking me out, and I didn't want to miss it when he did.

He, by the way, was Roy Stamos, this amazing guy who had moved to town over Christmas break. I'd been crazy for him since Penny's New Year's Eve party. I was hanging back from the others, waiting for my just-friends date to bring me something to drink. Roy broke away from the group of guys hanging around the food, walked up to me with a sprig of mistletoe, and pecked me on the cheek, right by the corner of my mouth.

"What was that for?" I whispered.

"For the mistletoe."

Before I could say or do anything else, he turned and walked over to Josie Randall and did the same thing. Then every other girl in the room. But I had been the first, and I knew that had to count for something.

Not that I thought for a second I had a chance with him. I mean, he was so . . . scrumptious. But then, a week ago, on the last day of school, I was cleaning out my locker when he'd passed, alone for a change. He'd done that hot-guy head nod—the kind where guys nod up instead of down? It's like the opposite of a nod. It's a don. Anyway, as he was passing, he donned at me and said, "Hey."

I played it extremely cool. I donned back and waved. I might have dropped a few books on my feet when I waved. And I may have tried to say, "Have a great summer," but instead said, "Hegratsum," because I was in so much pain from the torrent of textbooks.

I *may* have.

Maybe.

However ridiculous I'd felt at the time, my bumbling response must have been endearing because he had texted me three times since. And then, last night, he'd texted his first truly romantic message.

full moon 2night

It had taken me seven minutes to think of a good reply.

Yeah.

He responded immediately.

made me think of u

At first I thought it was a joke, something to do with how pale I am or how I'm as round faced as a *Peanuts* character. And, cruel fate being what it was, my dad had the unfortunate habit of calling me Moonpie. So I asked:

Really? Why?

so beautiful it glows 2

My affection for him skyrocketed.

I'd never had anyone look at the moon and think of me. I'd

never texted a guy for an hour about anything, let alone about how my beauty compared to the moon's. I had climbed out my window to sit on the roof and stare up at the moon between texts, wishing he were next to me. It had been magical. Then I'd asked my stupid question about a blue moon, and that was the end of my perfectly magical night of texting.

So now, here I was, the morning after the moon texting, and I still hadn't heard from him. Should I text him good morning? Or was that too . . . girlfriend-y?

Hey.

There. That seemed casual. Right?

I pushed Send before I could change my mind again.

The thing was, I didn't have much experience with guys before this. And by not much experience I mean, well, none. Penny's New Year's Eve party was the only time I'd seen any action, and that was just a peck on the cheek. A smoking-hot peck on the cheek, but still, I knew it didn't count as a real kiss. Come to think of it, that was also the night of my one and only official date, although, like I said, it was a just-friends date. I'd known Calvin forever. He had acne and snorted when he laughed, which I'd thought was kind of cute right up until he ditched me in the middle of our date to go to his friend's house and play video games. We hadn't spoken since.

So, yeah, you could say I had zero experience with guys.

"Hey, it's Darby! Hey, girl!"

Maya Johnson and Laeticia Marshall, two seniors I knew from church, were staking out a square of sand a few yards away. They had a cooler and folding beach chairs and everything. They were always at the beach in the summer. Like me, they didn't go off to summer camp. But unlike me, they didn't have much to do during the season.

"Isn't it beautiful today?" Maya asked as she expertly popped open her chair.

"Gorge. Perfect for the festival." I brushed my bangs out of my eyes and squinted up at the sun. "Y'all are coming, right?"

"For sure," Laeticia said. "Are you in it again?"

I nodded. "Unveiling's at seven."

"We'll be there."

There was an awkward moment where no one really knew how to end the conversation. We weren't good enough friends for them to ask me to join them or for them to join me. Maya kind of smiled and then angled her chair slightly away from me. When she sat down, I turned my head the other way.

I already missed Penny.

My phone dinged. Roy?

Dad.

TCL @ 11. Dont b late!

Bananas! I'd almost forgotten the monthly town council luncheon. It was quarter 'til eleven now. I jumped up and threw my red gingham button-up over my green tankini. My white shorts needed a good beating to get the sand off. I shimmied into them and stepped into my flip-flops. Had I brought mascara with me?

I searched my bag for some as I hurried through the parking lot, glad when I reached the shade of the sycamores on Garland Street because it was getting muggy and I didn't want to sweat through my clothes. I half walked, half ran toward the business end of town on the square.

Downtown Christmas was a sight to behold in the summertime,

decked out in all its glory. Fake snow was piled under store windows like it had drifted there on a polar wind; green plastic wreaths with giant red bows festooned every light post; and storefronts displayed their best holiday wares. Sure, we were hokey. But where else in the world could you go to celebrate the best holiday year-round? Tourists came to town for the seasonal attractions like our life-sized Snow Globe and the biggest Christmas festival in Kentucky that isn't held in December, and to see the town decorated like a full-scale ceramic holiday village.

It really was amazing. This year, we'd even made *Travel America*'s list of "Top Ten Best Small Towns South of the Mason-Dixon Line." I was extremely proud, not just of Christmas, but of my dad. As the mayor, it was an honor for him, too.

I hurried up Main Street, tying my hair into a neat ponytail as I dodged tourists. I waved to Mr. Johnson as I passed his toy store. He kept sweeping but made a duck face at me. I laughed; he'd been making faces at me since I was four years old. I hurried past the Vista Brody Christmas Museum, an old Victorian mansion on the square with a bright-red banner stretched across its little lawn, teasing the antique ornament collection inside. I stopped to check my reflection in a storefront window. I swiped some lip gloss across my lips and brushed my bangs to the side. Mrs. Jenkins called through the open door, "You look fine. Hurry, now! The luncheon starts in five minutes!"

Mr. Jenkins was on the town council, but he didn't make a move without talking to Mrs. Jenkins first. She probably already knew what Dad's speech was about and probably even who would eat what. Mrs. Jenkins knew everything about everything.

I headed for the diner on the corner of the square. The bells on the door jingled as I went inside, and the icy air hit me full in the face. Thank you, Lord, for air-conditioning. I stood in the blast and let the breeze frost the beads of sweat on the back of my neck while I looked around for the council and Dad. It being a Saturday, the booths were crammed with families eating brunch. Many of them were visitors who were in town for tonight's unveiling, but I recognized lots of faces. Being First Daughter in a town as small as Christmas meant I could name most of its citizens. There were the Hollisters, Mr. Steinman and his grandkids, Josie Randall from homeroom, and a few other familiar faces.

Mr. Grant, the owner of the Holiday Diner, was behind the counter, refilling coffee. He had a rim of silver hair that matched his walrus mustache. He caught my eye and nodded toward the doorway in the back corner, which led to the private party room. I smiled in thanks and headed that way. Mr. Grant was on the council, but he'd only be popping in and out while he served guests. He was Dad's number-one supporter, though, and would be fine with whatever decisions Dad made.

Dad smiled as I came in. "I'm sure you all know my daughter?"

Everyone laughed. Of course they knew me. I'd been First Daughter since I was four years old. Mrs. Mason from the post office had taught me to write letters; Mr. Gomez used to let me play in the bank lobby while Dad was in meetings; John Grant made my breakfast every weekend at the diner and at least half my dinners; Mr. Jenkins snuck me peppermints when he passed the offering plate at church; and Mrs. Goodwin took me back-to-school shopping in Louisville every fall. They weren't just people on the town council. They were my family.

Mrs. Goodwin stood up to give me a warm hug. "You smell like summer. Baby oil?"

"Just some sunscreen."

She looked me over as we sat down, and nodded firmly. "You look lovely."

"Thank you."

Mrs. Goodwin was my favorite, and not just because she took me shopping. Her curly black hair had streaks of gray that she refused to dye. Her dark-brown hands were super soft, and she never asked why when I stopped by just because. Mr. Goodwin had been gone since before I was born, but she talked about him like he was still nearby. And she was the smartest person I knew. She could talk to anyone about anything, and she never ever made me feel stupid for asking questions. Plus, she owned Blessings Bakery, so she always smelled like sugar and vanilla. Speaking of:

"I made you cookies." She opened the cranberry-colored box, and the smell of gingerbread wafted across the restaurant. "There's one for everyone."

She'd personalized them. I found mine right away. It was decorated with chocolate hair, blue candy eyes, a red piped dress, and green flip-flops on its round little feet.

"Well?" she asked.

I bit the arm off. The gingerbread was just the right amount of sweet and spicy, and it melted into my taste buds as I nibbled away. "So yummy."

"Oh, good," she said with relief. "I'm sampling them tonight for tourists. Thinking of starting a Christmas cookie mail-order business through our website."

"Really?" I said. "That's great!"

"Trying to capitalize on our newfound fame," she said with a smile. "Gotta strike while the iron's hot." She offered the box around the table. "Eat up."

Everyone else took theirs, and I noticed Dad's cookie had the same blue candy eyes as mine but a swirl of yellow hair. It looked just like him, down to the rolled-up shirtsleeves. The way he darted around, hair mussed from working so hard, he looked younger than fifty-five.

Mr. Grant came over to take our order—he brought me an Ale-8 with a swizzle straw in the neck of the bottle, just like he had at every town council luncheon since I was a kid—and then Dad started in on the business stuff. I opened the calendar app on my phone and checked the minutes of last week's meeting. There wasn't much new to discuss this week except the festival tonight. I knew we'd get to that quickly. Before I started taking notes, I texted Dad a reminder that he had a meeting in two hours with the board of tourism and an afternoon on the square shaking hands.

Mr. Gomez was just warming to the subject of the budget when my phone dinged.

I dropped it on the ground, reached down to grab it, and hit my head on the table as I righted myself, rattling all the flatware.

"Darby, are you all right?" Mrs. Mason asked.

"Fine, thank you. Sorry."

My phone dinged again. I quickly silenced it so Mr. Gomez could go on with his report.

hey . . . what r you up 2?

It was Roy! I may have squealed.

Dad cleared his throat.

"Sorry," I said again, remembering where I was. I smiled at everyone and hid my phone under the table.

As soon as Dad returned to his conversation, I texted back.

Eating lunch at the diner. What about you?

The response bubbles came up right away. He was answering!

on my way 2 beach

Seriously? I was *just* there, and now he's on his way? My heart sank. I could've seen him.

He sent another text.

what r you doing l8r?

Holy kiwis! Was it happening? Was *Roy Stamos* asking me out?

What should I say? I didn't have any plans besides the festival with Dad, but I didn't want to sound like a friendless dork. But if I said I *did* have plans, then he would think I was busy and wouldn't ask me out. Conundrum overload.

Probably just checking out the festival or something. What about you?

That was good. Not too specific, not too boring. I hit Send, held my breath, and pretended to be enthralled with whatever words were coming out of Dad's mouth—they could have been Swahili for all the attention I was actually paying.

If Roy *was* asking me out, what would we do? Hang out at Holiday Beach? I'd never gotten invited to hang out there after hours before, but I'd always wanted to. Maybe he'd ask me to go to the movies. I shivered just thinking of us sitting in a dark movie theater. Maybe we'd check out the festival together. That would be fun. We could look at window displays, get snow cones . . .

want 2 meet up or something?

Yes! He was asking me out! What should I text back? Obviously I'd accept, but should I just say *yes*, or was that too eager? He already knew I had a crush on him—he knew every girl had a crush on him. Should I say *maybe*? Should I wait awhile to answer?

Dad elbowed me, and I looked up.

Everyone was staring at me. "Yes?"

Dad raised his eyebrows. "I said, you need to be at the ceremony by seven."

"What ceremony?"

Dad looked at me like I'd grown antlers.

"Oh." I shook my head slightly. Roy's words were swimming in front of my eyes, but I needed to focus. "Right. Yes, of course. What time?"

Dad felt the back of my head where I'd banged it on the table. "Are you all right?"

"I'm fine. It should be a wonderful night." I smiled but inwardly groaned.

Don't get me wrong—I loved the festival, and I wanted to help Dad in any way I could; we were a team. But Roy had just asked me out, and I couldn't be in two places at once! I wanted to make up some excuse to get out of it, but I knew I couldn't. Christmas came first.

But what would I tell Roy?

The luncheon broke up as soon as everyone finished eating. Mr. Gomez was needed at the bank, Mrs. Goodwin had gingerbread to bake for the ceremony, and Mr. Jenkins had to get back to Mrs. Jenkins to fill her in on everything they'd decided.

John Grant came over and refilled our drinks. Dad and I

usually hung around for a little bit on weekends. He didn't have anything scheduled until the tourism board meeting.

"What's going on?" he asked me. "Are you sure your head is okay?"

"I'm fine," I assured him. "I just . . . um . . ."

I'd never had to ask Dad if I could go on a date before. I'd never needed to. But now, well, if I disappeared after the ceremony tonight without an explanation, he'd probably have Sheriff Lewis searching for me.

"I was wondering if I could sneak away from the ceremony a little early tonight?"

"What for?"

I set my fork down and tried to think how to answer that. Dad and I were close, but we'd only ever had hypothetical conversations about boys. "I kind of . . . got asked to hang out."

"By whom?"

"A boy."

Dad choked on his sweet tea. "You mean a date?"

"Kind of?"

"Who is it?"

"You don't know him."

"Does he live in town?"

"Yes, but—"

"Then I know him."

"Exactly!" I said, using this to my advantage. "You know everyone in town. Are there any psychopaths running around?"

Dad frowned. "No."

"Then he's okay. Just . . . please don't make me say. Yet. It's only one date."

"Where will this date take place?"

I shrugged. "He didn't really say. Probably we'll, like, hang out."

"Forget it."

"Why?"

"Because I'm your father and I don't like the way you say *hang out.* What does that mean? Is it some sort of girl code for 'necking'?"

"Seriously? *Necking.* What are you, like, old?"

"Decrepit." He pushed his plate away and looked at me with a tragic expression. "It's happening, isn't it?"

"What?"

"You're becoming a teenager."

"I've been a teenager for years."

"Not one who dates."

"It's just one date."

He folded his hands on the table and considered me. Suddenly, he was back in mayor mode. "We need to discuss a few ground rules. And it's probably best if we review the importance of—"

"We've covered the important stuff. Like, ad nauseam."

He shook his head. "Seriously? 'Like, ad nauseam.' What are you, a teenager?"

"Touché."

We studied each other for a moment, trying to guess the other's next move. His hair flopped over his forehead, and his eyes were bright with anticipation of the coming festival. He looked like a little boy waiting for Santa Claus.

"Okay, how about this?" I said finally. "You let me go out after the ceremony, and I'll be on laundry duty all month."

Dad smiled wryly. Laundry duty was always my offer when I really, really wanted something. He wiped his hands on his napkin, mulling it over. "Fine. But you have to text me where you are, you are not allowed to be at his house if his parents aren't home, and you can't get in a car with him until I've met him, whoever he is. And you have to be home by ten."

"Eleven."

"Ten thirty."

"Deal," I said before he could take it away. "Thank you."

He rose and kissed the side of my head. "I have to go if I'm going to make it to my meeting. See you tonight, Moonpie."

"I'm getting a little old for that one, aren't I?" I asked as he walked off.

"Never," he called back.

I smiled.

As soon as he was gone, I texted Roy back. This was shaping up to be the best day of my life.

Two

THE SNOW GLOBE IS THE TOWN'S MOST PROFIT-able attraction. The clear plastic bubble, inflated to roughly the size of a small hot air balloon, sat perched atop a stair-stepped wooden platform that looked exactly like the base of a snow globe. The Globe was custom-made by Night Sky Tents, a camping company out of Phoenix that specialized in bubble tents. Our Globe, with its thirty-foot diameter and nearly perfectly spherical shape, was the largest they'd ever designed. Inside, a snow machine circulated blizzard-force "snow."

Currently, the Snow Globe was hidden from curious onlookers behind a giant curtain. People had started lining up hours ago to get their chance to go inside the Globe after the unveiling and have their picture taken while the snow whirled around them. And for a price, they could order their very own hand-carved, miniature, collectible Christmas Snow Globe, complete with a miniature version of themselves inside. Only the first three hundred orders are guaranteed to be ready by December 25, so people from all over the place flock to Christmas when the Snow Globe is unveiled for the season.

Every year, a different business is selected by the council to sponsor the construction of the set inside the Globe. Last year, Mr. Johnson's toy store had the honor, and the Globe was piled with oversized packages and toys; tourists could sit astride the gigantic rocking horse or cuddle up with the six-foot teddy bear for their commemorative photographs and globes. It was beautiful, but my favorite Snow Globe was from the year I was eight. Christmas Creamery had turned the Globe into a sort of ice-cream land: the trees were made of waffle cones, and rock candy icicles hung from their branches; the "stream" looked like melted snow cream; and the mountains in the distance were chunks of chocolate. I still dream about that one.

This year, Nick Patterson's Holly Jolly Land amusement park had the honor of decorating the Globe. Letting Nick Patterson have his way with the Snow Globe was a risk; old Mr. Patterson had become something of a hermit after the death of his wife a year or so ago, and when he did show his face in town, it was twisted into a snarl. It was like he'd had a personality lobotomy or something. When I was a kid, he was always the life of the party, there during every town festival handing out balloons with Holly Jolly Land's logo stamped on them or giving out free day passes to the park, whistling. But now, he startled most people. He was kind of . . . off.

But like Dad had told the town council when they'd protested, Holly Jolly Land had been chosen fair and square, and that was that. If Nick Patterson wanted to sponsor the Snow Globe, he could. And, surprising as it was to all of us, Mr. Patterson had sent the sponsorship agreement back to the courthouse checked "yes" and signed with a flourish.

At seven, it was still eighty degrees outside, and I was sweating buckets as I pushed through the crowds on Main Street. The sidewalks and lawn in front of the Snow Globe were packed with people; the entire county seemed to have shown up for the unveiling, all of them pressing forward, hoping to get on the TV news. Those families waiting in the picture line had brought lawn chairs and picnic dinners and even their pets. Kids were running around and begging their parents for ice-cream money while they waited. A camera crew had come from Bowling Green and was set up next to Mrs. Marshall, the Globe photographer, on the raised platform to the right of the courthouse, where they would have a direct view of the unveiling. The cameraman panned the crowd, and people waved and cheered as he swooped over them.

I couldn't help it; I waved, too. Christmas was finally getting the attention it deserved. I'd always known it was the best place on earth, and now the country knew it, too. Okay, technically we were in the top ten southern towns, and the local news would only broadcast in the surrounding counties, not across the country, but it was something. My heart swelled with pride as I looked around the square.

Our downtown was magnificent tonight. The speakers hidden among the bushes and under gutters along the street played jazzy carols. After Dad's speech and the unveiling, the Christmas Community Choir would give a concert on the church steps as the people in line finally got to take their turns inside the Snow Globe. The twinkly lights that crisscrossed over the square blinked to life as the sun began its slow descent behind the courthouse clock tower, adding to the anticipation of the night. It was nearly time.

I must have said "excuse me" a million times until, finally, I reached the podium on the courthouse steps. Dad was already there, in the red polo shirt and hunter-green pants I'd told him he should wear instead of his usual jeans. I'd dressed up a little bit, too. I was wearing a mint-green sundress (not technically Christmas green, but I'd holidayed it up with red beads, red kitten heels, and my red-and-green-checked headband). I'd trimmed my bangs so they made a perfect line above my brows, and I'd curled my hair. I figured if Roy asked why I was all dressed up, I could blame it on the Snow Globe unveiling. That way, I looked nice but I had a cover so he wouldn't think I was trying too hard.

When I'd told Roy I would be free around eight, he'd responded right away:

cool just text me

And then he'd sent a wink emoji.

I may have sent three smiley-face emojis back. And a wink. I *may* have. Maybe.

"I'm here," I panted, fanning my underarms. The last thing I needed was sweat rings. I rushed up to Dad and the tall woman in a gray pantsuit he was talking to. "Couldn't get through the crowd, sorry."

I didn't recognize the woman. I stopped fanning my underarms. "Hello."

She nodded curtly and continued to address my dad. "As I was saying, Mayor, I'm from Frankfort, and I'm here on behalf of the—"

"I'll be happy to listen to what you have to say," Dad said.

"Some other time. Stop by the courthouse next week, and we'll talk. Right now, I have a Snow Globe to introduce!" Dad gestured to the waiting crowd. "The tourists are here to see Holly Jolly Land's beautiful scene. If you'll excuse me."

Dad took my elbow, and we broke away from the stranger, who looked put out.

"Perfect timing," he whispered to me, relieved.

"Who is she?"

"Not sure," Dad said. "Wants to talk about outside investment in Christmas while we're making a splash."

"Investment?"

"I don't know the details yet. For now, let's give the people a show, huh?" Dad said.

The red curtains stretched across the wire that spanned from the corner of the courthouse to the corner of the theater across the street, blocking the Snow Globe from the crowd on the square. We hung banners on the wire during the rest of the year. Black curtains backed the Globe in the courthouse parking lot beyond, and Dad barred the lot until the unveiling to keep people from getting close and peeking in that way. I followed Dad through the gap in the red curtains and got my first glimpse of the new Snow Globe scene.

Pandemonium.

A dozen or more people were hurrying around inside the bubble, putting finishing touches on the scene. Some had dripping paintbrushes, some had tools, and others had long cables over their shoulders. All of them looked frazzled.

Nick Patterson, the owner of Holly Jolly Land, was sitting on a lawn chair in front of the Globe, his left leg sticking out straight so that people had to step over it. His severe buzz cut coupled with his tangled mess of silver beard made him look like a schnauzer. I tried not to stare at the purple scar on the knobby knee sticking out from his camouflage shorts. His army boots were spit shined, and his striped socks were every color of the rainbow.

He barked orders into a sparkly purple walkie-talkie.

"Riya, no more glitter! The thing looks like a disco ball as it is! Think camouflage! Friendly fire is heaviest during wartime."

Riya Shah was a grade ahead of me at school, and a total diva. I was surprised she was working on the Globe at all. She turned to glare at us, her pink-tipped black hair whipping around, and stepped away from the Holly Jolly Land sign at the base of the platform.

"Charlie, you're running late! In 'Nam, late was dead! Are you dead?"

"Sir, no, sir!" called a voice from around the back of the Globe. Someone laughed.

"Uh, Mr. Patterson?" Dad said, approaching the old man. "How's it coming?"

"Eh?" Nick Patterson stared at Dad for several seconds before he recognized him. "Oh, hello, Mayor. Mayor's daughter," he said to me. "Coming along just fine. We'll be done in five minutes."

"Five minutes," Dad said, looking up at the Globe.

It was the worst Snow Globe I'd ever seen. The Holly Jolly Land sign on the base of the Globe was red-and-white striped, with what I think were supposed to be sprigs of holly at each end. They looked more like hemp leaves. Riya with the pink-tipped hair had sprinkled so much glitter on it all, it was hard to make anything out.

Inside, the set was built to look like an amusement park. The

Ferris wheel in the middle was easily the best part. At least it didn't look like it was about to fall over. But the roller coaster tracks winding through the scene were swaying slightly. Nothing was to scale, either. The carousel on the right was painted on plywood, and it looked good, but it was huge compared to the shrub-sized trees.

Front and center of the scene stood a huge replica of the North Pole, the swing ride from Holly Jolly Land. It was red-and-white striped, too, like a barbershop pole. The two swings that hung from it looked like they might have been from the actual ride at the park. It took up almost all the space in the Globe.

"It looks . . ." Dad's face was a strange mix of white and green.

"Sure something, ain't it?" Nick Patterson said. He lumbered to his feet and folded the lawn chair. "You can really sit in those swings."

"That's . . . good."

"Great for picture posing."

Dad cleared his throat. "I'm not sure it's quite sturdy enough."

"Too soft, the whole lot of you!" Nick barked. "It'll be fine. Just tell people not to sit too hard."

"Well—"

"Better get inside, honey," Nick said to me. "It's nineteen hundred hours. I'll have my man stand guard at the gate, make sure no one sneaks behind our lines. Johnson!" he shouted into his walkie-talkie, hobbling away. "Get your squadron out of there! It's showtime!"

Dad glanced at his watch. "He's right. Darby . . ." Dad watched Nick shoo people away from the Globe. "Go inside, and don't touch anything."

"Sir, yes, sir," I said, saluting.

Dad didn't laugh. "No, really. This thing looks like it's about to collapse. If we are lucky enough to avoid any incidents tonight, we'll have to hire someone tomorrow to go over it carefully and make sure it's structurally sound."

Oh, holy mother of kiwis.

"You get in there and be ready to smile and wave when the curtain opens."

"I know the drill. First Daughter, remember?" I gazed up at the huge Snow Globe. "It's not as bad as the year Big O's sponsored. Remember that?"

Dad raised an eyebrow. "Oh, I don't know. I thought the stack of tires was pretty festive."

"And the cases of oil. Don't forget those," I reminded him.

He smiled. "How old were you that year?"

"Five."

"Ten years." He sighed and shook his head. "That one wasn't on TV."

"It'll be okay," I said. "I'll wave so big no one will notice all of . . . this. What time does your speech start?"

Dad checked his watch. "Soon. They'll pull the curtain at the very end, say, seven thirty-five."

I checked my phone. That was more than half an hour. This was going to be a very long wait. But anticipation was half the fun, right? It was why we strung red curtains in front of the Snow Globe every year. The anticipation, the building excitement. And then—

Just the thought of *Roy Stamos* awaiting my text had me fanning my underarms again.

Dad gave me a fatherly look. "Have a good time tonight, and remember to be home by ten."

"You said ten thirty!"

"I did?"

Now I knew he was teasing. "See you at ten thirty."

He pecked the side of my head and took off.

Some kids were still gathering up their tools and leaving. I made my way around to the side of the Globe, stayed back, and waited. Riya and a red-haired girl named Glenda were laughing so hard they were crying as they walked by. Two guys ran past and threw glitter on them; they cussed and chased them with paintbrushes. A lanky guy with long hair loped past with a blond girl—I'd seen them around town before, but I didn't know them. They must've gone to the county high school.

They were so different from me. None of them were in red or green—the lanky guy wasn't even wearing shoes—but they all looked . . . festive, like they were at a party instead of working. They swirled past me to a rhythm that was entirely their own, covered in paint and sweat and glitter. Even though the Snow Globe was a disaster, one guy looked up at it with a proud smile before catching up to the rest of them.

When I couldn't hear them anymore, I drew closer to the Globe. It sat on stacked wooden platforms on top of a trailer bed the Christmas Ladies Auxiliary had covered with ruffled green skirts. As I climbed the rollaway steps to the trailer I ran smack dab into Calvin Sherman.

"Oh," I said.

Of all the people to run into tonight, it had to be Calvin. As in Calvin Sherman, my just-friends-date ghost of Christmas past, the guy who had taken me to Penny's New Year's Eve party. As in Calvin Sherman, who ditched me at the party without even telling me he was leaving early. As in Calvin Sherman, who had done nothing but glower at me from behind his glasses ever since, like I was the one who had been totally rude and inconsiderate that night for no reason.

That Calvin Sherman. Although he seemed taller than ever, and broader across the shoulders. His thick braids fell down his back, and there wasn't a trace of acne on his dark skin. He still had the same glasses and quizzical expression, like he was doing calculus in his head even though I knew he had multiple calculator apps on his phone. He held a bunch of fabric in one hand and a hammer in the other. He helped build the Snow Globe? Then he must work at Holly Jolly Land. How did I not know this about him? Somehow, I couldn't imagine buttoned-up Calvin with the group of people who had just left. He didn't fit.

As soon as he realized it was me, he made a face that was the square root of annoyed plus nowhere to run.

"Excuse me," I said, trying to go around him.

"You can't go in there yet, Darby." His voice was an octave lower than the last time he'd talked to me.

"Dad says I have to get in position."

"Right. Well, in that case"—he thrust the fabric at me—"Nick said to put this on."

I held it up. It was a khaki-colored Holly Jolly Land T-shirt that said HAVE A HOLLY JOLLY SUMMER! in camo-green letters.

"I can't wear this! It doesn't match my dress."

He shrugged.

I hadn't been this close to him in months. It wasn't that I hadn't seen him every day since our just-friends date, but I'd gone out of my way to avoid him in the halls at school since New Year's, which wasn't easy in a school as small as mine. I guess all the effort to avoid him had been a waste of time since here I was, a foot from him, and he still managed to stare over my head and completely ignore me. I stood on my toes and tried to make eye contact.

Nope. Infuriating. "Oh, fine." I glared at him as I pulled the T-shirt over my head and shoved my arms into the holes. "Happy?"

He glanced down at me but quickly looked away. "Please don't touch anything in there."

"Nice to see you, too," I muttered.

I went around to the back of the Globe. From this angle, it looked more like an igloo; because the interior of the Globe had to be constantly pressurized by an air pump, there was a tiny antechamber sticking out of the back. I went through the first door, and when it swung closed behind me, I pushed through the entrance to the Globe.

Inside, all the workers had abandoned ship. The smell of paint was extra strong, blown around by the air pump. Mr. Patterson really should have painted the set before he'd moved it inside; people would get headaches if they were in here too long. The snow was sticking to everything that was wet, which was pretty much everything in sight. The set didn't look *that* bad now that it was half-covered in snow. And the Ferris wheel really spun, which was kind of cool. It was also very wobbly.

There was nowhere safe to sit, and there was nothing to do. I was wearing the ugliest shirt in the history of ugly shirts, for the whole town and the TV cameras to see. And it really did clash horribly with my dress.

I checked the time. I still had twenty-five minutes to wait. I texted Roy.

You'll never guess where I am!

He texted right back.

where?

In the Snow Globe!!!

why?

For the unveiling.

want some company?

No, you can't come in—

Wait a minute. Why couldn't he?

Because I was the only person allowed inside the Snow Globe before the unveiling, that was why. In all the years I'd done this, I'd never let anyone in early. It felt wrong, somehow, even though I'd had people beg me to let them take a peek. It wasn't fair to the hundreds—or thousands, tonight—who had waited for the first look.

Roy wasn't trying to see the Globe, though. He wanted to see me. Me! It was different. Besides, Dad wouldn't reveal the Globe for at least twenty minutes. And we definitely wouldn't be seen back here behind the curtain. We could hang out, and he'd be out before the unveiling.

Delete, delete, delete.

OK cool. Come through the side curtain.

see u in a few

I raced back through the antechamber and ran out of the Globe onto the platform. I went to the curtain to wait for Roy.

He must have been close by. I didn't even have time to freak out or check my hair in my phone before he ducked through. The red velvet brushed across his black hair and tousled it.

I tried to shove down the moan rising in my throat. He had dimples deeper than Mammoth Cave, dark eyes, and somewhere between one and twelve tattoos under his oxford shirt and salmon-colored shorts, depending on who you believed. He was sixteen and about to be a junior, but in a lot of ways he seemed more than a year older than me. Maybe it was because he was from Lexington and I hadn't known him all his life, or maybe because he acted so mature; the guys in my grade would never flat-out smile at a girl like that.

He must have felt my gaze, because he looked my way. Our eyes met, and he smiled a leaning kind of smile that only climbed up one side of his face. The earth tilted a little more on its axis so that the entire world leaned with that smile.

Moan.

I sort of waved—no books in my hand to drop on my feet this time, thank you very much—and went up to him.

"Hey, Darby," he said. He stretched the *a* in my name out in a flirty kind of way.

"Hey, Roy." I tried to stretch the *o* in his name out, but it stuck to the roof of my mouth like peanut butter.

His smile climbed up both sides of his face this time, a full-on, all-teeth smile. And then he leaned forward a little so that his mouthful of perfect white teeth was closer to my ear and said, "You look beautiful."

"I do?" I said. I pulled on the front of my T-shirt and looked down at it. Of all the things to be wearing. At least later, on our actual date, he'd see my dress. I crossed my arms over the camouflaged words and peeked up at him from under my bangs.

His brown eyes locked onto mine.

Holy avocado, this was the definition of smoldering.

"You do."

I had to look away. I wanted to keep my face passive, but it wasn't easy when I also really, really wanted to squeal. "Thank you."

Roy nudged my shoulder with his. "You okay?"

He had green specks in his eyes. I'd never noticed that before. "I'm great. But you can't stay long."

"Why? Got another date?"

Another date? He thought this was a date? He thought this was a date!

I tried not to smile so big. "No, it's just, um, you know, the unveiling . . . I'm in it every year?"

"In the Snow Globe thing? Why?"

Sometimes I forgot that he wasn't from Christmas. He didn't know the traditions. "I've done it since I was four. I stand inside and wave when the curtain opens. That way, people can see what it looks like with someone inside."

"Oh. What a drag."

"It's fun. Really." I laughed at his expression until I realized I sounded like a drowning cat. "I love it. Being in there, waiting for the curtains to part, it's like . . . I don't know. It's cool."

"Cool." He looked up at the Snow Globe. From the side, you couldn't really see the set. "Why don't you give me the private tour?"

My insides melted as we looked deep into each other's eyes.

"Oh. Okay. Um, it's . . . right this way," I said, gesturing at the huge plastic bubble. What was I, a flight attendant? He knew where it was! It was right in front of us!

Get a grip, Darby!

I led him around to the front so he could get a head-on view of the scene, then stood back to watch him take it in.

He laughed. "This is terrible."

That laugh was so melodic it made my insides dance around. "Yeah."

"Hey!" Calvin Sherman had popped through the curtain and now marched up to us.

Ugh. This guy.

"What?" I snapped.

"You're supposed to be inside the Globe." He donned his chin at Roy. "He's not supposed to be back here at all."

"Yeah? Says who?" Roy asked casually, but there was an undercurrent of a challenge.

"Says me." Calvin stood up straighter.

"Who are you?" Roy asked.

This is why the just-friends date of Christmas past should never meet the crush of Christmas present.

Calvin gave him an "Oh, I think you know me" look and said, "You don't work at the park, and you're not in the Globe, so you—"

"I'll only be a sec," Roy said.

He had his hands shoved in his jeans pockets, but he leaned closer to me and gave Calvin that look, the one guys give each other that says, *Don't mess this up for me, man. I'm working on something here.* I don't know why guys think girls don't know what that look means. Even I, the inexperienced First Daughter of Christmas, knew.

Still, my heart did a flip-flop. It was the look that did it. I was the girl he was working on, and he was readily admitting it to another guy! Okay, okay, it was only Calvin Sherman, but still. It had to mean something, right?

Calvin seemed as surprised as me by this information. He looked from me to Roy and back again. He shook his head at me, like I wasn't worth the effort.

"Don't you have a president to guard or something?" I said.

Roy laughed. I made *Roy Stamos* laugh!

Calvin's eyebrows shot up. He almost looked hurt, and I felt guilty until he narrowed his eyes at me and then at Roy and said, "Don't know why you're wasting your time."

My mouth fell open, but he stalked off before I could say anything. How dare he!

"What a nerd," Roy said.

I turned to him. He had moved closer to me, and I could see that he had one eyebrow that was longer than the other. "I'm sorry about that."

"Dude's a jerk," Roy said, but he was smiling. "A president to guard?"

I shrugged. "He moves all stiff, like a Secret Service agent. And he never smiles."

Roy snorted. "Nice."

"We probably should be quick, though," I told him. "The curtains will open soon."

"No problem."

He was so laid back! I wanted to tell him that I could be laid back, too, but that probably wasn't a very laid-back thing to say, so I just thought about it really, really hard and hoped he picked up on the laid-back vibe I was sending out.

Inside, Roy examined the Ferris wheel up close and pushed one of the swings. But when he reached up to the roller coaster track, I said, "Don't touch! It's fragile. At least, that's what my dad told me."

Roy smirked.

"Sorry, it's no big deal," I said, going over to him. "I know you'll be careful."

He stepped around a shrub-tree thing, nearer to me.

"I loved Holly Jolly Land when I was a kid," I said.

He stepped closer.

We were nearly the exact same height, so when he did the trademark Roy Stamos smolder I got a straight-on view.

I had to break his gaze on purpose. "It's a, um, a great turnout for the unveiling."

He looked at the back of the curtain. "I know. I can't believe people show up to see a Snow Globe. This town is so lame."

"Yeah . . . I dunno," I said. "If I didn't live here, I'd probably want to visit some place where it's Christmas year-round. I mean, it's sort of awesome if you think about it. Magical."

"Not to me," Roy said.

"Yeah, not to me, either."

He looked sideways at me, and I cleared my throat.

"Well, I mean, not to me personally, but to *some* people, it probably is magical."

"You really believe it, huh?"

"Believe what?"

"That Christmas is the greatest place on earth and all that."

"Oh." I wasn't sure how to answer. Roy was from Lexington. He went to tennis camp for the entire summer and went to Europe on vacation and had probably eaten crazy exotic food like . . . haggis, whatever that was. I wanted him to see me as a girl worth dating, not some small-town girl who'd only ever been to D.C. once over spring break.

"I think it's special." I shrugged. I couldn't help myself. When it came to Christmas, I was all in. "People like to come here because they get something back they've lost out there in the world. And the town—we want to give tourists that feeling. That's why the season is so important. It's about spreading that magic feeling."

He smiled his leaning smile. "That's cute."

"Cute?" Cute was for bunnies.

"I like cute." He stepped so close we were sharing the same space. We weren't touching, but if either of us moved half an inch, we would be. Snow fell onto his eyelashes, which I had just noticed were extremely thick. And then, something about the air between us changed. It got warmer, and quieter, and there was a pull to it, like we were really at the North Pole and magnetic north was drawing us closer. That was the power of Roy Stamos's eyes.

I went to brush my bangs off my forehead, but Roy beat me to it. His touch was gentle, and his fingertips lingered on the side of my face.

"Is this for real?" he asked in a husky voice.

"I think so," I breathed. I leaned my face into his palm. "Don't you feel it?"

"Yeah, but it's not that cold."

"What?"

"The snow. It's not very cold." He plucked a flake from the ends of my hair.

"Oh, the snow? No, it's not real, it's man-made."

Roy smiled his leaning smile and moved even closer. "What did you think I meant?"

"I . . ." I couldn't make any words come out.

Never in any of my wildest dreams (and I'd had some very intense ones concerning Roy Stamos, let me tell you) could I have conjured up a more perfect setting to do something about the heartbreaking, throbbing crush I had on the most beautiful boy I'd ever seen.

"I thought you meant . . ."

"What?" Roy said, nudging my nose with his.

"This."

"Us," he said, nodding slowly. He brushed his lips against my cheek, right next to my ear. "Is this for real?"

I shivered. "This is for real."

"You know I'm leaving tomorrow." His lips danced over my jaw with every word.

"I know." I closed my eyes. "Tennis camp."

"Will you wait for me to get back?" His nose brushed across my cheek and lightly bumped mine.

"Yes. Will you wait for me?"

He kissed me.

Kissing Roy Stamos was like waking up on Christmas morning and finding everything I'd asked for under the tree—soft lips and sweet breath and no clinking teeth. I shivered. It was easy to imagine that we really were standing in the snow in some magic land. Oh, the feels! I put my hands on his face and pulled him closer.

Lights flashed behind my eyelids like lightning. Then more lights flashed, so bright I blinked.

To my left, the red-velvet curtain was open, and hundreds of people were watching me kiss *Roy Stamos*. Just feet away, Dad stood at the podium on the steps, next to Nick Patterson. I froze, pressed tight to Roy, my lips still against his, my hands still on his face.

"What's wrong?" he whispered.

"Um."

He opened his eyes a smidge. "Oh, man!"

He jumped back, and I went reeling. I stepped back to catch myself, but I stumbled against a shrub-tree. My arms went into windmill mode as I tried to get my balance. Roy reached out and caught my left hand. My right hand got caught in the chains of one of the swings. I tried to hold on to it and pull myself upright, but the North Pole was as rickety as it looked. It fell back into the Ferris wheel, which broke free from its stand and went careening into the roller coaster tracks. The North Pole swung around and knocked into Roy. Roy fell into me, and we both went down.

"Ow!"

Roy was facedown in the fake snow, half on top of me. I finally freed my hand from the chains and tried to push the pole off us. It was heavy, and I was pinned down.

"Darby? Are you hurt?" he asked.

"I don't think so. Are you all—"

Something metallic groaned overhead. I looked up and saw that the buckled Ferris wheel was teetering in my direction. I covered my face with my arms as pieces of track and Ferris wheel carts rained down on us. The last thing I saw was the giant wheel, falling over.

"Mother of kiwis!" I cried, and then something hit me on the head, and everything went black.

Three

THE HERALD WAS CALLING LAST NIGHT THE "Nightmare before Christmas in July." That was the actual headline. Then underneath a picture of me, midfall, pulling the set down, a caption read, "First Daughter Darby Causes Disaster."

There was video of last night's entire ordeal on the website, too, because everyone had had their phones out for the Snow Globe unveiling. Kids from school who barely talked to me were posting videos and pictures all over social media and tagging me and Roy. I couldn't bring myself to watch any of them yet. I had the feeling once I did I'd never want to show my face in town again.

I didn't have a concussion, but Dr. Hoey wanted to see me again in a week or so. I had a nasty goose egg on my forehead that was so tender even my bangs touching it felt like a million needles stinging me. By this morning, the pain was replaced by a throbbing headache. I woke to a quiet house; Dad had gone to church without me.

I climbed out of bed and went downstairs. Our old Victorian off Kringle Avenue is a beautiful white house with a red door to set off the wreath that hangs from a hook year-round. Sometimes I wondered what it was like to live in a house that wasn't decorated. Penny's house didn't have stockings on the mantle from January to December, and to me that was plain sad. She didn't have greenery on the stair rails or mistletoe hanging from her doorways, either. I'd slept over a million times, but going to the bathroom at night always creeped me out. Everything looked so naked and exposed in the moonlight. I preferred our year-round decorations and Christmas tree tucked into the corner of the living room (I changed around the ornaments to match the season; now it looked very summery with a starfish tree topper, little beach-ball ornaments, pink lights, and my favorite, the melting-snowman ornament).

Maureen O'Hara, my Himalayan cat, followed me all over the house, mewing, as I closed the shutters against the glare of the morning sun.

"Quiet," I whispered. "I have a headache."

I stopped in the kitchen for an ice pack, an Ale-8, and some pretzel sticks, and fell onto our worn-in white couch. I took a huge handful of pretzels and arranged them into a sunburst on the coffee table as I sipped my soda.

You couldn't get Ale-8 anywhere else in the country. It was brewed right here in Kentucky, so of course every store and restaurant in Christmas sold it. It helped that the ginger soda had a hint of cinnamon in the aftertaste, making it the perfect cold drink to pair with Christmas cookies—or a near concussion. I'd been addicted to it since I was old enough to use a bottle opener; there was a reason why we called it liquid crack. The sugar buzz was definitely helping ease my bruise.

Maureen O'Hara jumped lightly into my lap and turned a circle, pawing at my legs until she found the right place to curl up. I planned to stay there all morning. Maybe all week. I had to suck on the pretzels until they were mushy and didn't make any noise when I chewed. Maureen's purring was like a jackhammer in my ears. I even had to mute *The Andy Griffith Show* on Netflix because the sound was killer, but it didn't matter since I knew every line of this episode by heart.

I love *Andy Griffith*. No matter how complicated things get, no matter how much of a mess Barney gets Andy into, everything in Mayberry turns out all right in the end: they all sit on the front porch, singing a tune, at peace with the world.

I scrolled through the guide to my favorite episode, the Christmas one. It was the one where mean old Ben is trying to get arrested just so he can have Christmas with Andy and everybody at the courthouse instead of being all alone. I watched Ben try again and again to get thrown in jail, too stubborn to ask to join in.

Netflix counted down to the next episode, but I switched the TV back to the local news and closed my eyes. My head was pounding. I had a bruise on my side, too, where the North Pole had fallen on me, but it didn't hurt nearly as much as my head. Or my pride.

Roy hadn't been at Dr. Hoey's office half as long as I had; he had a few bumps and bruises, but nothing serious. I had been lying on the exam table, waiting for Dad or Dr. Hoey or someone to come back and help me up, when he knocked on my door.

"Come in," I had called weakly.

He had stuck his head through first. I'd never seen his hair messy; a huge curl fell over his forehead and grazed his long eyelashes. That and the blue bruise under his other eye, and he'd looked like an old-school rebel, fresh from a fight.

He'd smiled and I'd held out my hand, and he came in and took it. As he stood over me, I realized I was lying down. With a boy in the room. A boy who had kissed me. Oh, bananas. What did I look like from this angle? Did I have a double chin and weird lumps and rolls in places? I'd never thought about how I looked on my back. There was so much more to worry about with a boy around.

I'd tried to raise my chin so my face wouldn't look flat and fat around the edges and smiled like I wasn't even thinking about it. "Nice shiner."

He smiled. "Thanks. How's your head?"

"Concussion watch, but I get to go home soon. You?"

"Nothing broken, but I dinged up my shoulder pretty good. I hope it doesn't affect my serve."

My heart rolled up into my throat. "So, does that mean you're still leaving tom—"

"Sure, I'll be fine. Besides, I can't wait to get out of this place. I mean, you know, because it sucks. Not because of you or anything."

"Yeah, totally."

"So, I guess I'll see you around."

"Yeah, tot—I mean, sure."

He'd leaned over me, and his curly hair had brushed against my bangs as he drew closer until his lips pressed against mine and, oh, he tasted like caramel, and it was totally different to have some guy lean over and kiss you than it was standing up, and I'd wondered if there had ever been two people more perfect for each—

"Knock knock. Okay, Miss Darby, you can go— Oh." Dr. Hoey's lips twisted off to the side, like she was trying not to smile. "Sorry to interrupt. Thought you were headed home, Roy."

Roy stepped back, and our fingers untangled. "I was just, um, yeah, I am. Um." He glanced at me. "See you in August?"

"Definitely."

He'd given me a small wave as he left.

Dr. Hoey had busied herself with my chart until the door closed behind Roy.

I bit on my lower lip, and I could still taste him.

She came forward and helped me sit up. "Sorry," she said. She gestured around at the carnival wallpaper. "Not used to my patients having boyfriends visit."

"It's okay." I wished we could have had just one more minute alone together before he left for the summer, but at least our reunion would be that much sweeter since we'd only gotten these couple of stolen moments. Besides, there was always FaceTime and texts, and maybe I'd even go visit him some weekend when it wasn't too busy around here. Maybe—

"On that subject," Dr. Hoey said slowly, "you know you can always come to me if you need any information on birth control or—"

"It's not like that!" *Death, take me now.*

"Okay. But if it ever *is* like that—"

"It won't be."

She held up a hand in surrender. "Just so you know."

"I know."

Even now, lying on my couch with Maureen O'Hara, I was mortified.

The Christmas episode ended, so I flipped the TV back to cable while I wallowed in my embarrassment. Dr. Hoey had been my doctor since I was born, literally. Mrs. Goodwin said she's the one who took care of me when I was a baby. I was born early, and my mom died in childbirth. Dad was too upset those first few weeks to do much when he visited me in the hospital, so Dr. Hoey drove up to Lexington and watched out for me until I was discharged. With all our history, it was so weird to hear her talk to me about . . . that. Especially since she'd seen me kiss Roy in the Snow Globe and had gotten a private encore in her office.

Stupid interruptions.

Why did the most romantic moment of my life happen in front of the entire town? I guess I should have seen it coming, in concussion retrospect. Every important moment in my life had happened with someone in town to witness it.

Mr. Grant from the diner still told the story of the time I tried to fly after reading *Pippi Longstocking*. And Penny's father, who owned the Rite Aid off Route 12, sold me my first box of Playtex when I walked all the way to the highway because I didn't want to tell my dad I needed a ride to the drugstore.

It figured the entire town would see my first kiss. I closed my eyes and tried to imagine what it would have been like to kiss somewhere else, where I was just a girl who liked a boy and no one knew my name. Maybe at some bonfire out in the county with kids I didn't know, far enough away from the dancing flames that no one would see. It wasn't as magical as a Snow Globe, but we wouldn't be interrupted, either.

"The town of Christmas got quite an unexpected present last night when two teens—one of whom was the mayor's own daughter—were caught canoodling inside the town's life-sized Snow Globe during an unveiling ceremony," said a news anchor on the TV.

"What?" I cried. I sat up so fast Maureen O'Hara fell out of my lap with a hiss. The picture over the news anchor's shoulder was a blurry freeze frame of me and Roy kissing. The anchor's face was twisted into a patronizing smile as she began the story.

This wasn't happening!

"Mayor Bobby Peacher was giving the opening speech at the annual Snow Globe festival when the curtains suddenly parted to reveal the star-crossed lovers' tryst. Here's the video."

They showed the entire thing, from Dad's speech to Roy and me kissing to us falling to me blacking out. The part where I fell and brought the set down on top of me, well, let's just say I'm glad I was wearing clean underwear, and that they were a respectable pair that covered everything and not my pink polka-dot thong or something. I wished it hadn't been broadcast on television for everyone from here to Hazard County to see, obviously, but I'd take any silver linings I could get at this point, even if they were of the blue-boy-shorts variety.

"Fan-fruiting-tastic," I muttered.

The video ended, and the broadcast cut back to the anchor. She smiled and shook her dark head slightly. "What a night. Channel Four's field reporter Houston Durham caught up with Mayor Peacher this morning."

There was Dad on the courthouse steps! Oh, bananas, this was bad. He'd had to go into the office on a Sunday because of me. There wasn't the faintest trace of his boyish charm. He was frowning, and his eyes were squinted against the sun. A trickle of sweat ran down the side of his face as he read a statement.

"We regret the incident last night, and the town of Christmas wishes to extend its deepest apologies to the many families that traveled here to go inside the Snow Globe," he said stiffly. "I would also like to personally apologize to Mr. Nick Patterson and his entire staff at Holly Jolly Land. But Mr. Patterson is already beginning reconstruction of his scene. It will be up and running as soon as possible. Thank you."

The reporter watched Dad as he climbed the steps to the courthouse, and then he turned back to the camera. "Channel Four asked some of the residents of Christmas for their take on the incident. Here's what they had to say."

Mrs. Whitfield from Christmas Creamery appeared, a microphone thrust under her heavy chin. Her blue eyes shone as she gave her take in her deep voice. "Well, it's just a nightmare. The Snow Globe is the town's pride and joy, and those two young people just went and treated it like some lover's lane or something. It's near sacrilegious. That Snow Globe has been around for years. Kids today don't care about nothing."

I cared! I was devastated! I couldn't believe Mrs. Whitfield would think any differently; she knew how much I loved the Snow Globe.

Cut to Mr. Oates, who owned Big O's tires off the highway. When I was little, he used to lift me into a stack of tires in his showroom and let me pretend I was stuck in a well and climb out to safety. "Those kids sure caused us all a lot of trouble. Businesses expect to make a buck or two off tourists. It's why we do it in the first place."

What? We didn't have the Snow Globe to make *money.* We did it for the people. What was Mr. Oates talking about? A lump formed in my throat.

The screen cut back to the news anchor in the studio.

"Thank you, Houston. Sounds like the summer tourist season in Christmas, Kentucky, is off to a truly *bumpy* start." She smiled conspiratorially.

I turned off the TV.

This wasn't good. I had to do something! I couldn't let Dad down now. I had made a mistake, and it was making him look bad in front of the entire town. Worse, it was making Christmas look bad in front of western Kentucky! I had to make it right.

I tipped back the last of my Ale-8 and jumped to my feet. My head pounded and I got a little dizzy from bouncing up so fast, but I couldn't let an almost concussion stop me. I ran upstairs and changed into one of my best red dresses. I pinned my hair into a respectable ballet bun, brushed my bangs over the worst of my bruise, and applied extra deodorant. I'd need all the help I could get in this hot mess.

Downstairs, I stepped into my flip-flops, grabbed my keys and messenger bag, and called good-bye to Maureen O'Hara, who stuck her head around the corner to watch me leave. On my way out the front door my phone dinged. Roy?

I dug it out of my bag.

Nope. Facebook.

Ding. Instagram.

Ding. Snapchat.

Great. I muted my notifications and hurried to the square.

Four

THE COURTHOUSE WAS A STRIKING BUILDING, dark-maroon brick with a star on top of the white clock tower, lit up year-round. Many of the pictures of Christmas on *Travel America*'s Best Small Towns list featured the courthouse at the end of Main Street on the square, the line of tidy businesses and Christmas-themed storefronts like a row of sentries standing at attention down the avenue. That was the prettiest view of town, but I liked the view walking from our house up the residential end of Main. The houses sat deep in their yards, most with front porches and picket fences. Live oaks stretched across the street overhead, making a canopy of limbs and leaves that let dappled sunlight break through like glitter onto the pavement. The back side of the courthouse was as grand as the front, and it appeared slowly as I made my way toward it, the trees slipping into my periphery.

Inside, my footsteps on the marble echoed as I walked across the cavernous entrance hall. I went through the huge wooden doors opposite the main courtroom and walked down the hallway past empty offices of town clerks and record keepers. I climbed the wide, creaky staircase up to the mayor's suite, my goose egg pounding with every step. The smells of Lysol and musty books pressed in on me and made me nauseated because of my head. I pushed through the door to Dad's outer chambers and looked around.

The desk in the outer chamber was supposed to be for a secretary or administrator, but it was mine by default; Dad didn't have a secretary, so I did homework there while I answered the phone after school and planned Dad's schedule for the next day. In the summers, I spent a few days a week at that desk, helping with the season's festivals and events, when I wasn't sitting in the chair opposite Dad's in his office, across his huge mahogany desk.

Last year, I got to make the playlist for the Fourth of July in Christmas parade. This summer, I was going to finally convince Greg and Fran to let me play some holiday films outside on the huge brick wall of their theater, an idea I liked to think of as "Christmas Classics under the Stars." I'd been begging for years, but Fran said it would cut into their profits. I was pretty sure I'd just about convinced Greg when I talked about the money they could make selling concessions and maybe even VIP cushion reservations.

Today, my desk had a box of files on it, and a black blazer was slung over the chair. I didn't recognize either. Dad's office doors were shut. I couldn't remember the last time I'd seen them closed.

I went over and knocked as I opened the door. "Why are the doors closed? Are you—"

A woman was in his office, sitting in my chair.

Dad stood. "Darby, come in. I'd like you to meet Ms. Walker."

The woman turned and smiled at me. She had a blond bob that was so shiny I squinted involuntarily, and her thick black glasses seemed too big for her pointy nose. She set a black briefcase on the floor by her feet and stood up, and up, and up—she had to be six feet tall, in black ballet flats—and extended her hand toward me. I recognized her from last night; she was the woman who had been trying to talk to Dad before the unveiling.

"It's Marianne, as I keep telling your father."

I reached out and shook. "Nice to meet you." I glanced at Dad as Marianne Walker pumped my hand so hard my entire arm wobbled. "Are you—um, here on business?"

Marianne Walker's smile grew. "I am. I'm from Frankfort."

"Oh?" I stood up straighter at her mention of the state capital and smiled my campaign smile. "What brings you to Christmas?"

"I was just about to find that out myself," Dad said. "Darby, why don't you—"

"Way ahead of you." I pulled up the side chair from the far wall and sat next to Marianne. Marianne seemed a little taken aback; she turned to Dad. "Maybe you and I should speak privately, Mayor."

Dad winked at me as he sat back down. "It's fine. Darby does quite a bit of work around here. She's welcome to stay."

"All right." Marianne smoothed her black pants as she sat down. "I'm here on the governor's orders."

"The governor?" I said.

Marianne Walker pushed her glasses up her nose. "He asked that I come down here and offer my services to you, Mayor."

"And what services would those be?" Dad asked.

"Well, I don't know if you know, but I worked on the governor's campaign two years ago. I'm a strategist."

"I'm not up for reelection until next year. And unless something changes, I don't think I'll have very much trouble keeping the job."

"Everyone loves Dad," I explained to Marianne. "He's been mayor three terms already."

Marianne smiled warmly, but her tone was all business. "Oh, I'm not here for your reelection campaign. I'm here because your town is changing rapidly, and with the influx of people and money since Christmas made that top-ten list, you've been on the radar."

"Well, I don't know about that," Dad said with a laugh. "It was an honor to be chosen, I'm sure, but it hasn't changed the town much."

"Yet."

Dad's forehead creased. "Yet?"

"The list came out, what, four months ago?" Marianne said. She pulled a folder out of her briefcase and pushed it across the desk to Dad. "Since then, your population has increased one percent, Google searches of *Christmas, Kentucky* are up seven thousand percent, real-estate searches are up five hundred percent, and the four nearest hotels are booked for the entire summer tourist season."

Dad's eyebrows climbed his forehead as he read the report in the folder. "I had no idea."

"We know. That's why the governor sent me."

Dad looked up from the folder. "You came all this way to tell me in person something I could have read in an email?"

"I came all this way to spend the summer tourist season helping," Marianne Walker said. She pushed her blond hair behind her ear, revealing a jaw so sharp it could cut glass. "The governor believes with the right campaign, Christmas could become one of Kentucky's biggest tourist attractions."

I laughed. "Christmas? But we're just . . . Christmas."

Dad winked at me. Obviously, Marianne Walker and the governor were reading way too much into all of this.

"Not anymore," Marianne said. "If you're not careful, you could waste this opportunity. But worse than that, you could lose the town."

This got Dad's attention. "What do you mean, lose the town?"

Marianne looked out the window to Main Street below. "This town is gorgeous. *Travel America* chose it because it's successful in so many ways—no doubt because of your leadership, Mayor. It's the quintessential American town: your employment numbers are higher than the national average; your population is older than the average, it's true, but it's also got one of the lowest crime rates in the state; you have one of the most diverse populations, too, at twenty percent African American and five percent Hispanic; real estate is cheap; and your downtown is thriving."

She sounded like a textbook. "So how is Dad going to 'lose the town'?"

"If handled incorrectly, he could lose it to investors." Marianne leaned forward and turned the page of her report. "The two towns listed in last year's Top Ten that didn't make the list this year. Look at those figures to see why."

Dad spent a minute reading. I spent a minute deciding I didn't like Marianne Walker. Her business suit was so . . . big city. And that hair. Hair wasn't that smooth or shiny without at least an hour of prep. Who had that kind of time?

When Dad finished reading, he closed the folder and slid it back across the desk to her. "I see the cause for concern, but I don't think you understand. Christmas is not like Quigby or . . . Hobsgood. The people here aren't going to sell off their stores. The town council would never agree to restructuring our zoning laws just to make a few dollars."

I nodded firmly. Marianne Walker and the governor didn't know the people in this town. It was like I was telling Roy last night: We were different. Special.

Marianne nodded. "That's what the mayor of Quigby thought, too. She resigned last November. Moved to Charlotte after her town council voted nine to one to allow franchises to open on Main Street."

Dad sat back and stared at the ceiling.

"Have you been approached at all?" Marianne asked. "By investors or real-estate groups?"

Dad caught my eye. "As a matter of fact, I have. They're interested in building a shopping center or something. But as I've told them, I'm too busy with the tourist season to listen to any proposals at the moment."

Marianne nodded. "Whitman Group or Hearth and Home?"

Dad raised an eyebrow. "Whitman."

Marianne relaxed. "They're a good company. We've had a lot of success with them in developing some land in Frankfort. But their legal team is a beast; the town will need to make sure contracts are correctly structured."

"But like Dad said, the town isn't going to be selling any—"

"Hearth and Home are here, as well," Marianne interrupted. "I saw Joan Crowder at the unveiling last night. She single-handedly ruined Quigby. You don't want to entertain any offer she has for you. And there are dozens of others just like her."

I tried to catch Dad's eye, but he was lost in thought.

She cleared her throat. "Look, I'm excellent at what I do. The governor wouldn't have sent me if he didn't think it was necessary, believe me; I'm needed in Frankfort. But there's real potential for Christmas to become a huge tourist town without losing the appeal that makes it so unique." She paused and leveled her gaze at Dad. "There's also real potential for the town to turn on you if they feel you're not handling the changing dynamics. I can help you there."

Dad sat back and studied her for a moment. Then he glanced at me. "It doesn't sound like I have much of a choice, if the governor sent you."

Marianne didn't respond. I took that to mean Dad was right.

"I suppose . . . if this is really a concern, then I'm all for the extra help. So, welcome to Christmas."

Marianne's cheeks turned a pleased shade of pink. "Thank you."

"Darby and I will be happy to listen to any ideas you have."

I nodded and got to my feet. "Let's see if we can get you set up at a desk down the hall. Then, if you'd like, I can give you the lay of the town this morning and then—"

"Actually," Marianne said, settling back into her chair, "there's something else I need to talk to you about."

"What's that?" Dad said.

"Darby."

"Me," I said.

"Now that Christmas is so much on the radar—both by the governor's office and by the public—we need to discuss your role."

"My role?"

"Last night was an excellent opportunity for the town to gain some publicity. Your . . . incident was unfortunate."

I glared at her. "It was an accident."

"I'm sure it was. But what happened to the Snow Globe hurt the town."

"Excuse me, ma'am," Dad said in a calm but firm tone. "My daughter's personal life is not something we need to discuss."

"But Darby's personal life isn't personal at all. She's the First Daughter of Christmas—isn't that what they call you?" she asked me.

I didn't answer.

"And as the First Daughter of Christmas, you're in a spotlight all the time. You shouldn't be," she said bluntly.

"Darby didn't ask for that title," Dad said evenly.

Marianne smiled warmly at me. "I'm sure she didn't."

I crossed my arms.

"But the word around town is that Darby has her run of the place. And based on what I've witnessed in the last five minutes, it's true."

Dad's forehead creased. "What do you mean?"

"Well, I've never had a meeting with a public official and his child before."

She said "child" the way some misinformed people say "cat." And speaking as a "child" and Maureen O'Hara's owner, I resented it.

"I'm only helping my dad!"

"And that's very honorable, Darby, but maybe you shouldn't be helping quite so much. You should be out having fun with your friends, dating that boy you were kissing last night, being a teenager."

I wished the floor would open up and swallow me whole. A perfect stranger was talking to me about kissing Roy right in front of my dad. Seriously bananas.

Dad leaned forward and put his elbows on his desk. "As I said, my daughter's private life should be kept private."

Marianne nodded, and her curtain of shiny blond hair fell. "I couldn't agree more. Which is why she needs to stay away from the courthouse this summer."

"What?" I cried.

Marianne pushed her black frames up her nose and looked at me. "You need to be at major events, of course, but that's it. For now."

My mouth fell open. "No way! I have a job here! I run Dad's schedule and help plan the festivals."

"Most elected officials don't bring their daughters to work every day. It makes your father look weak."

I wasn't at the courthouse *every* day.

"He needs me here," I said, glaring at Marianne Walker. "Dad, tell her."

But he didn't. After a pause, I turned to him. "Dad?"

He was looking at Marianne, the crease between his eyebrows deep. "You really think it's that important?"

"I do. Mayor, you need to show your strength this summer. The way I understand it, the town loves you and Darby, but they see you as the poor single father who needs help raising his daughter—she's First Daughter because they think of her as their responsibility. That translates to weakness. If investors think they can railroad you, they will. Just ask the mayor of Quigby."

"Dad . . ." I said, but he held up a hand.

"We have to, Moonpie." He met my eye. "If it's what's best for Christmas."

He always knew what to say to convince me. And appealing to my love of Christmas was a surefire way to get me onboard. But it meant leaving Dad here with a total stranger.

"So what am I supposed to do all summer?"

"Well, that's easy," Marianne Walker from Frankfort said. "You should spend time with your friends."

"My best friend is at riding camp. She's gone until the end of August." I didn't say anything about my other friend going to tennis camp. Seemed the wrong place to bring up his name.

"Is it too late to join her?" Marianne asked.

"I don't ride," I mumbled. "I never did because . . ."

"Because why?" Marianne asked.

Dad cleared his throat. "Because she was always busy here."

Marianne nodded thoughtfully. Her glasses were *definitely* too chunky for her face. "Well, then. It sounds like a chance to make new friends. Have an adventure, even."

An adventure. More like me and Maureen O'Hara on the couch all day, watching *Andy Griffith*. I could barely contain my excitement.

"You could get a job," she went on. "I'm sure there are lots of places in town that will need extra help, what with all the tourists arriving for the season."

Dad raised an eyebrow. "That's not a bad idea, actually."

What. Was. Happening? "But if you want me to work, shouldn't I just work *here*?"

"It's just a suggestion," Dad said. "It would give you something to do. You like to be busy."

"Actually, getting a job out in the community might be a boon to your images," Marianne said. "If Darby works elsewhere, she's obviously not working here. It would be a reminder to the town that you're completely capable, Mayor, and that Darby isn't in need of constant supervision."

A job. "What a fun adventure," I mumbled.

Marianne smiled. "I'm sure you could find something more fun than worrying about budget meetings and zoning restrictions."

I liked zoning restrictions.

Dad seemed to guess what I was thinking because he gave me a sad smile. "For Christmas," he said.

I sighed. For Christmas.

Five

I SPENT THE NEXT FEW HOURS ON MAIN STREET, ducking into every business that might be hiring. If I was seriously going to have to stay away from the courthouse, at least I could be close by. Besides, I gave Marianne Walker from Frankfort two weeks, tops. She'd get bored with the small-town bit or get summoned home to the capital, and then everything would go back to normal.

Christmas wasn't going to change just because of a top-ten list and a couple of investors. Those other places were different; they didn't have Dad, for starters. Or pride in their town, obviously. Besides, Christmas had been the same forever; it would take a lot more than one busy summer and some local news publicity to change things.

Christmas had embraced its name since 1912, when Vista Brody started selling ornaments in Brody's Mercantile on Main. Christmas ornaments were still kind of a new idea back then, and when people came into town for supplies, they loved to look at Miss Vista's creations. Before then, Christmas was simply named after Zeb Christmas, the man who settled the town in the early eighteen hundreds. I loved to visit the museum once in a while and look at all the old pictures of Main Street back when it was just a couple of buildings and a dirt-packed road.

I went to the bakery first. If anyone would hire me, it was Mrs. Goodwin.

"Darby, darlin', what in the world are you doing here?" She brushed sweat off her forehead, leaving a smudge of flour behind. "You should be home resting!"

"I was wondering if you were hiring?"

"Hiring?"

I filled her in on Marianne Walker. She listened so intently she stopped rolling out gingerbread and leaned against the counter instead. "And this Miss Walker really thinks investors will be interested in Christmas?"

I shrugged. "So, can I work here?"

Mrs. Goodwin sighed. "If I had the money to hire you, you know I would—the publicity alone, having the First Daughter of Christmas here, especially after last night."

"After last night?"

"Girl, if we weren't on the radar before, we sure are now. That news anchorwoman made certain of it with her silly story, even if she doesn't know her butt from a hole in the ground."

"Mrs. Goodwin!" I laughed.

"Well, she doesn't. You didn't ruin anything."

"But you won't hire me?"

"Baby, I can barely afford to pay myself. I'm sorry."

"It's okay."

I stuck around long enough to have a scone, and then I went down to Evergreen Coffee Co. If I was going to be working, at least I could try for a place with free frappucinos. But Gavin, the manager, wouldn't let me fill out an application.

"Got to be eighteen to be a barista, Darb," he said. "Come back in three years."

"I could be eighteen."

"Yeah, if I didn't know you don't even have a driver's license yet. Not gonna happen."

I almost didn't wait around for my marshmallow crème frappe.

I got the same response at the Theatre Royale. Greg was at least nice about it. Greg was nice about everything but Fran, and with his slow drawl, even his complaints about her were sweet sounding. "Sorry, darling, but I only hire eighteen and up. What do you need a job for, anyway?"

"Long story," I mumbled.

He fluffed the deep part in his hair. "I tried talking to Franny about the VIP cushions."

"Yeah? Did you tell her my idea for concessions?"

He rolled his eyes. "She said people wouldn't pay for cushions or food if they could just bring their own from home."

"Maybe," I said. "But if you had, I don't know, like gourmet popcorn, or—"

"Girl, you know my sister isn't going to spring for gourmet anything."

The Christmas Cupboard was a no-go. Old Mrs. Lowenstein motioned around the store at the delicate display of china and pottery and said, "I don't think it would work out, Darby. The way you took down the Snow Globe set, well, you could cost me a bundle."

I knew Mr. Johnson hired high-school kids at the toy store; Laeticia Marshall worked there. I stopped in and found her trying to pick up after squealing kids as they ran circles around the train table. The mothers stood to the side, watching as they gossiped. When a boy with green goo on his face stomped on Laeticia's foot as he rounded the corner, her face squinched up in pain.

I backed out of there before anyone saw me. I couldn't imagine a worse job.

I tried the cleaners and an insurance company two blocks off the square, where lawyers' offices, a bank, and some other non-holiday, suit-and-tie businesses lined Prancer Lane, but I wasn't old enough there, either.

No way was I trying Taco Bell down by the high school. Gross. And I didn't have my license, as Gavin had pointed out, so I couldn't get to the highway to Rite Aid or Dollar General.

I plopped down on a bench near the diner and watched the red trolley unload tourists. It seemed like one woman did a double take when she noticed me and nudged the man nearest her. Maybe I was something of an attraction in town today because of the Snow Globe. Not that Marianne *Walker* was right about anything.

Then an out-of-towner with twin toddlers in a double stroller stopped on the sidewalk and glared at me. The strapped-in girl had an ice-cream cone that was melting all over her seersucker dress; the boy was fast asleep, a hat covering most of his face.

"We came all the way from Chattanooga," the woman said.

"That's nice," I said. "Are you enjoying Christmas?"

"We *were*." The woman scowled and thrust her thumb over her shoulder toward the red-velvet curtains that were closed against the street. "I stood in line five hours so my family could be one of the first three hundred in the Globe."

"Oh." I felt horrible. "I'm sorry."

"My husband took the last of his vacation days to be here."

She pushed the stroller away before I could think of anything to say.

I should probably issue an official apology, I thought. But then I remembered that I was supposed to stay out of the public eye and away from the courthouse. That was out, then. Still, I wished I could let people know how sorry I was.

The red curtains were hiding the Snow Globe from view. I wondered how it looked in the light of day. Were the same kids who were painting last night there trying to fix it? I bet they all hated me. I really wanted to tell them how sorry I was. At the least, I owed Mr. Nick Patterson an apology. It was his Globe scene, after all. But I didn't know how to even begin to say I was sorry.

Hey, Mr. Patterson, sorry I got embarrassed when the town saw me kissing Roy? Sorry I ruined your flimsy, not-so-great-to-begin-with set?

I sat there until the next red trolley pulled into view. I couldn't take another dose of whispers and disappointed tourists, so I jumped up and headed toward the red curtains. Maybe Mr. Patterson was around. I had to try, anyway.

As I reached the curtains, I paused to take a deep breath. What if he yelled at me? What if he hated me?

CRASH!

The boom rang out from behind the curtain. What the fruit cup? I stepped through.

The scene wasn't much different from last night's scramble to finish the set. There were people everywhere, but instead of the kids with paintbrushes, there were men with brooms and dustpans. And forklifts. And a Dumpster.

The Globe was a disaster. The Ferris wheel was splintered into wedges. The men inside were tearing the tiny trees out with ease and tossing them into a pile. They'd pushed the North Pole back to a standing position so they could work around it, but it looked in danger of falling again.

My heart sank. I had done this.

"Mushmelon," I muttered. I walked around to the side of the Globe to get a closer look.

"Darby!" someone called.

I turned.

Calvin Sherman was heading straight for me, and his face was way beyond Secret Service serious. He was wearing an army-green jumpsuit that was smeared with grease, carrying a huge wrench. I wondered if he actually worked with any of the tools he walked around with all the time or if he just carried them so people would think he looked manly.

"What are you doing here?" he practically shouted at me. His expression softened slightly when he seemed to notice the goose egg on my forehead. "Shouldn't you be home resting, where you can't make it worse?"

I was there to try to make it better, not that I had any intention of telling him that. Still, it hurt that Calvin Sherman, who used to be my friend, thought all I did was make things worse.

"I'm looking for Mr. Patterson," I said. "Can you tell me where he is?"

"Why?"

"That's between Mr. Patterson and me."

He glowered at me. "Mr. Patterson is busy. Go home."

Ugh. Why I had ever been friends with this guy was beyond me. Well, okay, before our just-friends date, he was the nicest guy I knew. He never snapped any of the girls' bras, and he paid attention in class, and he would hurry ahead to hold open doors. I always liked that about him. But then he ditched me at the party and woke up the next day as the Grinch and Scrooge and Mr. Oogie Boogie rolled into one. I got all icky-feeling just being in his vicinity.

I had to find Mr. Patterson, though. "Look, I need to talk to him, okay?"

"I'm not sure you should."

The arrogant asshat!

"Why am I even bothering talking to you?" I said. "I don't know why I thought you would help me. But you obviously won't, so I'll find Nick myself. Thanks for nothing."

I turned on the toe of my flip-flop and almost ran into Nick Patterson.

"Looks like you found me, honey."

His star-shaped purple sunglasses hid his eyes from view, but they didn't stop the icy anger from hitting me in the face like an air conditioner on high. He was wearing camouflage pants, a tie-dyed T-shirt, and a bandana around his neck today, and he held a folder in one hand and a bedazzled walkie-talkie in the other.

"I'm about ready to get back to base, Head Helper," he said to Calvin, waving him away with the folder.

"Yes, sir," Calvin said.

I glared at him until he was out of sight. Then I said, "Mr. Patterson, sir, I'm glad I found you. I was—"

"You. Follow me."

He limped back around the Globe to the curtains. He parted the gap, jerked his head toward the street, and said gruffly, "This is the way out, honey. Don't let me see you near my Globe again, hear?"

"Mr. Patterson, sir—"

"Name's Nick."

"Yes, sir. Mr.—Nick—I'm so very sorry about the Snow Globe. I didn't mean to cause a, um, a—"

"I believe the word you're looking for is *disaster*."

I winced. "First Daughter Darby Causes Disaster," *The Herald* had said. That's what Mr. Patterson thought, too.

"Right, that. I'm so, so sorry." When he didn't immediately accept my apology, I said, "Will you forgive me?"

"Don't know," he said.

"Oh." I took a deep breath. "Is there anything I can do to show you how sorry I am for the, um—"

"Disaster," he barked.

"Yes, sir," I said, and I tried to stand as still as possible, like soldiers in movies. "Is there anything I can do to show you I'm sincerely sorry?"

He pushed his sunglasses down his nose and peered at me. "Where's the other one?"

"The other one?" Oh. "He's at camp."

"Camp?"

"Yes, sir. But he's really sorry, too."

"You sure about that?"

"Of course. We both are very sorry."

"You two left a mighty big mess to clean up," Mr. Patterson said.

"Yes, sir," I agreed. "I'm sorry."

"Your father is giving us a week to rebuild. Nice of him," he conceded gruffly.

POP!

The sound made us both spin around.

Oh, no.

The North Pole had broken through the plastic of the Globe, opening up a long rip. All the air was leaking out of the bubble as it deflated. The handful of men inside scrambled to the exit before the entire thing collapsed. The last man darted out the door as the plastic sank to the base.

Well, monk fruit. This wasn't going to make things any easier for Dad or Mr. Patterson. I turned away; I had done that.

"Do you think—will you be able to patch that?"

"Negative."

I wondered how fast Night Sky Tents could get a replacement to us. How much would that cost the town?

Another something behind me crashed to the ground. I mentally cringed but tried to keep a straight face. "I'd like to make it up to you."

His eyes twinkled. "You'd make a good soldier if you weren't royalty. How old are you?"

"Fifteen."

"You really want to make it up to me, well, come by the park first thing in the morning. Oh eight hundred hours, and don't be late. You can start basic training."

"Basic training . . ." I glanced around. "Mr. Patterson, I didn't mean—"

"You said you want to make it up to me."

"Yes, by apologizing."

"Words don't fix my Globe."

"But I don't know anything about fixing the Snow—"

"Never done any manual labor? Operated heavy machinery?"

"No!"

Nick stuck out his jaw, snapped his suspenders, and said, "You certainly seem sturdy enough."

Sturdy? I preferred lovely. Sweet. Sugar and spice and everything nice.

"But—" I looked around at the Darby Disaster Zone. I hadn't expected this. I was just coming to apologize. Yet I needed a job, didn't I? Maybe working at Holly Jolly Land would be okay. "So, would I be working in your park or would I be fixing the Snow Globe or—"

"Oh eight hundred hours," Nick said again. He looked at me over the points of his star-shaped sunglasses and winked. "Don't be late."

I watched him hobble away. His cane had glitter on it, maybe from all the glitter on the Globe. Or maybe he meant for it to be there. Some of the kids from last night were sitting on the back of a pickup truck, eating doughnuts and laughing.

"Get back!" Nick swung his cane, and they all backed into

the truck bed, still laughing and talking. Nick slammed the tailgate and climbed into the passenger side. "Sherman! Let's go!" he shouted through the open window.

Calvin Sherman jogged over from the demolition crew and hopped into the driver's side. For some reason, I had the feeling he'd been listening to Nick and me talk. Maybe it was the way our eyes met in the side mirror as he revved the truck. He didn't seem happy.

Then again, he never seemed happy.

"Scrooge," I muttered.

What had I gotten myself into?

Six

THE NEXT DAY, I WAS UP EARLY TO SHOWER AND get dressed for my first day. I put on a red floral sundress, but then I looked in the mirror and realized manual labor might call for something . . . grungier. But these were the work clothes I owned. Besides, the dress looked great with my green flip-flops with the red bunches of holly at the thong—a nod to my new employer. I tried to get my hair to do that beachy wave thing, but it was too thick to do much more than hang there, so I clipped it back with my green barrettes.

At seven, I went downstairs and poured Froot Loops for me and muesli for Dad and put the milk on the table. He came out of his room at 7:05, the same as every morning. But today, he was wearing a tie.

A blue tie.

"Um, what's going on?" I asked.

"What?" he said. I gave him a look. "Oh. Ms. Walker and I are meeting with some state officials about the Western Kentucky Parkway exit."

That was fast. She'd been here a day and she already had meetings set up? "Dad, are you sure this is a good idea?"

He looked down at his tie as he poured coffee. "Too bright?"

"No, I meant . . . Are we sure about Ms. Walker?"

"Honestly, Moonpie, no, I'm not sure. But I've already had an e-mail from the governor's office this morning confirming Ms. Walker had arrived. And if the governor sent her, I have to at least make an attempt to cooperate, don't I?"

"I guess," I mumbled. "But what about the investor groups? Do you really think they'll try to buy up property in town, or—"

"You let me worry about Marianne Walker and the town and the investors. You focus on having a great first day at your new job."

"Yeah, okay."

"Why don't we have supper at the diner tonight? About six? You can tell me all about your first day, and I'll fill you in on how spectacularly we get turned down for the exit."

I smirked. "I can't believe she thinks you've got a shot."

Dad reached out and put his arm around me. "Well, she's right about one thing. You should be enjoying yourself. You'll still have plenty to do around town during Christmas in July. We can't have the parade without you. And there's the Twelve Days of Christmas Giveaways. You always like those."

I nodded. "Okay."

I spooned my soggy cereal down the garbage disposal and sighed.

"Anything else you want to talk about?" Dad asked, too nonchalantly.

"Like . . . ?"

"Like you and Roy Stamos?"

"Da-a-ad."

"Da-r-r-rby."

I sighed. "He left for tennis camp."

"Well, I have to admit, that makes me slightly happy. Giddy, actually."

I frowned at him. "His being away at camp doesn't mean anything. We'll still talk all the time."

"Ah, the promises of young love." Dad smiled. "Still, it's good for my nerves that you two have some distance between you. It's not easy for your old man to watch you fall head over heels for some little punk—"

"Stop!" I giggled. "He's not a punk."

"Either way, I'm glad this relationship will be moving slowly this summer. Snail slow. Glacially slow. Paint-dryingly slow."

Okay, so maybe being apart would keep things moving slowly between us, physically. But emotionally? We were already past the point of no return.

Dad pecked the side of my head. I ducked away and grabbed my purse off the table by the backdoor. "Yeah, yeah. See you at the diner tonight."

I walked up to the trolley depot, bought a fare card, and waited for the green line that ran to all the stops out in the county. A dozen or so tourists were waiting in line with me; I didn't recognize a single face, and no strangers seemed to recognize me today.

When the green trolley pulled up to the station, I hopped on, swiped my card, and grabbed a window seat. Holly Jolly Land was the last stop on the line. I just hoped I'd get there on time.

The trolley stopped at the Christmas post office first, where twenty or so people got off to tour the gingerbread-like building and send cards postmarked "Christmas" to their friends and family back home. The trolley rolled farther into the country, past dozens of red-and-green billboards advertising the shops in town.

I wanted to text Roy, just to say hi and see how camp was going, but I didn't want to be the one to break the seal on the texting. He would text when he had time. Besides, it had only been a day and a half. At least my new job—whatever it was Nick Patterson had me doing—would keep me busy. I was glad of that.

Of course, the flip side was not being at the courthouse. Maybe some kids would be glad to have a summer free of politics and fundraisers, but not me. I loved it. Okay, not the corny jokes and forced-laughter part of all the schmoozing, that was lame. But helping Dad? Fundraising? Organizing meetings and schedules and planning events? That was what I was great at. It was *all* I was great at. And whatever he said, I wasn't sure about leaving him in Marianne Walker's hands, governor's office or not. She didn't seem capable. Plus, she was so . . . un-Christmas.

The trolley stopped at Santa's Stables & Riding Trails ten minutes later. I looked around when the trolley didn't immediately set out again. Lots of people were getting off here, and it was taking a while. I glanced at the time on my phone. The trolley was taking longer than I'd thought. I'd have to remember that once I got a work schedule. This was going to be a thirty-minute trip each way, at least.

I couldn't wait to get my driver's license.

When everyone for the stables had disembarked, I was the only one left. The trolley driver glanced back at me in her rearview mirror. She sighed and muttered something under her breath as she edged the bus back onto the road.

It had been a few years since I had been to the park, but I could still recall the thrill I'd felt at seeing the flashing holiday lights around its gates. Dad used to take me every summer. I smiled, remembering the two of us running past the gate employees, who laughed and waved as Dad flashed our passes. Then we would shove through the turnstiles and emerge onto Santa Claus Lane, a red-and-white brick road that ran straight to Christmas "Lake," where the towering North Pole swirled from its island in the center.

The North Pole at the park was way taller than the one in the Snow Globe; it really did look like a giant barbershop pole, and the swings, attached to a gold ring, would rise until they were at the top of the pole, several stories above the ground. Around and around I would go, waving down to Dad every time I swept past.

Dad would spend every dollar in his wallet at the Reindeer Games Midway, trying to win the giant abominable snowman for me. Then I would drag him to Frosty's Freezefall. I loved to watch people drop from the platform above and free-fall 109 feet to the net below. Every summer, I would beg Dad to let me try it.

"You're not big enough," he'd always say. "You have to be fifty-four inches tall. See?" He'd point to the Frosty cutout, who had his stick hand stretched out to measure people. I never believed Dad, and I'd always go up to that stick arm, standing as straight and tall as I could but never reaching it.

I hadn't thought about that in years. By the time I was tall enough, Dad had stopped taking me to Holly Jolly Land. Maybe now that I had a job there, I'd finally get the chance to dive off the Frosty platform.

The trolley slowed as it passed the huge HAVE A HOLLY JOLLY SUMMER! welcome sign at the entrance to the park. I peered out the window to get a good look at it. The lettering was chipping away, and the waving Santa and Rudolph had graffiti sprayed across their faces. I wondered why the trolley driver had slowed down, but as we entered the parking lot I figured it out quick—right in the keister.

The trolley jolted so violently I almost hit my head on the seat in front of me. We bumped and dipped and swayed because of all the potholes. I braced myself, but even though the lot was nearly empty at this early hour, the trolley driver slammed on her brakes at the drop-off point a hundred yards from the entrance.

"This is as far as I go," she called back. "Ticket booth is straight ahead."

"Thank you," I said as I passed her.

"Mm-hmm."

I stood at the trolley stop and waited for her to roll past me. When she did, I got a clear view of the entrance. *This* was Holly Jolly Land?

There were still flashing lights around the edges of the gate. But some of the bulbs were burned out. The gate itself, once a bright holly green, was faded and spotted with rust. Tinny speakers played "A Holly Jolly Christmas" as a giant Santa statue rocked back and forth, waving.

In the distance, I could just make out the red metal tracks

of Rudolph's Wild Ride twisting and turning in the spaces between the trees. I imagined a car thundering by on the track above, spinning as it went. To the far right beyond the gates, the tiptop of Frosty's Freezefall was just visible over the treetops. I didn't think I'd like working there, but it would be fun to finally get to take a dive off the top.

"Here goes nothing," I muttered as I hurried across the lot to the gate. Where was I supposed to go, exactly? Nick Patterson hadn't told me where to meet him; would he be waiting out front? I didn't see anyone at the turnstiles—I guessed it was all automated now—so I went over toward the ramshackle ticket booth whose roof was in danger of sliding off, where I could make out the soles of large Chuck Taylors propped on the counter behind the glass. Whoever was in there would be able to help me. I wound up and down the chained-in aisles to find out.

A guy about my age belonged to the shoes, his stool leaning so far back his head and shoulders were propped up on the wall behind him. He was crossing his arms over his stomach, settling in like he was about to take a nap. His long hair fell into his face, but I thought I recognized him as the barefoot guy from the Globe unveiling.

A plastic name tag pinned at his chest read, *My name is* CHARLIE IN THE BOX*! How can I help you have a Holly Jolly day?*

I tapped on the glass.

Charlie-in-the-Box's nose twitched.

I tapped again, harder. "Um, hello?"

"Don't open until nine."

"I was wondering if you could tell me—"

"Daily admission is forty-five dollars." He rolled his head to the left so he could see around his shoes and said, "Season pass is a hundred and twenty-six bucks, a steal now that we're open daily for the summer. The pass lasts until Labor Day, when we go back to weekend hours only."

"I don't need a ticket," I said. "I'm here to work."

"You don't work here," said Charlie-in-the-Box.

"Oh, well, I'm new."

"Nice try."

"No, really, I am. Can you just let me in? I have a meeting with Mr. Patterson."

"Who?"

"Nick Patterson. The owner?"

"Crazy St. Nick?"

"Um, yes, if that's Nick Patterson. The owner of the park."

"That's him."

"Then yes!"

"Admission is forty-five dollars."

"I'm not here to visit, though!" I didn't like to do this, but it usually helped. I cleared my throat. "I'm, um, I'm the mayor's daughter?"

"Good for you, I guess," he said, rearranging himself to get more comfortable.

"Can you tell me where I can find Mr.—Crazy St. Nick?"

"Inside."

"Any idea where inside?"

"Probably he's like, you know"—he yawned and scratched under the hem of his shirt—"in his office or something."

"Okay . . . Can you tell me where his office is, exactly?"

He slowly lowered his feet from the countertop, and the stool creaked onto all four legs. He reached for something under the counter like he was moving underwater. Then he floated it through the opening at the base of the plastic partition. He leisurely leaned back again, set his feet on the counter, and rested his hands on his stomach.

"Past Frosty. If you get to the Indiana state line, you've gone way too far."

I snatched the map, made a face, and stalked off in the direction of the turnstiles.

"Can't do that," he called lazily.

I stopped and looked back. "Why not?"

"Don't have a ticket."

"But I'm here for work, not—"

He pointed to a little plaque at the top corner of the booth.

NO ADMISSION WITHOUT A TICKET
STAMPED WITH TODAY'S DATE
TODAY'S DATE IS: DECEMBER 24

The adjustable date on the sign hadn't been adjusted for five months. I sighed but went back to the booth. "Can I have a ticket . . . please?"

"Ten bucks."

"Seriously?"

"Seriously."

I reached into my pocket and pulled out what was left of my money after the trolley ride. "I only have seven."

"Seven it is, then."

"That's extortion!"

"Tell you what. If it turns out you really work here, I'll give you your money back. I'll even walkie-talkie Nick for ya," he said. "Let him know you're coming."

"Thanks *so* much." I handed over the ransom and took a ticket.

He smirked at me but then did a double take. "Wait, aren't you that chick from the Snow Globe?"

I looked down so my bangs covered my face. "Um."

"You are!" he guffawed. "You know, you got your ass handed to you by the Ferris wheel?"

"Yeah. Thanks," I said. I headed for the gate.

The music piping through the speaker crackled, and Charlie-in-the-Box's voice rang out. "It's a Holly Jolly day here at Holly Jolly Land! HEADS UP! We have a special visitor here today. You might have seen her most recent work on the SQUARE. She's the FIRST DAUGHTER of CHRISTMAS and stunt-woman extraordinaire!"

I turned to glare at him.

He gave me the thumbs-up. "If you missed her last show, stick around. Word is, she's performing HERE this summer. This is Charlie-in-the-Box, reminding you to enjoy the ride."

I stomped off, thoroughly annoyed, and pushed through the turnstile.

The park was in worse shape inside than outside. Santa Claus Lane looked shabby, with weeds growing up between the red-and-white bricks. I turned in a circle as I walked, taking it all in. Most of the storefronts were just that—fronts. Only one housed an actual store, the Holly Jolly T-shirt Shop, where you could buy neon shirts, blinking red noses, or a pair of antlers. A soft-serve ice-cream cart sat on the curb, the red-and-white-swirl umbrella about to topple the entire thing over. At the end of Santa Claus Lane, the North Pole still stood proudly on its island in the center of the lake, just as I remembered it. Well, almost; its golden knob was tarnished, and it seemed to be peeling in places.

It was nearly summer in the South, and the weather knew it. Baking in the sun, the candy-cane-striped brick path reflected the morning heat. There wasn't even a hint of a breeze. Sweat beads appeared on my forehead as I fanned myself with my map. When I went to swipe them away, I pushed against my bruise where the Ferris wheel had hit me. The pain had mellowed some, but it still thudded like a heartbeat.

When I finally looked down at my map, the words swam slightly. I squinted, trying to focus on the cartoonish drawing and ignore the headache. The Away in a Manger Petting Zoo was a new addition since the last time I was here. So was the Dreidel, Dreidel, Dreidel ride.

But where was Nick's office? I was hoping for a dot that said "Nick Patterson," but no such luck. Charlie-in-the-Box had said near Frosty, but that didn't really help much. I decided to just head that way and look around.

At the end of the lane, same as I remembered, was the wooden signpost that pointed to all the major attractions. The Reindeer Games Midway and Rudolph's Wild Ride were to the left in Holiday Land. The Babes in Toyland area, where the kiddie rides were, lay beyond the lake. To the right was Frosty's Freezefall in Winter Wonderland.

I took the path to the right of the lake—which was much smaller than I remembered . . . and green from algae. Ugh! I didn't even want to think about the germy water. My hands needed sanitizer just from imagining it. In my memories, the lake was sparkling blue and as big as the ocean, and Dad and I would be out of breath by the time we reached the end of the line for the swings. I wondered if it really had been that way or if my little-girl eyes had seen what they wanted instead of what was really there.

I had to stop and reevaluate my map as I passed the Christmas Carol-sel; I'd taken a wrong turn. I looked around for someone I could ask for directions, but this part of the park seemed deserted. Great. I doubled back to the lake and finally found the shrub-lined path to the Winter Wonderland area.

Okay, okay. If I were Nick Patterson, where would I be? I turned in a circle, taking in the Candy Mountain Confectionary, the path to the petting zoo, and the entrance to Frosty's Freezefall. As I turned, my eye caught a few people disappearing around the side of the confectionary. All of them were in uniforms.

I went around the side of the building. Sure enough, there was a dirt path that wound into some deep brush. A cardboard sign read, NO CIVILIANS. SOLDIERS ONLY.

This had to be it.

I hurried down the dirt path. It was eerily quiet in the woods once I lost sight of the back of the candy store. The path twisted and turned, and I had to take a deep breath because there was something unnerving about walking into the woods all alone. I was so spooked that for a split second I thought I saw a goat running through the brush to my left, but when I looked back there was nothing there. I shook my head and hurried forward. I didn't want to be back here alone, but this was the way all those people had gone. Right? I hadn't missed a fork in the dirt path or anything. I was just about to turn back when the woods cleared enough to reveal a low, cinder-block building. It was painted khaki green and was so covered in ivy and bushes it was nearly invisible. But the brown door was still swinging shut. I jogged to catch it before it closed.

Inside, the low drop ceilings were covered in water spots, and fluorescent lights cast a greenish glow on everything, including the brown industrial carpet that smelled like mildew. The big open space, which was like a break room, had a microwave on a stack of milk crates, a vending machine, and mismatched tables scattered throughout.

Several people sat around the room, all in different costumes. A huge guy was fast asleep on top of a table while another kid in a snowman costume threw his oversized snowball head into the air and caught it over the guy's face; several girls from my high school, in matching blue snowflake dresses, were laughing at him; a few fairies at a round table by the vending machine were painting their nails.

I didn't see Nick Patterson.

"Who are you?" said a sharp voice.

It was Riya Shah. She was in a long beige tunic, the waist tied up with a rope, carrying a shepherd's hook. Her olive skin was flawless. She would've been a convincing shepherdess if her black hair hadn't had pink tips. She was standing with Glenda, the redhead from the night of the Snow Globe. Today Glenda wore red-and-green lederhosen and elf shoes.

Glenda's turquoise eyes were taking me in from head to toe. Everyone turned to stare at me, and I had the urge to suck in my stomach and smile my biggest smile. They looked me over in that way girls do when they're trying to be intimidating—and succeeding in this case.

Fan-fruiting-tastic.

"She's the First Daughter of Christmas, remember?" Glenda said.

"Oh, ri-i-ight," said Riya. "I didn't recognize you without your tiara."

I forced the smile to stay on my face, a trick I'd learned campaigning with Dad. Just smile and nod, don't let them see that they're getting to you, and above all, keep circling back to the message.

"You ruined our Snow Globe," Riya said.

"Yes," I admitted. "I feel horrible about it." I looked around at the others. The girls in blue snowflake dresses were glaring now. "Can you tell me where—"

Riya's dark eyes narrowed. "I worked, like, all day on that thing."

"All damn day," Glenda agreed.

"Us, too," said the fairies with the nail polish.

"I'm so sorry," I said with my most humble expression. I looked past them to everyone else and said, "I didn't mean to destroy it. It was an accident."

A few of the snowflake girls shook their heads in disgust. The snowman turned away from me.

"I broke four nails." Glenda held out her hands to show me that half her turquoise nails were gone.

"Um, can you tell me where Nick is?"

Riya popped her gum and said, "Why?"

"I have to talk to him."

"Why?" she asked again, glaring at me. "Did you come with a lame-ass apology for him, too?"

"No, I—"

"Come to break something else?" a snowflake girl called.

"No, I'm—"

Riya stepped closer. "Then why?" *Pop.* "What are you doing here? Shouldn't you be, like, leading a parade or something?"

Glenda giggled.

I waited a beat, willing my hands to stop shaking. Riya popped her gum again, and I couldn't help but think of the bursting Globe every time she did it.

"I'm here to work."

"St. Nick gave *you* a job?"

"Yes, I did."

Nick Patterson stood in a doorway across the room. He took a long sip from a khaki canteen, wiped his mouth with his hand, and burped loudly. Then he shouted like a drill sergeant, "Get to your posts! The gates are opening!"

They all cleared out like someone had shouted "fire!"—Riya glaring back at me as she went. Even the guy who had been snoring on the tabletop jumped up and dashed for the exit.

Nick pointed at me with his thumb. "Come on in, honey. On the double."

Seven

NICK'S SHIRT WAS NEON YELLOW AND SHOUTED HOLLY. JOLLY. GOLLY! in trippy white letters. He sat behind an old green metal desk, hands folded, glaring at me. Was he waiting for me to say something?

"Um, good morning."

Nick swiveled his chair around to a metal storage cabinet with a combination lock. As he spun the dial, he said, "What time did I tell you to be here?"

"Eight," I said.

"What time is it now?"

"I don't— Um." I checked my phone. "Eight seventeen?"

Nick opened the cabinet and dug inside, saying, "If you are ever late to work again, you are fired."

"The trolley took longer than I thought," I explained.

Nick spun around with a vacuum-sealed bag in his hands. He

leveled a hard stare at me. "That's the last excuse you'll give me. Understood?"

I bit down on the tip of my tongue to keep from arguing. That wasn't fair at all.

Nick took my silence as assent. "Good. New business, then. Today is training day." He tossed the bag to me, and I barely caught it. "This is your park-issued uniform. You are not allowed to wear it outside the park. You may not appear on the park grounds during work hours *out* of uniform. Your entire uniform must be worn at all times on park property. You can change into or out of your park-issued uniform in the designated locker rooms. Understood?"

"Yes, sir," I said.

"Locker room and heads are down there," he said, pointing down a short hallway.

Heads?

"Leave your cell in your locker; phones are not allowed in the field."

I nodded.

"Take a look at the flow chart."

He pointed to a huge laminated poster on the wall. The top said HOLLY JOLLY LAND CHAIN OF COMMAND in bold letters. There were two lines marked OWNER. One had NICK written in, the other, LANH. Mrs. Patterson had been gone almost a year; maybe he couldn't bring himself to erase her name. Lines underneath these blanks branched down to five sections, each a different color.

"The red column is for attraction attendants, green for maintenance, yellow for concessions, and so on," Nick told me, offering me a green dry-erase marker from a Santa mug on his desk. "That empty line at the bottom of maintenance will be you."

I looked at the green section and followed the lines all the way to the bottom, where, sure enough, there was an empty line marked HELPER.

"Helper?" I asked. "In maintenance?"

Nick nodded and held the green marker out farther. "Write your name, please."

"Mr. Patterson, wouldn't—"

"Nick."

"Yes, sir. I think I would be more of an asset as a ride worker."

"Attractions are full."

"But—" I racked my brain for an idea, anything at all that would get me out of working on a maintenance crew. "I don't know anything about mechanics or engines."

"Helpers don't do mechanical work." He shook the marker at me, but I didn't take it.

"I'm great with numbers," I said. "I could work in the office, here, do your accounting or—"

"Look, honey, you're the one who said you wanted to clean up your mess."

"Sure, but I didn't mean—"

"Didn't mean what?" he said. "Didn't mean you wanted to do anything so menial?" He raised an eyebrow at me. "I need help in maintenance. You really want to clean up your mess, you'll work there. Take it or leave it."

For a split second, I considered leaving it. This place was a dump, it took forever to get out here on the trolley, and the people hated me. But I really did want to make it right; I wasn't used to being disliked around town—or responsible for a disaster. Besides, what else was I going to do all summer?

I sighed, took the marker, and wrote my name at the very bottom of the chart.

"It's imperative you follow chain of command," Nick said. "To break chain would result in anarchy, and we can't have that. If you have a problem, you go to your immediate superior, the department head. Understood?"

I followed all the green lines back up. My department head was . . .

"Calvin Sherman?" I groaned.

Nick's lips twisted off to the side, but he didn't respond. "You'll need a maintenance map," he said, opening a squeaking drawer in his desk. "This is not for civilian eyes. It has the codes so you can speak to your squadron without worrying about enemy ears. Do not give away the codes to civilians, foreign or domestic!"

The way he said it, like they were nuclear codes or something, made me laugh. "Got it."

He didn't smile; he stared at me, hard, until someone knocked on the door.

"Enter!" Nick barked.

Calvin opened the door and stuck his head in. "Nick, man, did you hear the mayor's—" He caught sight of me and stopped short, staring.

Nick waved him in. "I was about to radio you."

Calvin entered and stood at nearly perfectly rigid attention. He was wearing those ridiculous coveralls again, and his glasses were smudged. "What's going on?"

"Need you to train our new employee."

Oh, mother of kiwis both human and fruit. No. No, no, no, no!

"What?" Calvin cried. "You hired *her*?"

"That's right."

"But she . . . she—"

"She deserves a second chance," he said. "Like all of us."

Calvin sniffed and crossed his arms over his chest.

"Can't someone else train me?" I asked Nick. "Please? Maybe someone a rung or two up the chain of command from me? They might have more insight into my . . . post."

"Yeah, Nick, come on, man," Calvin said. "I don't have time to babysit the First Daughter for you this week. We've got real work to do."

"You've been given orders!" Nick barked, his eyes sharp as cut stone. "Unless you'd both like to be relieved of duty?"

Calvin fell as quiet as I did.

"That's what I thought," Nick said. "So, you will shadow your department head," he said to me. "At the end of your basic training, he will report your progress to me. If we feel you are capable, you will be an official employee."

"How long does . . . basic training take?"

"As long as it takes."

My skin crawled at the nonanswer. "What's the average?"

Nick's beard twitched. "You average?"

"No, sir, I just want to make sure I complete basic long before then."

Calvin snorted.

"Hey!" I said. I can't believe I used to think that snort was endearing.

"*If* Calvin's report is poor, you will repeat training until you are up to the standard we expect here at Holly Jolly Land," Nick continued. "Once you are an official park employee, you will receive your name tag. Until then, you are Santa's Candidate Helper."

I didn't even get to use my name? What the heck?

"I assume training is paid?" I said.

Nick laughed a deep, rich laugh that came from his gut, the kind you couldn't fake or stifle. "Brass tacks! Just like your father!" He wiped his eyes. "You're on the clock, honey, don't worry. Now get out of here, both of you."

"I'll wait outside for you to change," Calvin muttered. He marched out of the room.

Nick was already looking at some paperwork.

"But—"

"I said you're dismissed!" he growled. "Get to work."

I brushed past Calvin without a glance on my way to the dressing room. Inside, I found an empty locker to use and tore open the sealed bag, hoping for something cute like the lederhosen elf outfit Glenda wore, or even one of those blue snowflake dresses.

As I held up my uniform, my heart sank.

"You have got to be kidding me."

Khaki-green coveralls. Khaki-green utility belt. Khaki-green tank top to wear underneath. There was nothing festive about this! No berry red or holly green. Just ugly khaki green on top of uglier khaki green.

Plus, Calvin and I were going to match.

I drew the line at the heavy work boots. I shoved them back into the bag; I'd wear my flip-flops.

I took a deep breath and looked at myself in one of the

mirrors. I looked ridiculous. And fluffy. Nothing about this getup was flattering. In the right outfit, my curves were out of control. In this stiff, canvas material, all my curves melted together to make a big lump of khaki ick. It didn't help that the jumpsuit was made for someone much taller than me. I had to roll up the sleeves and the cuffs. The belt was heavy and bunched up all the extra fabric at my waist.

I went out, self-consciously pulling on my collar; I was already hot in this thing. Calvin was waiting for me by the door, and as soon as he saw me, he took off without a word. It was a vast improvement over him speaking, so I enjoyed the silence while it lasted.

He power walked all the way back up the dirt path to the park. I had to practically jog to keep up with him. As we crossed the bridge connecting Winter Wonderland to Babes in Toyland, he finally spoke.

"So. Number-one thing you need to know to work here?" He went around the side of a building to a door marked MAINTENANCE. "Safety always comes first. A safe park is a happy park."

I stifled a laugh. After the shoddy work he'd done on the Snow Globe, he had the nerve to talk to me about safety?

"What, you think that's funny?" Calvin demanded.

"No, it's—"

"See, that's the problem hiring someone like you, Darby."

"Someone like me?"

"Yeah, somebody who doesn't really care." He took a ring of keys off his tool belt and flipped through them until he found the one he was looking for and shoved it in the lock. "Someone kind of spoiled."

"I am not spoiled!" I cried. "You don't know anything about me."

"Yeah? I know how you got that scar," he said, pointing to the back of my hand. "And I know you hate grape Skittles."

A weird mix of feelings churned in my stomach: I was annoyed that he thought he knew me just because he knew some trivial things like junk-food preferences, but also kind of touched he remembered the time I cut my hand on the slide in fourth grade. I'd cried and cried, but he'd walked with me to the school nurse and told me stupid jokes while she cleaned me up.

"Just because you know things about me from back then doesn't mean you know me now," I argued.

He pushed his glasses up his nose. "I'm pretty sure I do."

I was pretty sure I'd never hated anyone so much in my entire life. "Whatever. I'm here to help, so—"

"Like you helped the other night? If you had listened to me and kept Roy out of the Snow Globe, none of the rest would have happened."

People who always thought they were right had to be kowtowed to. That's what I learned from taking minutes at many, many, many town hall meetings. Whenever old Mr. Varney stood up to complain about taxes, Dad smiled and nodded and said things like, "Excellent point, Vern. I'll make sure we look into it."

He never did, but it kept old Mr. Varney from going on and on. So, I pushed a smile onto my face and told Calvin what he wanted to hear. "Fine. Safe park equals happy park. I'll make sure to remember it. What else do I need to know?"

His forehead knotted. "Why are you making that face?"

"Just because *you* don't know how to be friendly doesn't mean I don't."

He shoved open the maintenance closet door, and smells of bleach and ammonia wafted out. "I know how to be friendly."

"Yeah?" I said. "That why you've been a jerk to me for months? Because you're so friendly?"

His eyes flashed behind his lenses. "Maybe you're too friendly, ever think of that?"

"What does that even mean?" I demanded. "It's a crime to be nice to people now? That doesn't make any sense."

"No?"

"No!" I said. "What are you—" I pinched the bridge of my nose and tried not to scream. "You know what? How about you train me and we'll leave it at that?"

"Fine." He leaned into the maintenance closet and pulled out a purple janitor cart packed with cleaning supplies, including a broom and dustpan, a covered garbage can, and two buckets of soapy water, each with a mop. He pulled a dripping purple-handled mop out of one bucket. "This is the M-O-P."

"I beat you in the spelling bee in second grade," I snapped. "It's a mop, I get it."

Calvin shook his head. "This isn't just a mop. The regular mops have red handles like your other one. This one is the M-O-P—the Mop of Puke."

He pushed the handle of the mop toward me, but I quickly leaned to the side to avoid touching it. It fell to the ground. "That's disgusting!"

Calvin shrugged. "That's the job."

"Nick told me I would be working maintenance!"

"You will be. You're a helper, which means you *help* by cleaning up messes around the entire park. You can start in Holiday Land, but make sure you circle through Babes in Toyland every hour or so. Little kids make the biggest messes."

"You have got to be kidding me."

"That's the job, Darby." He hurried on before I could protest anymore. "Take a look at your tool belt. Everything you'll need is on there, including this." He pointed to his own belt, to a purple sparkly walkie-talkie that didn't match anything else. "This is the only form of communication allowed on park premises. If you need to talk to someone, you radio. Maintenance is on frequency one. Don't bother me unless it's life or death. I'm busy today."

"I thought you were training me today."

Calvin sized me up. "Do you really need me to train you to mop? Figures you'd expect someone to hold your hand."

"No!" I said, glancing at his hands. He had long fingers, and even though they were covered in grease at the moment, I could tell that he'd recently clipped his fingernails. "I just thought—"

"When you radio someone, use your full title. And don't cuss on the radio—the parents can hear you, and they get mad about it. And say *over*."

"Say what?"

"Like this." Calvin took his walkie-talkie from his belt. He stared at me as he said into it, "Head Helper here. Anyone need the M-O-P today? Call Santa's Candidate Helper. She starts basic training today. Over."

Someone responded at once. "Attendant Jamarcus to Head Helper: What's the Candidate Helper's frequency? Over."

Calvin was still staring at me, and a self-satisfied little smirk lifted the corners of his mouth. I had to look away. "One, Attendant Jamarcus. Over."

A split second later, my walkie-talkie screeched, and Jamarcus said, "Rudolph's Wild Ride to Santa's Candidate Helper: Need you to check in once an hour, please. We get a lot of six-two-fours over here. Over."

"What's a six-two-four?" I asked Calvin.

He grinned, the first real smile I'd seen on his face since last December. It made his eyes squinty behind his glasses. "You have a list of codes on the back of your maintenance map."

I took my map from my belt and flipped it to the back. He was right. There were dozens of codes. I skimmed the list until I found it. *6-2-4: Puddle of Puke.*

And beneath that? *6-2-5: Puddle of Pee. 6-2-6: Pile of—*

My stomach churned as I looked up at Calvin. "Seriously?"

The morning sun now whited out his glasses, so I couldn't see his eyes.

"Tell me!" I demanded.

Calvin laughed. "Yep, looks like you've got plenty of training to do. I'll come check on you in a few hours."

When I didn't move, he picked up the M-O-P from the ground and shoved it into my hand. I could practically feel the germs traveling from the handle to my palm. I wondered if there was any hand sanitizer in my tool belt.

"You are a total—"

"Careful. If you want to finish basic training ahead of the curve, you better get to mopping."

I had never been so hot in my entire life. Or miserable. Or sweaty. Or filthy. My first puke encounter (excuse me, my first 6-2-4) was at the Ferris wheel at the end of the Reindeer Games Midway. I'd had to run to the nearest bush and nearly gagged up my own 6-2-4.

The ride-attendant guys had cracked up. Stephan Gill was one of them. We'd had geometry together last semester. You'd think he'd be nicer to me since I'd let him copy my homework once or twice.

"That's been there since yesterday afternoon, but we didn't have anyone working cleanup yesterday, so we left it. Glad you're here today, Darby. It was getting rank."

Since. Yesterday. Afternoon. What was it about boys that they'd rather look at—and smell—vomit for an entire day than clean it up themselves? Gross.

I wheeled my cart down the midway past some carnival-type rides. The ring-around-the-antler toss had a small crowd, and there were a few people trying to shoot balloons off a wall to win the same old stuffed abominable snowman dolls my dad tried to win me when I was a kid. The games workers were dressed in straw hats and bowties like at an old-timey fair. Most of them were sitting on the counters, fanning themselves with maps and looking bored. Once they recognized me, though, they perked right up.

"There goes the First Daughter of Christmas," called a kid I didn't know; he must have gone to Liberty County High.

Hailey Barnes hollered at me as I passed, "I worked on those trees for weeks, *Darby*."

"I'm really sor—"

"Save it."

"But I—"

"No one wants you here."

Tell me something I don't know.

I stared straight ahead and hurried through the midway. I got lost in the crowd coming off the bumper sleighs and tried not to cry.

"Don't listen to them," a somber voice boomed from speakers behind me.

I turned around and saw the blond girl from the Snow Globe leaning into the microphone at the Dreidel, Dreidel, Dreidel spinning-cups ride across the midway. She had a book in her hands.

"They're just bitter crybabies!"

"Screw you, *Jane*!" shouted Hailey.

Jane gave her the finger and went back to reading.

I pushed the M-O-P over to her. The DREIDEL, DREIDEL, DREIDEL sign overhead was blue and white with a gold menorah painted in the middle and spinning dreidels on each end. The ride itself was basically a Tilt-a-Whirl, the fair ride with the spinning cups and wavy floor that spun like a record. A punk-rock version of "Sleigh Ride" was blasting at eardrum-piercing volume from speakers overhead. The one family on the ride looked a little green, like they'd been spinning a long time. I had the feeling I would be cleaning here a lot.

The girl—Jane—didn't look up from her book, *A Moveable Feast*.

"Um, thanks," I said.

"Yeah, dude."

"Is that any good?"

She shrugged and turned the page. "It'll do."

Her long hair was a tangled mess, a few tiny braids running here and there through it. She was barefoot, and her peasant shirt was too short at the wrists.

"Everyone here hates me," I said.

"Yep. We worked hard on that dumb thing." She turned a page. "You broke our toy and then showed up in our backyard to play. What did you expect?"

"I'm sorry."

She cut her eyes at me. Up close, they were a kaleidoscope of colors. "Yeah, well, the North Pole was kind of flimsy, I guess. Still. Our toy."

"I understand," I said. "I'm trying to make it right."

She put her book down, stood up, leaned into her microphone, and cried, "Okay, losers, ride's over! Stop spinning your dreidel—Hey! That means you, dude in the ugly polo! Yes, you, don't look around, you're the only dude in a polo!"

The man was about Dad's age, and he was smiling in an embarrassed sort of way while his kids laughed at his pink-and-blue checks.

"Wait for your car to come to a complete stop before you

unbuckle," she shouted. She pulled on a lever by the microphone and the ride slowed to a crawl. "Do not, I repeat, DO NOT try to exit while the dreidel is still spinning or you will die a painful death!"

She turned to me. "Darby? Right?"

I nodded.

"Holly Jolly rule number one, Darby: no good deed goes unpunished."

I wasn't sure if she was messing with me or not. "What's rule number two?"

She shook her head. "Can't tell you. Gotta earn it."

I took the back path away from the dreidels so I could avoid the jeers from the midway workers. A footbridge that ran to several of the ride exits cut a path over the shallow edge of Christmas Lake. I hoped it came out in Babes in Toyland or somewhere far from Hailey Barnes and her angry glare.

Halfway across the bridge, I pushed my cart to a stop. I needed a minute to catch my breath. And swallow the lump in my throat. I went over to the wooden railing and peered down at the algae-covered lake. Was this really how my summer was going to go?

I leaned against the rail, completely drained. The railing leaned with me, bowing under my weight. It leaned so far I nearly fell into the lake.

"Whoa!" I said, hopping back. The last thing I needed today was to fall into that water. I grabbed my cart and hurried off, suddenly unsure just how safe the wooden slats under my feet were. This place was seriously falling apart!

It turned out not just 6-2-4 made my stomach churn. There were spills and soggy popcorn and bird poop to attend to. From the looks of the park, no one had mopped since last year. Not to mention the litter I was constantly sweeping up. Or the messy bathrooms, which I was supposed to check in on once an hour. From what I could piece together, there was no other janitor—excuse me, *helper*—for the entire park, just an after-hours cleaning crew that came a few times a week. I was literally up to my elbows in filth.

By the time I got to the Christmas Carol-sel, the sun was straight up in the sky and the park was crowded with tourists. The guy working the ride saw me coming and pointed toward a blue spot outside the exit gate. A little girl with blue slushy all over her front was crying nearby as her mom tried to clean her up with a tissue. That explained the electric-blue puddle.

Before today, "The Twelve Days of Christmas" was one of my favorite carols. But the high-pitched children's version blasting from the carousel was grating on my nerves. I had heard the entire song seven times already, and if this blue puke didn't come up soon, I was pretty sure I would be destined to spend the rest of eternity in Carol-sel Hell with twelve puddles of puke, eleven M-O-Ps, and a partridge in a pear tree.

I squeezed the M-O-P through the ringer again and tried one last time. I scrubbed that floor so hard blisters popped up on my palms where I was gripping the handle. The peppermint swirl tiles would forever be stained blue if I didn't get this stuff up, quick, but it was so hard! I stopped mopping and wiped my arm across my face, accidentally pushing against my goose egg. Between the smells, the sights, the pain in my head, and the heat, everything was getting fuzzy around the edges.

I dunked the M-O-P into the bucket, spun it around, and found myself face-to-face with Calvin. He looked me over, leaned to the side to glance at the puddle, and raised an eyebrow.

I looked back at the blue ground. "It's the best I can do—"

"First of all, you always need to put up the caution sign while you're working, Darby," he said.

"What sign? You didn't tell me—"

Calvin reached around me for a tall CAUTION: WET SURFACE sign attached to the bucket cart. He unhooked it and stood it up next to the spill. "I didn't think I had to break it down into baby steps for you."

I watched him study the blue spot. "Did you try bleach on that?"

I held up my hands. "Does it look like I have any bleach on me?"

He made his "bah humbug" face, took hold of my tool belt, and pulled me toward him.

"Excuse me!" I cried, shoving his chest. "What do you think you're doing?"

He smelled like sweaty puke. Oh, wait, that was probably me.

He gave me a steely look as he ripped open one of the Velcro pouches on my belt. While holding my gaze he pulled a hotel-sized shampoo bottle out and held it up. "Undiluted bleach."

I snatched it from him. "You could have told me about it sooner."

"My bad. Do you know what to do with it?"

I bit back a retort and squirted some directly onto the ground. I knew plenty about bleach—I'd been doing laundry for years. Sure enough, everywhere the bleach landed the blue disappeared. I hated that he was right, and I hated that he was smirking, and

I *really* hated that now he was going to stand there and watch me mop.

I swished the M-O-P across the stain as fast as I could. When I finished, I turned around and caught him checking out my coveralls.

"Yeah, I know, my uniform is dirty. That's what happens when you mop up bodily fluids all day." I choked on the last words. The day was catching up to me, and I shook my head. How was I going to do this all summer? "I can't believe I took this stupid job," I muttered.

Calvin sighed. "Then why are you here?"

Like I would tell *him* about Marianne Walker and her claim that I was in the way at the courthouse. "Why do you care?"

His eyes narrowed. "Clean your mops in the slop sink, dump the trash, empty the buckets, then you can go for the day. Be back at eleven tomorrow."

"Gee, thanks."

I headed toward the maintenance closet before he could retort. It had been the worst day of my life, and I had to come back and do it again tomorrow? Not going to happen. I pinched the bridge of my nose, remembered what my hands had been touching all day, and yanked them away. I had to talk to Dad; once he heard how awful this place was, he'd let me come back to the courthouse.

"Hey, aren't you forgetting something?" he called.

"What?" I snapped.

"Sign."

I stomped back over to him and grabbed the yellow sign off the ground. Then with as much dignity as I could muster, I turned on my flip-flopped heel and strode off, pushing the M-O-P and bucket. I had never hated someone so much in my entire life.

"Hey!" Calvin called after me.

"What?" I growled, spinning back around. He was watching me with his stupid Secret-Service Grinch face.

"Welcome to Holly Jolly Land."

Eight

THE SAME DARK-HAIRED TROLLEY DRIVER FROM that morning sat behind the wheel, thumbing through her phone. She wasn't pleased to see me; it looked like she was taking a break out in the parking lot where no one would bother her. There wasn't anyone in line at the Holly Jolly Land stop, and I finally had to knock on the door to get her to open up.

"Where you headed?" she asked as I swiped my pass.

"Back to town."

She wrinkled her nose. "What's that smell?"

I held up a plastic bag I'd gotten from the office. "My uniform."

"You work here?" she asked. "That mean you're going to be riding out here every day?"

I nodded.

"Great," she grumbled. She pulled the doors closed and cranked the trolley up. "Take a seat near the back and crack a window.

I don't want my trolley smelling like a toilet." She turned the air vents toward her face.

I was too exhausted to care. My feet were killing me, and I had major blisters where the thongs of my flip-flops fit between my toes. My back and shoulders hurt from mopping, and my neck was sore. The goose egg on my forehead was throbbing, but it wasn't nearly as bad as the bruise on my ribs.

I leaned against the window and let the hot air blow my hair off my face. I would have fallen asleep if the ride hadn't been so bumpy.

I decided to break the seal and call Roy. I knew it had only been a day and a half, but I needed to talk to someone who would care that I'd had a miserable day. I didn't really expect him to answer. But when he did, he sounded so happy, I felt instantly better.

"How's camp?" I asked.

"So awesome, Darby. All my friends are here. It's like I never left."

"Oh, that's—that's great." I stared out the window at the rolling hills. We were passing the Elams' place, the one with the red barn and all the quarter horses in the pasture.

"I wish you were here, too," he said. "Then it would be perfect."

My insides turned to banana mush. "I wish I were there, too." I sniffed back tears. "So much."

"What's wrong?"

I didn't want to complain, not when he was saying romantic things. "I just miss you."

"Yeah, I know what you mean."

"August is so far away."

He hesitated. "I might come home for the Fourth of July."

"Really?" That wasn't so bad, just a month away.

"Pretty sure."

He was coming home to see me. Some of the tiredness from the day lifted off my shoulders like birds taking flight. "That would be—"

"Hey, JACKSON!" he shouted away from the phone, but it still made my ear hurt. "No, man, hold up, I'm coming!" He laughed. "Shut up, it's not like that. Hey, Darby?" he said back into the phone. "I gotta go."

"Oh, yeah, okay."

"I'll text you, okay?"

"Okay. Have a great—"

He was already gone.

I chose a playlist and let Boyz II Men croon in my ears the rest of the ride home. This thing with Roy was going to be harder than I'd imagined. I knew there would be days we wouldn't talk at all, or not very long, like today. I'd expected the deep longing to sit deep inside me, but I didn't expect it to feel like indigestion.

I tried to convince myself that the Fourth of July wasn't so far off.

At least it was a fantastic time for him to come home. That was the weekend the town kicked off Christmas in July. There was the parade, and the concert in the square, and everyone who came home would hang at Holiday Beach at night . . .

I must have dozed off, because the next thing I knew, I was back at the town depot and the driver was hollering at me from her seat up front.

I took an earbud out. "What?"

"Isn't this your stop?"

"Oh. Yes, thank you."

She shook her head and turned back to the front. As I passed, I said, "See you tomorrow."

"I'll be counting the hours."

Since when were people so rude?

I practically crawled the five blocks home. I wanted to collapse in my bed and sleep for a million years even though it was only three in the afternoon, but I was supposed to meet Dad for dinner at the Holiday Diner. Besides, at that point, I could smell myself. Yuck. So I soaked in a bath that was half Epsom salt. Who knew mopping all day would be so strenuous? Maybe it was all the walking; I'd probably crossed the park twenty times. Not that it was that big. In my memory, it had been huge, each land a million miles away from the next.

I had to talk to Dad. Maybe I could convince him to let me come back to the courthouse. If Marianne Walker was as big city as she seemed, his day had probably been a nightmare, too. I could only imagine how awful it must have been for him to go to that Western Kentucky Parkway exit meeting with the state highway commission. Marianne was out of her mind; the last time Dad had tried to get an exit off the parkway, they'd laughed him out the door. Christmas was too far off the highway to deserve its own exit, they'd said. Besides, the Liberty exit just ten miles down wasn't *that* far out of the way.

If I knew Dad, he would be as ready for me to come back to the courthouse as I was. Marianne could stay and help with the investors, that would be fine. But she didn't know anything about small-town politics, much less anything about our town. Christmas wasn't the kind of place that would jump on some bandwagon for excessive growth or allow some big conglomerate to come in and capitalize on what the people here had worked so hard to build from the ground up. I knew it, and Dad knew it. He needed me back by his side so Marianne Walker wouldn't mess up everything.

This negotiation with Dad would be as smooth as Kentucky silk pie.

The diner was again packed with tourists. I wound my way up to the Formica bar and grabbed the two stools on the end. Mr. Grant didn't see me as he went up and down the counter refilling drinks and dropping burgers in front of customers. It was just as well; I couldn't decide between corn puppies or a Hot Brown. As I scanned my choices, I noticed the menus were brand-new. They were the same layout as before, but they were crisp and fresh off a laminator. And the prices seemed a bit higher.

Dad came in a few minutes later. He was beaming as he made his way to me. He put his briefcase on the counter and loosened his bright-blue tie as he sat down. "How was your day, Moonpie?"

"It was—" I began, but he was scanning the menu, whistling.

Why was he whistling?

"What's going on?" I asked.

Mr. Grant hurried over then. "Hello, Mayor. Usual?"

"With lemonade tonight," Dad said.

"Darby?"

"Hot Brown and an Ale-8."

He hurried to the window to place our order. "Peacher burger and a Hot Brown!"

He brought our drinks back, but he didn't bring my usual swizzle straw with my Ale-8. Before I could remind him, he was gone again.

"I wonder if he's out of my special straws?" I asked. "He seems preoccupied, doesn't he? Dad? Dad!"

"Hmm?"

He was staring at the counter, lost in thought, but the deep crease between his eyebrows wasn't there; he was planning, not worrying. What had happened today?

"Sorry, Darby, what?"

"Nothing." I swigged my drink and watched him from the corner of my eye. "How was your day?"

"Good!"

"Good?"

"Great, actually. Turns out, Ms. Walker is much more of an asset than I'd predicted."

"Really."

He beamed. "We got the exit!"

I nearly dropped my drink. "Whaaa! How?"

"Marianne knows three of the people on the board. In fact, two of them owed her because she got them their jobs as a thank-you for campaign contributions. It was the easiest negotiation I've ever done."

"Really."

"They're going to submit the proposal for approval later this month, with construction slated to start this fall. This time next year, we'll have an exit."

"That's great," I mumbled. I forced a smile. "Great."

"I think this is really going to work out well." He stirred his straw around his glass until a cloud of sugar and lemon pulp made a whirlpool around the edges. "And you! You didn't have to sit through boring meetings all day. Working on a roller coaster must have been like a breath of fresh air after all these years sitting in the stuffy old courthouse."

"Well, actually . . ." I said as he smiled at me without a trace of concern. "Mr. Patterson assigned me to the maintenance crew."

He laughed. "What do you know about maintaining a park?"

"Not much."

"Do I need to give him a call?" he asked, snapping into mayor mode. "Pull some strings and get you on a ride? Maybe the North Pole swings? You used to love those when you were a kid."

"No, that's not—"

"It's no trouble," he said. "I have to update him on the Snow Globe anyway. Night Sky Tents says it will take them a month to manufacture another globe bubble. We'll have to unveil the new set after the Fourth of July."

A month? Add it to the list of ways I'd ruined the summer season.

"Why don't I just mention to Mr. Patterson that you'd rather be working on a ride or something? After all, you're the First Daugh—"

"No, please don't," I said firmly.

The last thing I needed was to give the kids at the park *another* reason to be angry. If someone got bumped off their ride just so I could have an easier job, they'd hate me even more than they already did. Besides, I didn't want a better job at the park. I wanted my job at the courthouse. But apparently Marianne Walker had secured her position with Dad. I was out.

Mr. Grant brought our dinner over, and this time he stayed to talk.

"Like the new shirts, Mayor?" He motioned to the front of his hunter-green T-shirt, where there was a white illustration of the outside of the diner. He turned, and across the back in white letters, it read:

HOLIDAY DINER
Christmas Cheer All the Year

"Catchy," I said.

"Twenty bucks apiece," Mr. Grant said. "Got bumper stickers, too. They've literally been selling faster than my hotcakes today."

"Really?" Dad said.

"Sure. Folks are snapping them up. I've had a lot of people wanting to know if I ever thought of selling online."

"T-shirts?" I asked.

"And the stickers and our maple syrup."

Dad and I shared a look. Mr. Grant used Aunt Jemima syrup. He seemed to guess what we were thinking because he added, "Started making my own. It's got peppermint extract in it to give it that Christmasy flavor. Bottling it in mason jars. I just sold a case to a couple from Ohio!"

"That's great, John," Dad said.

"Who knows?" Mr. Grant went on. He rubbed his walrus whiskers. "Maybe I'll franchise. Holiday Diners from here to California. I could make a fortune."

First the price increases on the menu, and now franchise talk? Maybe Marianne Walker was onto something. Maybe people in town really would jump at opportunities from investors.

Speaking of Marianne Walker, Dad started in about her just then, and I felt nauseated. So what if she was right about the parkway exit? Okay, and maybe even about the investors? That didn't mean she was right about my not working at the courthouse all summer. Right? I tucked in to my cheesy open-faced sandwich and tried to drown him out by listening to the clinking of plates and the laughter of families in the booths behind us. The hairs on the back of my neck stood up, though, when I thought I heard a nearby table of out-of-towners whispering about me.

"It is! It's the girl from the Globe! She's with the mayor!"

"You should say something. She needs a good talking-to."

Great. Even the tourists recognized me. I put my knife and fork down; I couldn't eat when I had a lump in my throat.

Mr. Grant came to top up our drinks. When he left, Dad turned to me with a huge smile that faded as he searched my face.

"Is everything okay?"

"People are staring at me," I mumbled.

Dad glanced around. "Who? No one is staring."

"Not when *you're* looking. This is torture. They're all mad at me about the Globe."

Dad frowned. "They'll get over it. Besides, now with news about the new exit, well, that will help ease any bad feelings."

The new exit. That Marianne Walker helped Dad get.

"Yeah, maybe."

"And you out at Holly Jolly Land, well . . . being out of the public eye will probably help, too. I think Marianne was right to suggest it."

"Great."

"Don't you like the park?"

I shrugged.

"You loved it as a kid."

"I remember." Which reminded me. "Hey, Dad? Was it kind of dirty back then? Like, was the lake full of algae? Were the rides pretty run-down?"

"No, not that I recall."

"Well, it is now." I thought about the broken front gate, and how most of the plantings were brown and dying. "It's sad, actually."

Dad frowned. "I had been hoping the Snow Globe advertisement would give Nick's place a boost. I hadn't realized he was struggling with the upkeep. I guess she would have been the one to take care of those sorts of things."

"His wife?" I remembered her. She was a Vietnamese woman with a wide smile. When she laughed, her black-and-silver bob bounced around her shoulders. I felt a twinge of sadness for Nick Patterson as I remembered how he was before she died. He was strange back then, sure, with his crazy clothes and penchant for treating everyone around him like soldiers, but she kept him reined in. And happy. They were always laughing. "I didn't realize she was the one who ran the place."

"Well, they were a team, but Mrs. Patterson kept everything in line, starting with Nick." Dad's smile faded. "I guess Mr. Patterson doesn't have anyone to help him keep the place going anymore."

"That explains a lot," I muttered.

Dad nodded and dipped some fries in ketchup. "Be kind to Mr. Patterson. He's a nice man. Different, but his family has been in Christmas for several generations."

"I will." I suddenly felt sorry for Nick. Maybe there was something I could do to make the park better. Maybe I could offer to—

"And you'll let me know if the work is too hard? I'm sure if I just mentioned it to Mr. Patterson, you could work a different—"

"No. It's fine."

He searched my face, and I had to look away.

"Is there anything else going on?" he asked.

"Nope." I couldn't ask him now. Not when everything seemed to be going so well for him. I plastered on a wide smile. "Everything's great."

He knew my campaign face as well as I knew his. "Is it Roy? He'll call once he gets settled in at camp."

"No, it's not—I talked to Roy earlier."

"Already?" Dad's eyebrows shot up into his blond hair. "Are you two going together now?"

Going together? Fathers.

"It's not like that."

"Then what's wrong?"

I took a breath. "It's just that I had a really hard—"

"There you are, Mayor!"

Marianne was behind us, her black glasses slipping halfway down her sweaty nose. "You have a meeting with the Whitman Group on Sunday afternoon."

Dad grinned. "That was fast. I can't believe you got that worked out!"

I gasped. "You scheduled a Sunday meeting? Dad!"

My father never worked on Sundays—not officially. He liked to spend a few hours every Sunday morning at his desk, catching up after we made a rushed trip to the early service at church, but he never scheduled meetings or did public appearances. He said if God got a break, so did he.

"Just this once," he said. "Marianne thought it would be a good idea for me to meet with them as soon as possible."

"Why the rush?" I asked, pointedly not looking at Marianne.

"Because the town council is meeting with the tourism board the following Friday," Marianne said. "The more information and time your father has to prepare for the tourism board meeting, the better."

The tourism board met monthly to discuss upcoming events, talk logistics and marketing, and listen to proposals for new ventures. How fast was Marianne moving this thing forward if she wanted Dad to have a proposal ready next week? And why did she have to schedule a Sunday meeting with the Whitman Group? I couldn't even go along; I had to work Sunday!

Dad grinned at my baffled expression. "Isn't she a gem?"

I nodded and swiveled my stool back to my Hot Brown. "Yeah. Definitely."

"Speaking of gems," Marianne said. She squeezed between me and Dad and thrust her phone at him. "I got a doozy of a tip this afternoon from a friend at Whitman. One of their primary interests when meeting with you is to get an idea of zoning restrictions."

"Zoning for what?" Dad asked. He took his reading glasses out of his shirt pocket and squinted at the screen. I accidentally on purpose knocked Marianne's bony arm as I leaned over to read along with Dad.

"They want to build a *mall*?" I shrieked.

"Shh!" Marianne skimmed the diner. She was so tall, she barely had to turn her head to see the entire place. "There are ears open all over. Hearth and Home representatives are at the table behind you."

I looked back. The investors stuck out with their dark blazers and sleek hair, the same way Marianne did. Outsiders looked so starched. The collar of Marianne's crisp blue shirt was as stiff as if she'd just gotten it from the cleaners. Everything about her was sharp edges.

"They didn't hear me," I muttered.

"Marianne is right," Dad said. He donned his head at the table behind us. "You never know who's listening."

Tears pricked the backs of my eyes. Marianne was right? Marianne was a gem? I didn't have a chance in Christmas of getting back into the courthouse for the summer now. Thanks to her, I was stuck mopping up messes while Calvin Sherman stared me down all summer.

"You brainstorm a list of questions you foresee the board of tourism having," the *gem* said to Dad. "I'll check in with the County Commissioner's Office and work on a zoning report. See you first thing in the morning. Bye, Darby!"

Dad smiled as she walked away. "Isn't she something?"

"She's something all right," I muttered.

"What'd you say, Moonpie?"

I chased my Hot Brown with the last drops of Ale-8 so I'd have an excuse not to answer.

Nine

"IF YOU ARE STUCK, KEEP YOUR FOOT ON THE *pedal, turn the wheel all the way to the left, then all the way to the right."*

"If you are stuck, keep your foot on the pedal, turn the wheel all the way to the left, then all the way to the right."

"If you are stuck . . ."

I absolutely hated cleaning at the Bumper Sleighs. The line was always long because only nine of the fourteen cars worked, the entire place smelled like gas fumes amplified by a thousand because of the ninety-degree weather, and, worst of all, Glenda worked the bumper cars.

Her voice sounded nasally even over the loudspeakers. And all she said, over and over and over and *over* was—

"Ifyouarestuckkeepyourfootonthepedalturnthewheelallthewaytotheleftthenallthewaytotheright."

She glared at me the entire time I was cleaning.

I ignored her and kept my head down. Especially since, today, to make things extra fun for me, Riya was there, too, on her break. She'd brought Glenda a granola bar to snack on between bursts of yelling into the microphone. She was using her shepherd hook to pull out cars that were jammed in the corners of the track. And she was glaring at me, too.

I'd been working at Holly Jolly Land for nearly a week, and by Sunday I was exhausted. Who knew sweeping and mopping could be such a workout? Plus, now that Dr. Hoey had officially declared me concussion-free on my recheck, Calvin had added to my workload; I was also in charge of wiping down all the railings, doors, and metal surfaces around the park. Degreasing and de-germing, he called it. I called it torture, and he glared at me. He was always glaring at me, and telling me every little thing I did wrong, and reminding me to use bleach, and asking if I was following safety procedures, and ordering me all over the park to clean up one mess after another. For someone who hadn't talked to me since New Year's Eve, he sure was making up for it now. The only thing he hadn't told me was how hot metal is to the touch under a blazing sun on a ninety-degree day. And that's the one thing I wished he had said to me this week, because I didn't know until I'd burned the feeling out of my fingers.

Ninety degrees, and it was only June. I couldn't imagine what July was going to be like. I'd sweated off about five pounds in my heavy coveralls since my first day. I'd figured out a few things, though. Like, since I wore the tank top underneath, I could tie the arms of my coveralls around my waist and wear them like huge pants. It kept me cool, but I was getting bronze shoulders while my legs stayed pasty. I'd figured out that most of Winter Wonderland was shady, so I cleaned that side of the park as soon as I got to work in the afternoons. I spent the slightly cooler evenings in the wide-open sunny parts of Babes in Toyland and Santa Claus Lane.

Loath as I was to hang up my flip-flops, I'd also started wearing sneakers to work. I hated the way my feet felt trapped, and I really, really hated the feel of socks, but at least my toes weren't pruney from puddles anymore. It was slightly better for my toes to be smooshed inside shoes than covered in blisters and spatter from the M-O-P bucket, I had to admit.

As I swished my purple-handled friend over a stubborn grease stain from somebody's spilled French fries, I wondered if Roy had texted me back. I'd texted late last night on the trolley ride home from work, but he hadn't answered. He had probably been at a campfire sing-along or hanging out with all his friends in the woods or something. Sometimes, on the trolley, I dreamed about asking the driver to keep going past the gates of the park and heading straight for Indianapolis, where his camp was.

"Santa's Candidate Helper," Glenda screeched into the microphone. "You missed a spot."

She pointed to an imaginary speck to my left. Riya laughed.

I swished the M-O-P in the vicinity she was pointing, dunked it back into the bucket, and wheeled past them with as much dignity as I could muster.

Around seven, while I was wiping down the railings of Santa's Scrambler, Nick Patterson nearly careened into me in his bright-red golf cart.

"Whoa," he said as he braked. "Easy, girl."

I was going to retort when he reached out and patted his cart. "Gotta work on that landing with Blitzen here."

He pushed his purple star-shaped sunglasses onto his forehead and stared at me. "You're still here."

"Yes."

"Have to admit, didn't think you'd last a day."

"Why?"

"You're soft."

Last week, he'd called me sturdy. I wondered which was more of a compliment. Or, in his case, which was more of an insult.

"Guess I should've realized you'd stick," he went on. "Guilt's a good motivator."

"I'm not here because of guilt," I said. "I'm here to make up for the—"

"Disaster."

I sighed. I didn't need to be reminded of the catastrophe that had brought me out here to work in the first place. Like I could have forgotten if I wanted to. Even in my greasy coveralls, random people came up to me while I was mopping to tell me I'd ruined their lives. One woman followed me across the park, complaining she had a miniature globe for every year all the way back to 1985, and now, thanks to me, her collection was ruined.

"Mr. Patterson—"

"Nick."

"I'm sorry I broke the Globe," I said for the twenty-seven thousandth time. "I know how much it meant to you and everyone who works here."

"Any sign of the enemy?" Nick asked abruptly.

"The enemy?" I looked around and saw a few happy-looking families strolling here and there. Attendance seemed light today.

His eyes were slightly unfocused as he looked me over. "They're coming. Be ready."

Before I could respond he pushed his sunglasses back into place, hit the gas, and guided Blitzen into a U-turn in front of a group of startled stroller moms. They leaned forward to shield their children, who were in no real danger.

"You can't save them!" Nick shouted as he drove off. "There's no saving any of us now! We're surrounded!"

The moms huddled together, probably to discuss the crazy owner of the park. I went back to daydreaming about Roy.

At closing time, "The Little Drummer Boy" playing across the park screeched to a stop, and Charlie-in-the-Box's staticky voice blared through the speakers. It was the same old announcement I'd heard every night for a week.

"Thank you for visiting Holly Jolly Land. We're closing in five minutes, so make your way to the entrances before we release the holiday hounds. Just kidding. Or am I? Have a Holly . . . JOLLY . . . *NIGHT*!" Then he added in a near whisper, "Charlie is adorable."

Wait. What was that last part? I wasn't sure I'd heard him right.

I unstrapped my little bottle of hand sanitizer and cleaned my hands and forearms. I'd had to switch some things around on my belt to accommodate my nonissued contraband, but it was well worth it. If I could have figured out a way to carry enough of the germ-killing gel around to douse my entire body with it every hour or so, I would have.

I had to finish scraping and scrubbing the area beside the Ferris wheel—apparently, little kids liked to hock their gum from the top, trying to hit people's heads. I couldn't leave until my work was finished. Besides, I wanted to avoid the crush of people in the locker rooms. They all hated me, and I didn't need another dressing-down today.

When I scraped the last pink loogie off the ground, I turned my cleaning cart toward the maintenance closet. After taking care of my final chores to get ready for the next day, I closed my cart inside and shuffled to the bunker, dead on my feet.

I changed clothes in a hurry and made my way through the empty park. It was actually kind of pretty at night; all the rough edges disappeared into the dark, and it looked the way I remembered from my days here as a kid. Even shoddy Santa Claus Lane seemed prettier at night. Dim lights glowed through the windows of the false storefronts. I wondered what actually was behind them—only the one on the corner was a real shop. Maybe Nick stored supplies behind them or something.

Curious, I took the path beside Lost and Found that wound behind the storefronts. As soon as I turned the corner, I heard voices.

"No, dummy, we have to put braces on it or it won't stand up!"

"But last time—"

"Last time the entire thing fell apart."

I peered around the corner. Huge military-grade lanterns lit up the darkness, making the construction site as bright as day. Hailey Barnes and the freshman who worked Santa's Scrambler were arguing over a stack of plywood. Beyond them, a handful of employees, including Steve Gill and Jamarcus Allen, were painting a red Holly Jolly Land sign. They were rebuilding the Snow Globe scene.

Hailey caught me. "What do *you* want?"

"Um, I was just— I heard voices." I cleared my throat. "Do you need help? I could—"

"Forget it! We wouldn't be stuck doing this if you hadn't ruined the first one. Get lost." She glared at me, then whipped around and yelled, "Stop gawking and get to work!"

They all went back to painting like I wasn't there.

I slipped away, forcing back tears. Why had I even bothered? Of course they wouldn't want my help. They hated me.

As I headed through the main gates, I was feeling thoroughly sorry for myself. I'd been ousted from the courthouse and shunned here. I didn't fit anywhere this summer.

Charlie-in-the-Box was just locking up his ticket booth as I passed.

"Hey, First Daughter Darby, hold up."

I sighed. "What?"

He slowly pulled money out of his pocket and handed it to me. It was paper-clipped to a gum wrapper that said *Dar-Dar* in a neat scribble.

"Oh." I hadn't expected to see my seven dollars ever again. "Thanks."

"Yah. Meant to catch you on your first day," he said. "Sorry for taking it, but, you know. Figured if you were scamming me I should get something for the old man."

"The old— You mean for Nick?"

"Yah."

So he wasn't just pocketing it. Huh. Maybe Charlie-in-the-Box was all right. "Well, thanks."

"My pleasure."

I was already at the curb when I remembered. "Hey, Charlie?"

"Yah?"

"Was it just my imagination, or was something different about the closing announcement today?"

He puffed up with pride. "Noticed that, did you?"

" 'Charlie is adorable'?" I quoted.

"Subliminal messages, man. I'm trying them out for . . . research purposes." He tipped an imaginary hat. "Until we meet again, Dar-Dar."

"Good night . . . Char-Char."

He grinned like the Cheshire Cat.

The trolley stop was deserted, so I sat down to wait in the orange pool of the streetlamp for the next ride. I wondered how often a trolley came through after nine. I'd never been at the park so late before; my chores today had taken longer than I'd realized. The lot was nearly empty, with only a couple of cars and a rusty truck parked in the employee section a couple of rows away. I realized I might be in for a long wait, so I texted Roy.

I miss you.

Delete, delete, delete. I didn't want to start off that way. Besides, if his phone was lying around in his cabin, someone might see my text on his screen. I didn't want to embarrass him.

How's camp going?

Delete, delete, delete. I sounded like his grandmother or something. What would Roy say if he were texting me? I scrolled through our old messages. The last time he'd texted me first, it was the thing about the full moon. I looked at the sky, but no luck. There was a sliver of silver in the black sky, but "Waning moon tonight" didn't have the same ring to it.

I typed in my old standby and pushed Send before I could change my mind. It wasn't original, but it had worked before.

Hey.

"Hey," said a deep voice behind me.

I shrieked and spun around, my heart thundering in my ears. I wielded my phone like a knife, ready to fight. Was it a killer? A kidnapper? A maniac loose from a mental institution?

Nope. It was Calvin.

I lowered my phone. "You scared me!"

His lips twitched. "Sorry."

"What are you doing, sneaking up on me like that?"

"I didn't sneak up on you. I walked up to you."

"Why?" I demanded, angry now that the fright was wearing off. "What do you want? Did I forget to wring out the M-O-P or something?"

He made a face at me that was the square root of annoyed plus get-over-yourself. "I just thought you should know the trolley made its last pickup at nine thirty."

I checked the time on my phone: 9:52. Well, fan-fruiting-tastic. It was at least seven miles to town, and I didn't want to walk down the highway in the dark. I sighed and pulled up Dad's name on my phone. I wondered how long it would take him to get out here.

"Come on." Calvin gestured toward the truck a few rows over. "I'm going your way."

Why was he being nice to me?

"My father doesn't let me ride with people he doesn't know."

Calvin rolled his eyes. "Your father has known me since you

and I were in preschool together. Besides, I think he'd rather you get a ride with me than sit here in the dark waiting for him."

He was right, and I hated it. I grabbed my bag of sweaty clothes and marched toward his truck. "Fine."

"Fine."

The passenger door was locked. I waited for the clicking noise to signal he'd unlocked it with his remote, but none came. Instead, he came up and unlocked it with his key and then opened the door for me. I glanced at him and wondered what he was setting me up for.

He waved me in. I clambered up and was about to say thank you when he grumbled, "You're *wel*come."

Ooh, he drove me kiwis.

We rode in silence. The night was country dark, different from dark in town, where even at night there was a glow around the horizon from Main Street stores. It was the kind of dark that went on and on, swooping up and down over the rolling hills. No cars passed us, and the only light came from his headlights, cut off by each rise in the road.

After a few minutes, he reached out and flipped on the radio, and an old New Edition song came on. I nodded along. I had this on my playlist.

"You know Bobby Brown didn't sing on this track," I said.

"What do you know about Bobby Brown?"

"I know he didn't sing this song."

He laughed, and he snorted, and that made me laugh.

"What?" I laughed.

"You."

"What about me?"

"You think you're so—"

My phone dinged, and the screen turned on and lit up the interior of the cab.

wassup?

It was Roy! I keyboarded right back at him.

Hi! Nothing, I just got off work. How's camp?

No response. I cleared my text bubbles so he wouldn't think I was still writing to him in case he was waiting to see what I said first.

"That your boy?" Calvin asked. He was staring out at the road.

"It's Roy."

"I know his name." He chucked his chin at my phone.

"You think you know everything about everything," I muttered.

If he heard me, he ignored me. "Tell him I said what's up."

"Um, no? We're having a conversation."

"About what?" He glanced at my phone, but I quickly angled it where he couldn't see it.

"That's private."

"Right," he snorted. "Because y'all talk about anything important."

"Excuse me?" I snapped. "We talk about all kinds of things."

"Really? What kind of music does he listen to?"

I hesitated.

"What's his favorite book? Where does he want to go to college? How many—"

"What's your point?"

"Y'all don't talk about nothing."

I glared at him, but I don't know if he could tell in the dark. "He likes indie," I invented. I'd never seen him with a book, so maybe . . . "He hates to read. He wants to go to UK."

Silence. There. Maybe I'd finally shut him up. I looked down at my phone, but Roy still hadn't responded.

"What about him?" Calvin said.

"What?"

"Does he know you like nineties R&B? Does he know you don't like pizza or that you watch that dumb Barney Fife mess, or—"

"Andy Griffith."

"Whatever," he said dismissively. "Does he know anything about you?"

"Of course he knows me."

"No, he don't."

"So, maybe he doesn't know 'Darby Trivia.' That doesn't mean anything. He knows me. He knows the important stuff."

"Yeah, right," he snorted. "Because you're so willing to let people in."

"What's that supposed to mean?" I demanded.

"It means, you really are the Globe Girl. You keep everyone at a distance."

"No, I do not."

It wasn't even close to true.

"Really? Who do you let in?"

"Penny."

"Penny's at camp. Like Roy. Who doesn't know anything about you."

"He knows plenty about me!"

"Like what?"

Like how my lips feel against his. And what I think of the moon.

"Why'd he leave you for the summer?" Calvin asked.

"He didn't leave me. He's at—"

"—*tennis* camp, partying it up, saving you for when he gets back and doesn't have any other options because no girl in her right mind wants anything to do with that clown."

"He is not partying all summer, and he is *not* a clown!" I cried. "Him being away doesn't change anything between us. We're as close as ever."

"That why he hasn't texted you back yet?"

"How do you know if he's texted me or not?"

He pointed to a reflection on my window. The light of my phone turned the glass into a perfect mirror in which he could see my screen. I closed my phone and shoved it in my pocket.

"You're an ass."

"Maybe I am. But I'm the ass giving you a ride home. He's the ass stringing you along."

"He's not stringing me along, but whatever." I crossed my arms and stared out at the dim lights of town rising from the horizon. "It's none of your business, anyway."

"Yeah, what do I know?" he muttered.

We rode down Kringle Avenue in silence. Calvin pulled to a stop in front of my house, and I yanked on the door handle. I couldn't wait to get as far away from him as possible.

The door wouldn't budge. I made sure it was unlocked and then tried again. Nothing.

"You have to pull up on it," he snapped. "No, up. Up, not down."

"I'm trying!" I said, pulling on the handle. "It won't *go* up."

"Here," he said. He unbuckled, slid across the seat, and reached across my waist with his left hand to grab the handle. "You have to pull it toward you, then up, and then—"

It still didn't open.

"See?" I said. I turned to glare at him, and his face was so close our noses almost touched. I swallowed and leaned back, but there was nowhere for me to go. I was stuck between Calvin Sherman and a busted door.

His eyes locked onto mine. I'd never noticed the flecks of gold in them before. Usually, all I saw were his glasses and deep scowl. But he wasn't scowling now. He was looking at me like—

"I'll go around and open it from the outside," he said in a low voice. "Hang on."

As soon as he slid over to his side and out the driver's door, I took a deep breath and leaned back. What the cantaloupe balls was that? Why was he looking at me like he wanted to . . . No, there was no way. He hated me. He'd been a jerk to me since New Year's. He hadn't wanted to—

The door opened and I nearly fell onto the curb. I grabbed the seat to steady myself and climbed out. I kept my back to him as I yanked my bag from the floorboard, determined not to look at him until there was at least ten feet between us.

When I turned toward my front walk, he backed up. He was staring at his shoes, probably as mortified as I was, worried that he'd given the wrong impression.

"Thanks for the ride," I called as I ran up the front steps. I had a hard time getting the key in the lock because I could feel him watching me. I finally managed the lock and went in and slammed the door shut behind me.

I leaned against the inside of the door and sank down to the wood floor. Maureen O'Hara padded up to me and rubbed her face against my arm until I petted her. When I finally heard the roar of the truck engine as it pulled away from the curb, I sighed.

"What. The. Bananas."

Maureen O'Hara meowed.

Ten

THE NEXT WEEK AT THE PARK, I AVOIDED CALVIN, and he avoided me. Crazy St. Nick was nowhere to be found, probably hiding out in his air-conditioned office. I kept my head down and did my work, and I ignored the taunts Riya, Glenda, and the midway workers threw my way. Jane from the dreidels was the only one who was at least civil toward me. She would nod or say hi when I came by her spinning cups to clean.

One afternoon when Hailey Barnes threw popcorn all over a spot I'd just cleaned up, Jane came over, hiked her peasant skirt over her knees, and crouched to hold the dustpan while I swept it up.

"Thanks, but you don't have to do that."

"Rule number one," she reminded me.

"Still not going to tell me rule two?" I asked.

She raised an eyebrow as she plucked the last piece of popcorn from a crack in the walkway. "Gotta earn it."

Charlie-in-the-Box's messages were my only distraction. He obviously had it bad for someone, but I didn't know who. His messages were sweet but also a little sad. Yesterday, he'd broken through "Here Comes Santa Claus" with:

"It's four p.m. Do you know where your children are? Your sunglasses? The love of your life? Could be *in the box* at Lost and Found on Santa Claus Lane. So go claim that special misfit. This is Charlie, reminding you to enjoy the present that is the present. Have a Holly Jolly afternoon."

On Friday morning, I was bored of *Andy Griffith* reruns, but I didn't have to be at work until two. I stepped into some flip-flops and headed to town. I hadn't planned to go to the courthouse. I hadn't stopped by to see Dad in a while; I'd been too busy with work, and, okay, I was also avoiding Marianne "the gem" Walker at all costs. But curiosity got the better of me, and that's where my feet carried me once I got to the square. I took the creaky steps up to Dad's office two at a time.

The outer chamber had been so transformed, I hardly recognized it. My desk was covered in papers and huge white rolls of land plots and blueprints. A gigantic whiteboard leaned against the back wall, covered in slanted cursive that I could barely make out. The window seat where I did homework during the school year now overflowed with stacks of folders and file boxes.

I marched past the mess to Dad's office and knocked. No answer. I pushed the door open and found an empty room. Dad's office, at least, was exactly the same. That was good. We'd only have the one room to clean out when Marianne went back to the capital, where she belonged. I wondered when that would be. She'd said she was just here for the season. Technically, the season lasted until Labor Day, but the last of the festivals happened in late July. August was just a sweaty month of clearance sales and lingering tourists. Maybe Marianne wouldn't be one of the stragglers.

I went and sat in Dad's huge leather chair. When I was little, he used to let me play mayor while he met with officials in the conference room. I'd bang my pencil like a gavel—as a kid, I didn't really know the difference between a mayor and a judge—and order imaginary people around.

There was a picture of my mom on his desk, and I'd talk to her sometimes. Like when Jamie Holloway called me fat and shoved me down so hard I skinned my knees, I went to her and cried. When Penny went away to camp for the first time and I had to stay here for the Snow Globe unveiling and Fourth of July parade and all the other events during the season, I went to her to complain about Dad. And that day I'd had to walk all the way to the Rite Aid on the highway because I was too embarrassed to ask Dad to buy my Playtex, I went to her and told her how much I needed her.

It wasn't the same as having a mom to hug me and tell me everything was okay, but she was the only mom I had. And usually, just talking to someone helped, even if that someone was long gone. Even if all I had of that someone was an old picture in a frame.

I touched the frame now. "Hi, Mom."

She had dark hair and was short like me. Dad said we had the same smile, but I had no way of knowing. She was staring off into the distance in the picture on his desk, deep in thought, holding her round belly. She was pregnant with me, so I guess I was in the picture, too.

Mrs. Goodwin told me once that my parents had known it was

a high-risk pregnancy since Mom was forty-one. I didn't know how I felt about knowing that.

"I got a job," I told Mom. "But I'm still keeping an eye on him."

I hung around for a few more minutes, but it wasn't fun sitting in Dad's chair when he wasn't there. I didn't even know where he was. Less than a month ago, I knew every minute of his day, every meeting on his schedule.

I walked down Main Street for a while, looking in store windows. The sidewalks overflowed with tourists, though, window-shopping and drifting in and out of the stores, and it was too hot to get brushed against and bumped into. I ducked into Evergreen Coffee Co., stood in line to order my marshmallow crème frappe, and finally found a tiny table crammed against the front window.

Gavin brought my drink a few minutes later, but he didn't have time to talk. He gave me a rushed greeting and hurried off to the next table. I'd never seen the place so crowded. Usually, the summer rush was a trickle. This was a deluge.

A strange feeling crept across my skin as I watched the crowd. I pressed my palm against the warm window; I wanted to melt through it like Alice through her looking glass. But I couldn't. Out there . . . that was my town. I'd learned to tie my shoes on Mr. Johnson's stoop. When I was eleven, Penny and I had gotten to go to town all by ourselves to get ice cream, and we'd talked with British accents because it felt more grown-up.

But I didn't know a single face. All these tourists—there were more than ever. Strangers crossed in the middle of the block and honked their horns and turned the Main Street of my memories into some kind of fun-house version. I didn't recognize this place.

Without thinking about it, I texted Roy.

Christmas isn't the same anymore.

I sent it and then a second one.

Without you, I mean.

Even if that wasn't really what I'd meant.

He didn't text back, but I didn't expect him to. He was probably at serving class or taking a test on his backhand or whatever it was they did at tennis camp.

I sent a pink heart before I could change my mind and hoped he'd smile when he saw it later.

I couldn't wait to see him over the Fourth of July weekend—only one more week. I could practically feel his arms around me again. I closed my eyes and pictured him, leaning closer and closer until my vision was filled with those long eyelashes . . . and his dark eyes . . .

The picture shifted: Hazel eyes that studied me. Dark skin. A heavy brow. Soft, smooth lips.

My eyes flew open. What. The. Bananas? Why was I thinking about kissing *him*? I took a long, long, long drink of my marshmallow frappe to cool off.

"Hey, Dar-Dar!"

Charlie-in-the-Box, Jane, and Hailey and Jamarcus from the midway games were standing just inside the door.

"Oh. Hey, guys," I said.

Hailey Barnes looked positively contemptuous. Jane, however, waved. I waved back.

"Can we join you?" Charlie asked. "There's nowhere else."

"Um, sure, but there aren't any more ch—"

They pushed their way through the maze of tables, grabbing random empty chairs as they came. Somehow, they all squeezed onto three chairs. Jane half sat on Charlie's lap, her long legs reaching the floor anyway. Charlie beamed up at her, but she didn't seem to notice.

Hmm.

"Not mopping up at the park today?" Hailey asked. Her sun-kissed auburn hair flipped out just under her ears. She was so tan, her entire head looked like a caramel apple.

"She works afternoons," Jane said. "Right?"

"Just like you," I agreed.

Hailey made a face. "You're not like us."

"Can it, Hailey," Jane said. "It's too hot to get worked up."

"True. And you're already smokin', so . . ." Jamarcus said.

Hailey giggled as he rubbed his nose against her cheek. He was a year older than me, and was the biggest flirt at Christmas High. Hailey seemed enamored, though. She blushed when he dropped his arm around her, but then her face went stony when he asked, "What are you drinking, Peacher?"

Before I could answer, Jamarcus took my drink from my hand and took a long sip. And by long sip, I mean he sucked it dry, dipped his finger into the bottom for the whipped cream, and licked it off while giving me a sexy smile.

Hailey looked ready to jump across the table and strangle me. I hadn't done anything! I couldn't help it that Jamarcus was thirsty. Or that he was a huge flirt.

"Hey, Dar-Dar," Charlie drawled. "Do you work the Fourth?"

I shook my head. "I have the day off because of the parade."

"No way!" Hailey said. "How did you get the day off? You're just a grunt!"

"I'm, um, in the parade," I mumbled. The privileges of being

First Daughter weren't something I wanted to advertise around people from work.

"Figures," Hailey said.

"That's cool," Charlie said. "Life's a parade, you know. Better to be in it than rain on it."

"Um, I guess."

"We all go to Holiday Beach to watch the fireworks after the park closes," Charlie told me.

"Oh. That's cool."

"Anything's better than hanging with the touristas," Jane said.

"You should come," Charlie said.

"What?" Hailey shrieked. "Forget it, it's Misfits only."

"She's a Misfit," Jane said. She looked me over. "Aren't you?"

They all stared at me.

"What's a Misfit?" I asked.

"We are," Jane said. "All of us who work for Nick."

"You know, the Island of Misfit Toys . . ." Jamarcus prompted. "From *Rudolph the Red-Nosed Reindeer*?"

"Where a Charlie-in-the-Box is a sentry," I said. I knew my classic Christmas TV shows.

"Exactly," Charlie said.

Misfits. I liked it. "I didn't know that's what we were called."

"*We* are Misfits," Hailey said, gesturing to the four of them. "You're not even close."

"But I work at the park," I said.

"Only because you have to." Hailey smirked.

I stared out the window to avoid her gaze. I knew she hated me for the Globe, but I didn't know what she wanted from me. I'd apologized. I was working at the park. What else—

Wait. What?

Dad was going into the diner across the street. Mrs. Goodwin and Mr. Gomez were right behind him. What were they—Oh! It was Friday! I'd almost forgotten about the town council luncheon because I'd been so busy with work.

I jumped up. My knee knocked the table, and my empty cup rolled.

"Watch it!" Hailey said.

"Sorry," I said. "I have to go."

I hurried to the door.

"Bye, Dar-Dar!" Charlie called.

I crossed at the corner and ran to the diner. I *knew* there was a reason I'd wanted to come downtown today. Somewhere in the back of my exhausted brain, I must have subconsciously remembered it was council-meeting day. Dad would be so happy to see me!

The diner was packed as usual. Mr. Grant was too busy to nod me toward the meeting room, but I made my way to the back, pushing through the closed door. I was startled to find a much larger group of people sitting around the table, including Mr. *and* Mrs. Jenkins, Mr. Gomez, Mrs. Goodwin, some other people from town, some strangers, and Marianne.

Dad was just taking a seat at the head of the table, clearly getting ready to start the meeting.

"I think most of you know Darby," Dad said, smiling. He gestured me over and said to the group of strangers at the opposite end of the table, "For those who don't, this is my daughter."

I felt the blood rush to my cheeks as they stared at me, looking as confused as I felt. "I'm sorry, I thought this was a council luncheon."

"We're meeting with the board of tourism today," Dad said.

"Oh." Right. Marianne had mentioned something about that, hadn't she?

"Come sit, Darby," Mrs. Goodwin said. She patted an empty chair next to her. "You can take the minutes."

"Oh, that's not necessary," Marianne said. "I can—"

"I'd be happy to." I quickly sank into the seat by Mrs. Goodwin, and she winked at me.

Dad and Marianne shared a look. Why were *they* sharing a look?

"So, hello, everyone," Dad said. "To introduce our guest speaker, I wanted to say that I've met with the Whitman Group, and I admit, I was skeptical at first. After hearing them out, though, I think they have some excellent ideas for how they'd like to invest in our town as it grows."

What the kumquat was happening? Since when was Dad on board with inviting developers into our town? I knew Marianne had set up that meeting for last weekend, but Dad hadn't said a word about it at home. I hadn't asked because I didn't want to hear him go on again about how amazing Marianne was. Now I wished I had at least broached the subject. I was totally lost.

"The landscape of Christmas is changing," Dad went on. "I think it's important we adapt before something happens to force our hand. So, may I present—"

"Just a minute, Mayor. Food's up." John Grant hurried into the room with a tray of plates on his shoulder. My stomach growled; I could use a Peacher burger and onion rings right about now. But he didn't bring us the usual.

"Kentucky Caesar," he told us. "Blanched kale and collard greens, anchovies, and a lemon vinaigrette. Testing out some new menu items."

"Doesn't this look . . . interesting," said Mrs. Goodwin as John served the other side of the table.

"Very." Mr. Gomez speared a drenched leaf with his fork and watched the yellow goo drip back to his plate.

When Dad realized John Grant was waiting for us to give it a try, he cleared his throat. "Why don't we eat while we listen to the presentation?"

Several people nodded, relieved.

"May I present Harris Bradley of the Whitman Group?"

Harris Bradley wore a breezy blue dress and had a smooth voice with a lilt to it that matched the handkerchief hem of her skirt. "Thanks," she said to the polite round of applause. "I'm so honored to be here today. This town is by far the most welcoming we've ever visited, and let me tell you: as representatives for the Whitman Group, we have been to a *lot* of places."

She smiled while she talked, and what she said went over like sticky sweet syrup to me. She went on and on about the beauty of Main Street, the quaintness of the courthouse square, and how impressed she was by our town's sense of community. I was so bored, I was tempted to eat my salad. Instead, I pushed an anchovy through the sea of dressing until she mentioned the Snow Globe festival—which she'd seen.

"It was a shame the Globe scene was destroyed. Things like that can set a town back if not properly attended to. But it seems your fine mayor is doing his best to appease the community."

My face grew hot. It wasn't the nicest thing anyone had ever said. When she smiled at me, I narrowed my eyes. Mrs. Goodwin patted my knee under the table.

After talking about our fantastic town a little more, she went into her sales pitch. "Mayor Peacher is right that the landscape is changing in Christmas—or it will be. Because of your recent publicity in *Travel America* magazine, Christmas is about to boom. Whether you're ready for it or not."

She held up a stack of papers, a picture of a pretty little town on top, and showed it around like a teacher showing her class the pictures in a book.

"This is Greenbriar, Virginia, two years ago, about three months after *Travel America* put them in their top-ten list of best small towns on the East Coast. Looks a little like Christmas—well, it's not as lovely, but it's nice. And this is Greenbriar today."

She moved the next picture to the front of her stack. The town was almost exactly the same. What was the point? A tiny murmur of confusion rose from the table.

Harris Bradley smiled and held up a finger. "Not much has changed, has it? Not downtown, anyway. What you can't see is that Greenbriar was interested in commercializing on their newfound fame. They partnered with the Whitman Group and expanded their potential. Today, the town has a brand-new shopping promenade, a fantastic inn that stays booked from May to November, and high-end specialty stores."

She showed us a picture of a promenade. A long pedestrian lane had a Starbucks in the foreground and a movie theater in the distance. Chain stores and restaurants lined both sides of the street. It was packed with people.

Several board members *ooh*ed, including Mrs. Goodwin.

What was happening? Were people in town really that willing to trade in the charm of our town for a multiplex when we had the Theatre Royale?

Thankfully, John Grant reappeared from the kitchen with the second course, breaking up the lovefest. Harris Bradley's smile faltered as he stepped in front of her to clear the salad plates.

His walrus mustache withered when he saw the still-full plates, and he sounded strained when he said, "Second course, burgers."

His guests looked relieved until he added, "Salmon patties with candied beets, bok choy, and teriyaki glaze."

Dad turned a gray color when John served him an orange burger dotted with green and purple things and coated with a brown sauce.

Marianne smiled weakly. "Thank you, Mr. Grant."

John passed out the "burgers" and kept the last one for himself as he took a seat at the far end of the table.

Harris Bradley waited until he was situated to continue. "In partnership with the town, we opened The 'Briar last year. It's become the premier shopping destination of southern Virginia, and it draws nearly a million visitors a year. And in case you wondered, yes, that equals more money for the businesses on their Main Street, too. Not to mention the tax benefits of a complex like that."

Half the table was poking at the fish, not paying her a bit of attention. She quickly switched to another picture of Greenbriar's downtown. "Take a closer look. There are more people on the streets. The signs are updated, the benches on the corners are new. Their town has improved, but it hasn't lost its essence. That's what the Whitman Group can do for Christmas."

She nodded to one of her associates, who immediately stood, his arm full of folders. He walked around the table, passing them out, starting on the side opposite me. Everyone eagerly took a folder, anxious for an excuse not to eat.

"The Whitman Group is very interested in partnering with Christmas in a similar venture," Harris Bradley said. "But yours would be a completely unique promenade that is, you guessed it, Christmas themed. You could meet Santa year-round, ice-skate on an outdoor rink in the summertime, and visit stores that want to have holiday outposts right here in your town. Yankee Candle has already offered to open a Christmas-scents-only candle store. Belk is in talks with us about opening an outlet store."

"Belk!" squealed Mrs. Delgado.

The man passed the final folder to Mrs. Goodwin. I leaned in and looked at it over her shoulder.

It was dark navy with a thin gold border, *The Whitman Group* in tasteful gold letters across the middle. Mrs. Goodwin flipped it open. Inside, there were plans for a promenade, complete with an aerial watercolor sketch. Mrs. Goodwin flipped through to look at a page labeled *Tax Benefits*.

Harris Bradley watched us all with sharp eyes as we took in the contents of the packet. I glanced at Marianne. She was smiling at Dad, and Dad was smiling at her.

"Any questions?" Harris Bradley asked a few minutes later.

A dozen hands shot into the air. Ms. Bradley pointed to Beth Meyers, the school nurse who sat on the tourism board. "Could you tell us more about the tax benefits?"

Ms. Bradley went on and on.

I tuned her out and started eating my burger, which actually was surprisingly tasty. Others around the table followed my lead and started nibbling away.

Mrs. Goodwin got a turn, and she asked a question that showed she clearly wasn't as enchanted as everyone else. "Wouldn't this mall draw business away from town?"

"Well, to call it a mall is to do it a disservice. It would be a promenade, a haven, if you will, for tourists and locals alike to enjoy in one centralized location."

"One centralized location?" Mrs. Goodwin repeated, frowning at Ms. Bradley like she'd just asked for gluten-free, dairy-free cake. "You mean, like, oh, I don't know . . . a town square?"

Several people laughed.

"The promenade would enhance Christmas, not take away from it."

"Drawing business away from downtown doesn't take away from it?" Mrs. Goodwin pressed.

Harris Bradley's smile froze into place. "As I said, the shopping complex would serve to enhance. There is no room downtown for more shopping. There is no room for more parking. The town needs both. On page twenty-four, you'll see the income potential that is lost every year during Christmas in July. Not to mention the other ten months of the year that the town neglects to utilize for growth. Tourists come to town with full pockets in July and December, and they leave with full pockets. They want modern stores and conveniences *as well as* the old-timey feel of town. There is room for both—in two separate locations."

She fielded one question after another as a busboy and a smiling Mr. Grant cleared the mostly empty entree plates. As servers brought coffee and dessert, the questions kept coming: What about residential growth and development? Would there really be guaranteed space for our shops in the new complex? What did "other retail and hospitality sites" mean? When would the mall break ground? How long would it take to build? What about roads?

Ms. Bradley had an answer for everything. Except nobody had asked the obvious question. I kept waiting, but for once I was embarrassed to speak up.

After an hour Marianne stood and said the meeting needed to adjourn. People actually groaned, as if they were enjoying themselves. Why did she get to decide when the meeting ended? She wasn't on the council or the tourism board, or even part of the Whitman Group. She had no horse in this race. Why was she suddenly in charge?

"I have one last question!" I said suddenly. I didn't want Marianne dictating the flow of a Christmas meeting.

Ms. Bradley blinked, but smiled indulgently. "Of course. Darby, was it?"

"Yes. Where do you plan to build this . . . promenade?"

"In Christmas," Harris Bradley said, and everyone chuckled.

I forced a smile. "No, I meant where, exactly, in Christmas? You promised to put it far enough from Main Street that it won't compete. But you also said it would offer easy access back to town. And on page twelve, you promise to put it within three miles of County Road 243."

Several of the adults frowned down at their folders, then up at Harris Bradley.

"Excellent question," Mrs. Goodwin said. She, too, looked expectantly at Ms. Bradley.

Ms. Bradley hitched her smile in place again. "Well, I cannot legally divulge any of that information at this time. But we do have some locations in mind that fit every stipulation of the proposal in your hands." She smiled around the table. "It's not our first rodeo."

The board took her at her word. The tension in the air dissipated at once. Mrs. Goodwin, however, seemed more keyed up. "Of course, you need the proper permits and approval from the town council."

"Of course," Ms. Bradley said breezily. "We are in the process of working out the specific terms of our partnership. We can't move forward without the support of the town. That's why we're here, meeting you all. My card is inside the packet. My number is listed there, along with my email. Or, you can reach me at the Third Inn, where I'm staying while I'm in town for the season. Thank you."

She sat down to raucous applause.

Dad stood, rubbing his hands together, that excited, kid-waiting-for-Santa delight in his eyes. "If the board will cast votes on whether to move forward with the proposed plan sometime over the next few weeks and let me know if they vote in favor, we'll approach the zoning committee at their next meeting, which is held on . . ." For a second, Dad looked to me. Usually, I was the one with the schedule. But I didn't have it anymore.

"July nineteenth," Marianne said.

The meeting ended, but people stayed behind to chat with Dad and the Whitman Group delegate. I hung back with Mrs. Goodwin.

"Well, this ain't good." She sighed.

I agreed. "I can't believe Marianne ever convinced Dad to meet with these people in the first place." I threw daggers at Marianne, but of course she didn't feel them. She was too busy laughing and talking to Mr. Gomez and Ms. Kirchner.

"Oh, I can," Mrs. Goodwin said. "She's young and ambitious and convincing. And pretty."

"It's not like that!" I exclaimed.

"You're right, I'm sorry, sweetie." She rubbed my arm. "Are you doing all right? I haven't seen you much this season."

I shrugged, because I didn't know if I was all right or not, but also because I didn't want to be consoled or patronized. Dad wasn't on board with the promenade because Marianne was pretty. He wasn't that shallow. Besides, Dad had never really been interested in anyone. Plenty of women around town had stopped by over the years with casseroles and cakes, trying to win his heart. But he had never paid them any mind. Why would this be different?

"What can we do?" I asked.

"I s'pose there's nothing to be done except wait. Maybe the board will veto this thing."

We shared a look. They'd vote in favor; Mrs. Jenkins had dollar signs in her eyes, and Mrs. Delgado was still clamoring on about Belk.

"Well, maybe the zoning committee will," Mrs. Goodwin said. She was chairwoman of the committee; the fierce look in her eyes said she'd be voting a solid *No.* "There's not any place that fits the bill. I think they're bluffing, hoping we'll overlook the promises they've made about a location."

"But we won't."

Determination settled across her dark brow. "Not a chance in hell."

I giggled. She only cussed when she was mad at her cakes for not rising. And then there was that time in church when she dropped her Bible and it echoed across the congregation; she'd said a four-letter word that day, and it had echoed, too.

The people trickled out of the meeting room as I waited around for Dad. When it was finally only Mr. Grant and Marianne left, I went over to them and said, "Dad, can we talk?"

"What's up, Moonpie?"

"Um, alone?"

"Oh, sure. John, I'll see you tonight."

"I'll be there to beat y'all as soon as the last customer pays."

"With aces in your apron!" Dad cracked, and Mr. Grant shook with laughter.

They played poker every few weeks with Mr. Gomez and Greg from the theater and some other men in town who had been friends since elementary school.

John headed for the kitchen, still roaring with laughter. Marianne stood by, looking completely out of place in her ballet flats and black pantsuit.

"I'll, um, head back to the courthouse," she said when I stared her down. "Darby, it's good to see you. How's your—"

"It's fine."

She cleared her throat. "Well, Mayor, see you later."

When she was gone, Dad gave me a disapproving look. "You were rude."

I didn't disagree. "Dad, how could you?"

He raised an eyebrow. "Want to try that again without the tone?"

I sighed. "Why didn't you mention anything about the investors?"

"I didn't know you were so interested. You've been busy with your friends and your new job all summer. I thought since you hadn't asked you were glad to be free of all the politics and everything."

"Free?" I cried. "I'm not free of anything! I'm miserable at work, and I don't have any friends at all! Marianne pushed me out of my place here, and now—"

"She didn't push you out," he said.

I was so angry I was shaking. That's the part he wanted to address first? I didn't want to talk about her. "I can't believe you're going to let some strangers come to town and build a mall. What about town pride, and tradition?"

"It's because of my love for this town I'm doing this!" Dad said. "You know how much this place means to me. If it's going to grow, I'd rather have a hand in the way it changes than let it get run over."

"It doesn't have to change just because *Marianne* says it will."

Dad smiled. "Change doesn't have to be a bad thing, does it? Sometimes it's necessary. Like you."

"Me?"

"You're growing up. Out there working, having . . . adventures."

I knew what he was referring to. "Da-a-ad."

He held up his hands. "I'm just saying, change is sometimes a good thing. Growing is a good thing."

"I guess." I sighed. I kicked at the checked floor with my toe.

"Maybe you're miserable at work because you're fighting it," Dad said. "Don't spend your entire summer working there just to make up for the Globe."

"That's the only reason I got the job in the first place!"

Dad nodded. "I know that, but now that you're there, you might as well enjoy it. I bet you can find something you like about the park. Don't kids from school work out there?"

Calvin's face popped into my head, first at a distance like when he scowled at me during work and then up close like when our noses almost touched in his truck. I shook the image away. "They hate me for breaking the Globe. And they think I'm a snob."

"Then they don't know you," Dad said. "Let them get to know you. You don't have to hold them at arm's length. It's okay to let people in."

My skin crawled, and I scratched my arm. It sounded a lot like what Calvin had said to me when he gave me a ride home. But since when did Dad say stuff like that? He was always the one shaking hands with a big grin, no matter what. Watching him was how I learned to plaster on the smile. Now he was all . . . mushy. I wondered if he was letting Marianne in, but I couldn't bring myself to ask. Maybe I didn't want to know the answer. Or maybe I already did.

Eleven

FRIDAY, JULY 2, KICKED OFF THE BUSIEST WEEK-end of the season, and the overflow even trickled out to Holly Jolly Land. The park was more crowded than it had been all summer—and hotter. By three o'clock, the thermometer was scraping 101, and cleaning the metal railings was absolutely unbearable.

I had never been so glad to get a call on my sparkly walkie-talkie of doom.

"Santa's Candidate Helper, this is Dreidel, Dreidel, Dreidel, come in, over," said a crackly girl voice.

Jane worked the dreidels. I yanked the walkie-talkie off my belt. "This is Darby. What's up?"

"Need you to come take care of a three-oh-three, over."

A 3-0-3? I hadn't heard of that one yet. I checked the codes on the back of my map, but I couldn't find it anywhere.

"What's a three-oh-three? Over."

Jane seemed to hesitate. "Uh, why don't you just head this

way, Santa's Candidate Helper? We'll talk in person, over. And hurry."

"I'm on my way over, over." I sighed. If she wouldn't even say, it had to be something really disgusting. I feared the worst.

I'd never heard a punk version of "What Child Is This?" It kind of worked. Jane didn't have her nose in a book today; she was scanning the crowds.

When she saw me, she shouted, "Finally! What took so long?"

"Where is the, um, three-oh-three?" I said, not asking the more pressing question: *What* is it? "I didn't see anything by the gates."

"Hang on." She hit the Off switch for the ride. When the dreidels came to a stop she hustled the riders toward the exit.

Then she went over to the entrance gate, but instead of opening it, she flipped over a cardboard sign that read, BACK IN TWENTY.

The handful of people waiting in line groaned.

Jane groaned back at them. "It's an amusement park, people. Go amuse yourselves elsewhere!"

As she loped back to me, she rolled her eyes. "Sorry about that. Come on."

She stepped over the wall of the control booth and headed down the midway toward Winter Wonderland.

I hurried to push my bucket cart around and go after her. "Where are we going?"

"Three-oh-three." She sped up, and I had a hard time keeping pace with her. She glanced at me. "Ditch the M-O-P. You won't need it."

"What exactly is a three-oh-three?" I asked after I'd found a spot to park my cart.

"No idea," she said. "I just needed your help and I didn't want anyone to hear why."

"Oh. Okay. Um, it's not anything, I mean, will we get in trouble, though?" I asked. "I'm on the clock, and I don't know if Calvin will like it if I take a break or—"

She shielded her eyes with her hand and stared at me. "I'm not on a break, Santa's Candidate Helper. I'm assisting you with an emergency three-oh-three. Petting zoo, come on."

We took the less crowded route past the North Pole instead of winding through Babes in Toyland.

When we were close enough to the petting zoo that I could smell the sweet stench of manure and hay, I asked, "So, what is it you need my help—"

Riya met us on the path. When she saw me, she flipped her hair off her shoulder and put her hands on her hips. "What the hell, Jane? You brought the little princess?"

"She can help."

Riya glared at me but didn't say anything else as we made our way past the entrance of the petting zoo. The path wound around and came out on the backside of Babes in Toyland. Sometimes I came this way when I got radioed over to the Holly Bally Pit, where kids could bury themselves up to their necks in red and green plastic balls.

We headed to the ball pit now; a handful of people were gathered around the edges, taking pictures and laughing as they pointed at something in the center. A few Misfits were among them, trying to move them away.

Riya and Jane shared a look and rushed toward the ball pit.

"What's going on?" I called as I ran to keep up.

"Frank," Jane said.

Frank?

We approached the entrance. The Misfit working the pit, a freshman named Ava, breathed a sigh of relief. "Thank goodness. We got all the kids out—"

"Anyone hurt?" Jane asked, scanning the pit.

"No, a lot of criers, though."

"Moms or kids?"

Ava made a face. "Both. What now?"

"Get everyone away from here," Riya said. "Get Cleo and Hannah to help you block off this area. We'll get him out."

Get who out? Frank? I searched the pit, but I didn't see anyone. Was someone stuck inside?

"But Kyle says we should—"

"Kyle doesn't know jack," Riya snapped.

"Hey!" said a guy in the crowd.

"Shut up, Kyle! Everyone out!" Jane cried. "We'll radio when you can come back."

The Misfits scrambled to get the remaining onlookers away from the pit railing. As soon as they left, Jane and Riya surveyed the pit.

"Do you see him? Is he mad?"

"Near the back." Jane pointed to the far left corner. "Wait for it."

I watched, and sure enough, some of the balls were rustling, like someone was hiding there.

"I'll go around," Riya said. "Try to get him to come this way."

"Give Darby your hook, maybe she can pull him out."

Riya rolled her eyes but offered me her shepherd's hook.

I didn't take it. "Um, guys, who's Frank?"

Neither of them answered me. Jane said, "When I open the gate, follow Riya around but stop over there by the ladder. When she scares him, see if you can get the hook around his neck."

"His *neck*?"

"If you can reach him, hold him down. But be careful, he kicks." Jane clipped her walkie-talkie to her peasant skirt and opened the gate. "Go!"

Riya stuffed the hook into my hands and took off around the red padded edge of the pit. I followed. What in the world had I gotten myself into? And who—or what—was Frank?

"Stay here," Riya hissed when we reached the ladder into the pit. It looked like the white plastic ladder on the side of Penny's above-ground pool. I wondered if the ball pit was really just a pool half buried in the ground.

Riya hurried around to the back corner, moving silently but quickly. When she got to the corner where the balls were rustling, she knelt down, poised to spring, and nodded at Jane.

Jane held up one finger . . . two fingers . . . three fingers—

Riya punched both arms into the pit and swirled them around so fast balls flew into the air.

Frank was immediately on the move. At first, I only saw the balls undulating where he cut a path away from Riya, but then I saw flashes of brown fur. And horns. And then I saw his eyes: vertical slits of black in yellow.

Frank was a goat? A miniature goat? Why was there a tiny goat in the ball pit?

"Nehhhhh!" Frank brayed, butting the balls away from his face as he headed for the very center of the pit.

"Get him, Darby!" Riya shouted, snapping me out of my shock.

I grabbed hold of the ladder, leaned forward, and stretched out the shepherd's hook. The ladder, however, wasn't attached to the sides, and I belly-flopped into the Holly Bally Pit.

"Get him!" Jane said as I tried to get to my feet.

"Where is he?" I shrieked, turning in a circle. The last thing I needed was to get butted in the backside by an angry goat.

"Your right!"

"I see him!" I reached for him with the hook, but I missed. He turned and headed toward Jane.

"Bombs away!" Jane jumped into the pit, too, holding her nose like she was going underwater. She landed on her feet, but Frank turned back my way, *nehh*ing.

This time I was ready. As soon as he got within arm's reach, I grabbed for him.

I got him around the middle, and he bucked. No doubt confused and afraid, he fought me so hard it was impossible to hold on.

"Help!" I cried.

Riya jumped in, too, and she and Jane raced toward me and Frank. Jane grabbed his horns to stop him from shaking his head. Riya pulled off her rope belt and made a leash. She tied it around his neck.

Somehow, we managed to get him out of the pit. I'm not sure how; there was a lot of brown fur and kicking hooves and swearing on Riya's part. But we managed. Jane held the rope while Riya and I climbed out, and we led Frank around the edge of the pit and out the gate.

We got all the way down the path to the petting zoo before

anyone spoke. Riya rubbed her side and said, "When he's mad, he's strong for a little goat."

"Yeah," Jane said. "Don't underestimate a *pygmy goat*. Easier than last time, though, thanks to Darby."

"Whatever." Riya popped a piece of gum into her mouth and pulled Frank through the gate to the petting zoo. "Later, losers."

When she was gone, I asked, "Last time?"

Jane considered me. "Frankincense is an escape artist. Gets out at least once a month, usually heads to the woods to eat. But sometimes he ends up in the park, scaring the moms and butting the kids."

I remembered back on my first day, when I thought I'd seen a goat in the woods but had brushed it off, thinking I was seeing things in the heat.

We headed back up the path.

"Thanks, dude," Jane said when we reached the Ferris wheel, where I'd left my bucket and cart. "I'd say you earned it today."

"Earned what?"

She smiled. "You'll see."

I went back to mopping and emptying the trash, but I did it with a grin on my face. Not that cleaning the bathrooms or scraping gum off the ground was fun, but for the first time, I felt part of things. It helped that the other employees were nice to me. At Rudolph's Wild Ride, Jamarcus came over and said hi. The ice-cream-swirl girl gave me a cone on my break, and when I cleaned the midway, Hailey didn't throw anything at my head.

By closing time, I was in a pretty great mood, considering I'd swum through a pool of sticky plastic balls with a mad goat. As I finished up by Santa's Scrambler, I felt eyes on me. I turned and saw him across the way, staring.

"What?" I asked.

He shrugged and kept watching while he wiped some tool with a dirty rag. He had grease on his temples and the bridge of his nose where he'd pushed his glasses up his sweaty face. His braids were tied back in a thick ponytail at the base of his neck, and oil was smeared on the front of his coveralls. Why did he always look like he'd been working so much harder than anyone else around here?

"What are you watching me for?"

He shrugged again, looking me over as he leaned against the low railing.

"Your uniform is dirty, too," I said. "In case you're about to say something about mine."

"I wasn't."

"I put the sign out."

He nodded.

"I used bleach."

He kept watching me.

"What then? What am I doing wrong now?" I demanded.

"I didn't say you were doing anything wrong."

"But?"

"You've got a short fuse."

"I do not!"

He smirked and pushed off the rail. "Yeah. You do."

"You know what?" I said.

"I know a lot of things."

He got under my skin like no one else on the planet. "Talking to you is like doing a puzzle, you know that?" His haughty smile made me want to scream. "Did you want something?" I asked through clenched teeth. "Or are you just hanging around to annoy me?"

His face went stony. "Nick wants to see us in his office."

"Why?"

He shrugged. "Finish up. I'll let him know you're on your way."

"Asshat," I muttered as he sauntered away. His legs were too long, and I didn't like the way he walked in a very straight line. I didn't like the way his braids swished, and I definitely did not like the way my stomach knotted up when he was around. Ever since he'd driven me home, I'd done my best to avoid him, but I hadn't been able to erase him from my imagination.

The bunker was packed with people clocking out for the night and grabbing their paychecks from the messy stack on the break table. Glenda flipped me off as I walked by, but Riya just turned away. Well, that was an improvement. Jamarcus and Hailey and some of the midway workers waved. Jane and Calvin were having a close conversation. When she saw me, she smiled, and Calvin went into Nick's office.

What was that about? I wondered if the two of them were—No, he wasn't her type, not that I knew what her type was. But I doubted it was buttoned-up, tucked-in, super-serious Calvin Sherman. Was it?

I hesitated before I knocked on Nick's office door. Why did I care if Calvin was Jane's type? He wasn't *my* type.

Calvin opened the door and stood back to let me in. I avoided his eyes.

Nick Patterson was leaning on his cane, looking at the pictures on the wall. Most of them were of his employees—the Misfits—but some of them were of him and Mrs. Patterson. He rubbed his eyes and turned to us.

"How's basic training? Have you got a handle on it?"

I looked down at my sneakers. They were covered in blue stains. My back and neck were killing me. The blisters on my hands were hardening into calluses. And today, I fell into a ball pit with a mad goat. But it had been . . . fun.

"She's doing a good job," Calvin said.

I glanced up at him. Did he mean that? He was standing at attention, staring straight ahead, but there wasn't any sarcasm on his face.

"Is she, now?"

"She works hard."

Nick twinkled at me. "Had a feeling you would."

My mouth turned up at the corners a little. "I'm trying."

Nick opened the top drawer of his desk and pulled out a badge. "In that case, this is for you."

He held out an official name tag.

Hello! My name is ________________ ! How can I help you have a Holly Jolly day?

"Fill in your name, and don't forget to wear it at all times in the park," Nick ordered. "You're an official employee now."

I pinned it to the front of my filthy coveralls. "Thank you."

"Thank *you*," Nick said. "I appreciate your work ethic. The paths haven't been this clean since . . ." He cleared his throat and glanced at the photos on the wall again. "For a long time now."

I smiled. "I'm glad. So, does this mean I'm off M-O-P duty?"

Nick and Calvin shared a look. "We could use some help with repair work, if you think you're up for it."

I didn't know anything about machines or tools or . . . anything, but I wasn't about to say that. I'd watch carnival-ride-repair YouTube videos all night if it meant getting away from the M-O-P. "Absolutely."

"Good. Consider yourself promoted," Nick said.

"Thank you."

"Except you also still have to keep doing the job you're already doing. Because we don't have anyone to replace you."

"Oh," I said.

"You're dismissed. Head Helper, I need a word with you."

"Okay." Calvin held open the door for me.

As I passed I said, "Thanks."

He blinked. "Yeah."

Out in the break area, Jane immediately appeared at my side. She'd already changed into her street clothes. She was wearing holey fishnets under her cutoffs, and she'd torn the sleeves off her flannel shirt. I felt extremely grimy in my coveralls. Charlie-in-the-Box was right on her heels with a puppy-dog look on his face. His T-shirt said UNICORNS ARE REALER THAN YOUR LATTE. Jamarcus was with him, too.

"Rule number two: you gotta earn it." She smiled. "You earned it."

"What the flying freak are you talking about?" Jamarcus asked, but then he saw my badge. "You have a name tag!"

"Yeah, I—"

He cupped his hands around his mouth and shouted so loudly

I had to cover my ears, "Hey, everyone! First Daughter Darby is officially a Misfit!"

Jamarcus wriggled his eyebrows at me, then quick as a flash, he lifted me up and spun me around in a circle. If I were an inch or two taller, my head would have hit the soggy drop ceiling. Everyone clapped and whooped. Hailey put her fingers in her mouth and whistled. Even Riya golf-clapped while Glenda looked between us, confused.

My cheeks felt like they would split in two. I was a Misfit. And I liked it.

As Jamarcus spun me around, I saw Calvin coming out of Nick's office. He crossed his arms over his chest and smiled at me. Our eyes locked, and I couldn't look away. Something in his gaze turned warm, and I felt dizzy.

I tapped Jamarcus on the head. "Put me down."

He lowered me, and I hurried to the locker room to change and hide until everyone cleared out. It was just the excitement of the day. First the 3-0-3 and then getting promoted, that was it.

On the trolley ride home—I made sure to be on time to catch the nine thirty—I texted Roy.

Are you still coming for the 4th?

He didn't answer until I was walking home.

pretty sure

My heart somersaulted into my ribs as I texted him back.

I can't wait ♥

Twelve

THE CHRISTMAS IN JULY PARADE DIDN'T START until eleven, so I spent the morning procrastinating. I toasted a few slices of cinnamon-raisin bread and spread extra brown sugar and butter on top. I nibbled away, starting at the corner and working my way around in a spiral. I used to pick out the raisins first, but now I left them in. I liked the way they added a new flavor every bite or so.

I'd gotten pretty good at eating breakfast standing up. I couldn't remember the last time I'd eaten at the table. I went to the fridge for something to drink. We only had the orange juice with extra pulp—Dad's favorite—so I drank an Ale-8 while I read the festival coverage in this morning's issue of *The Herald*. Today's events kicked off with the 10K fun run. The race started at the post office, wound through some of the prettier countryside on County Road 243, and ended at Holiday Park. Thankfully, Dad never made me get up early enough to partake in this particular tradition, although he had left hours ago to help set up water stations and then give out medals to all the participants after the finish line.

Roy hadn't texted since Friday night, and I was dying to know if he was in town yet. Would he be at the parade? Would he see me in the lead car? Jane had reminded me last night at work that everyone hung out at Holiday Beach to watch the fireworks. Maybe we'd stop by, although I was a little worried that my partner in the Globe destruction might not be so popular with the Misfits.

I finished eating and went to get ready. I'd bought a new dress online last week especially for today. Last year, I'd worn a red-and-white-striped dress with green trim. This year, I'd picked something on theme that wasn't quite so over-the-top Christmasy, a grass-green sundress with white flowers on it and thin straps that crisscrossed in the back. I wore beaded brown flip-flops. I wanted to wear my hair down, but the weather app on my phone said it was already ninety-six outside. So I put it in a braided topknot and swept my bangs to the side. At least it showed off my tan.

I'd also bought a new swimsuit—a vintage-inspired blue one that I hoped brought out the color of my eyes—and new sunglasses. That was another benefit of working at Holly Jolly Land: I got a paycheck, something I hadn't gotten from my hours at the courthouse. Dad always bought me whatever I needed, but it felt so liberating to be able to buy things I wanted with my own money. I threw my new suit and sunglasses, a towel, sunscreen, and some lip gloss into a beach bag for later.

The parade route started in front of the high school, and it took me nearly fifteen minutes to get there because of the crowds. Dad was already enthroned high on the back seat of John Grant's old red-and-white Chevy Bel Air. Mr. Grant was behind the wheel . . . but why was Marianne in the passenger seat?

"You look beautiful," Dad said when he saw me.

"Thanks, Dad."

He scooted over to make room for me on the top of the seat. Someone had thrown a furry white blanket over the seat backs. It looked like a skinned polar bear. I shoved my beach bag into the space between the front and back seats where no one would see it.

Marianne turned in her seat to look us over. "Mayor, your tie will flap around in this breeze once we start moving. Here, let me." Her blond bob was sleek and shiny as always, curled under at the ends to frame her features, but it fell across her face as she reached into her bag. "I have a hairpin that will work as a tie clip, here." She tucked one side of her bob behind her ear and smiled at him as he took the hairpin.

Her glasses were still too chunky. I looked away.

The usual huge velvet Santa bag sat on the back seat between our feet, filled to the brim with candy to toss to the kids in the crowd. Not peppermints or rock-hard jelly beans, either; good stuff: mini Snickers, Reese's, and Hershey's, Fourth of July candy canes, and tiny boxes of red and white Nerds.

"All set?" John Grant asked after a few minutes. The conductor of the Christmas High School marching band at the head of the parade signaled they were ready to go.

"Let's get this show on the road," Dad said.

"Wait!" Marianne said. "I almost forgot." She handed us each a slow-dissolving Whitestrip for our teeth. It was an old campaign trick. Teeth were whitest during the actual bleaching process. Dad and I pressed them onto the top rows of our teeth and handed Marianne the wrapping.

"Good thinking," Dad said with a huge smile.

I sat up straighter and blinked hard. *I* was the one who had first started giving Dad Whitestrips before events. She was stealing my life! First my job, and now my dad? I should have gotten to the parade route sooner, and I should have brought my messenger bag with me. I had extra Whitestrips in it, plus a tiepin for Dad's floppy tie, a battery-operated fan, and some bottled—

"I have some waters, too," Marianne said, holding up two bottles. "In case you get thirsty. And, Darby, do you have on sunscreen? You're so pale, and the sun is scorching today."

I was not pale, not after a month mopping in the sun. Just because I was still lighter complexioned than her didn't make me *pale*.

"Marianne, what would we do without you?" John Grant said as she hopped out of the car.

She blushed. "See you all at the end."

"Bye," Dad said. He watched her until she disappeared into the crowd.

She was wearing a pink sundress. It was too bright.

As the lead car, we followed right behind the marching band. They began to play their medley of patriotic and holiday music, and it was so loud I couldn't hear myself think.

Somehow, in only a few weeks, I'd forgotten certain things about being First Daughter. Like how hard it was to smile nonstop for an hour. Or how my shoulder started to ache after twenty minutes of waving. Or how hot the car got in the sun. I had puddles of sweat in the most unfortunate places, like the small of my back and the base of my bra.

The fun part was tossing handfuls of candy to the kids in the crowd. As we turned up Main Street, the crowds grew thicker. Whenever my waving arm needed a break, I grabbed a handful and tossed it to the crowd, even if I didn't see any kids.

Some people called out to me as I passed.

Old Mr. Oates stood near the front, his UK ball cap pulled low over his eyes. He waved at me and called in his deep voice, "Glad to see you again, Darby!"

I waved back. I hadn't seen him in ages.

My butt hurt from riding on the back of the car. The "bearskin" helped some, but it made the backs of my sweaty legs itch. I wriggled a little, trying to scratch without actually scratching, a smile on my face as I tossed red, white, and blue candy canes into the crowd.

"After this, we need to go shake some hands for a couple hours before the pie-eating contest," Dad said to me. He had to practically shout to be heard over the marching band, but he managed to do it with a smile on his face.

"Sounds good," I said. I hadn't been around town much this summer. It would be nice to see everyone.

"And I thought we might invite Marianne and the Whitman Group to join us to watch the fireworks tonight," Dad said.

"I can't," I said, tossing some Nerds to a little boy on the curb, hoping I'd spot Roy somewhere along the way. "I have plans."

"You made plans for tonight?" He sounded hurt.

"Yes. Why?"

Dad waved at someone on his side of the street. "Happy Fourth of July!" he cried. Then in a slightly lower voice, he said, "I'm just surprised. We usually spend the Fourth together—"

"Working," I reminded him. His smile faltered slightly, and I felt terrible. I hadn't even thought about spending the day with Dad. "I was going to meet some friends at Holiday Beach around five, but if you want me to stay with you—"

"No, you go ahead," he said. He threw more candy into the crowd and called, "Merry Fourth of July in Christmas!"

Main Street was dressed to the nines. The windows were frosted with canned snow, every door had red, white, and blue wreaths, and the lampposts were wrapped in patriotic garland in anticipation of the big day. Tourists carried little American flags and red-and-green paper fans that they furiously beat against the thick heat.

I craned my neck to look at the bakery's window. Mrs. Goodwin went all out for Christmas in July, and I wanted to see what she'd come up with this year. Sure enough, there was a huge Santa cookie in the window, sporting a spangled top hat, pointing at the tourists. In frosting across the plate, Mrs. Goodwin had written, *Uncle Santa wants YOU to have a Merry Fourth of July in Christmas!*

The entire town was donning its gayest apparel for the season. Main Street looked like a huge, shiny present, just begging to be opened. But it all seemed so . . . plastic. Maybe I had grown accustomed to the general shabbiness of Holly Jolly Land, but the perfectly landscaped bushes and precisely pruned flowers that lined Main Street were so different from the modest plantings at

Holly Jolly Land. As we made our way down the final stretch of the parade route, I realized downtown Christmas was more like an amusement park than Holly Jolly Land was.

I glanced at Dad and asked through a bright, still-dissolving-Whitestrip smile, "How are the mall plans coming?"

Dad waved to someone in the crowd and said behind his own pearly whites, "Still working out details! Marianne has been a god-send."

We crept forward until we came to the final block before the courthouse. I'd thought the sidewalks were packed down Main Street, but the mass of onlookers waiting here was mind-boggling. There were easily five hundred people. It was like the entire county had shown up. They were crammed onto the sidewalks, cheering and waving.

As we pulled to a stop, a chorus of voices shouted, "Dar-Dar!"

I grinned when I spotted them. Jane, Charlie, Jamarcus, and some other people from work were waving at me from in front of the coffee shop. I waved back and threw them as much candy as I could.

"Friends of yours?" Dad asked, looking back as we passed them.

"Yeah," I said. "From Holly Jolly Land. They're great, you'd like them."

As the car slowed to a stop behind the courthouse, I caught Dad searching my face, with noticeable pride in his gaze.

"What?" I asked.

He shook his head. "Nothing. Go have fun."

"Oh, we're not meeting until later, it's fine. I'll go with you—"

"Moonpie, no, you go."

I kissed his cheek and ran to meet my friends.

Jane passed me a cup of ice, the little pebble kind that crunched just right in your mouth. We'd filled a Styrofoam cooler before we'd come to the beach. Most of it had melted around the edges of the cooler, but the cold felt good.

I'd had the best Fourth of July of my life. Jane and I had window-shopped down Main, so I got to see some people from town after all. This afternoon, we'd driven out to Santa's Stables with Charlie and Jamarcus for the pie-eating contest. Charlie had participated, and he still had a purple nose, chin, and forehead from digging into a blueberry pie face-first. I'd laughed so hard all day that my sides ached. We'd eaten BBQ and ice-cream sandwiches from the gas station out on County Highway 12—Mr. Delgado smoked ribs, chicken quarters, and Boston butt in his barbeque pit right behind the station. We'd smelled it from a mile down the highway, and we were practically drooling when he piled our to-go boxes high with pulled pork, slaw, and homemade sauce. Then we'd spent a couple hours splashing around and lying in the sun at a secret swimming hole at the creek out past Mr. Lowenstein's back field.

The sun had sunk behind the treetops nearly an hour ago, but summer days don't go down without a fight. The sky was still streaked with hot pink on that side, but over the town behind us, it was slate blue, the crescent moon a promise of the night to come.

We had gotten a fantastic spot under the palm trees planted near the deeper end of the water, away from the families with little kids. We'd been camped out about an hour, holding spots for the other Misfits who wouldn't arrive until after work. Hailey, Riya, and even Glenda showed up, but they spread their towels on the opposite side of the midway guys, which was fine with me. They'd been nicer to me—that is to say, they weren't calling me names anymore—but I wasn't sure I would ever want to be great friends with them. Jane and I sat with Jamarcus and Charlie and Hannah, one of the snowflake girls. She and Jamarcus were playing some card game that I couldn't follow no matter how hard I tried; I think they were making it up as they went. Charlie was drawing a bird on the side of the cooler with a Sharpie, nodding slowly to a beat in his head.

I checked my phone again.

"He'll be here," Jane said. "If he's got any sense at all."

"Who?" I said, quickly stashing my phone under my leg.

"The guy you're waiting for." Jane studied me. "It's a guy, right?"

"Um."

She nodded and pulled her T-shirt over her bikini. "Are you meeting him?"

I busied myself with my own cover-up—my green dress from earlier because I hadn't thought to bring a T-shirt; I wasn't sure I even owned a T-shirt besides the FIGHTING REINDEER shirts the school gave us for football games.

I had texted Roy a couple of times—okay, seven—throughout the day. I didn't know what time he would be back. We hadn't set an exact time to meet, and for all I knew, he was looking for me in town. Maybe he was with his family for the day and just thought he'd see me for the fireworks. Either way, I didn't want to miss him just because he didn't know where I was.

I hoped he'd text me soon. I wiggled my toes until they were half-buried in the snow-white sand and checked my phone one last time just to be sure before I shoved it in my beach bag.

"He'll show," Jane said again. She scooted closer to Charlie, and his face went totally euphoric when she pushed his hair out of his eyes so he could see his canvas better. "Right, Charlie?"

He squinted at me before going back to his bird sketch. "Yeah. You're rad, Dar-Dar."

"Thanks, Char-Char." Anxiety crawled over my skin like ants. "What if he doesn't turn up, though?"

Jane nodded at someone behind me. "He already did."

I froze. He was here? He was here! "Oh my bananas. Do I look okay?"

"Oh my whaaa?" Jane said.

I didn't answer. I slowly turned to look over my shoulder. I hoped my hair wasn't too messy.

I scanned the crowds of families with little kids and the older couples and the tourists, but I didn't see him. "Where?" I said to Jane.

"Right there."

I didn't see him anywhere. "Where is he?"

She pointed at a family about twenty feet away. "There!"

The two smallest kids were maybe five and six, jumping up and down around their mom; there was a girl about middle-school age talking on her phone; and standing next to his dad, nearly as tall, was Calvin Sherman.

I whipped back around to Jane. "Calvin?"

She frowned. "Isn't that who you've been waiting for?"

"Calvin?" I cried. "No!"

"I thought you were into him. Y'all flirt all the time."

"WHAT?" I nearly shrieked. "We do not!"

She gave me a "c'mon, dude" look. "You two are practically crackling."

"We can't stand each other," I said. "He's the biggest jerk to me! All we ever do is yell at each other!"

"It's a love/hate thing," Charlie said sagely as he added long feathers to the bird's tail. "Sometimes, when people are too immature to handle their feelings, the attraction comes out as dislike."

"I'm *not* attracted to Calvin." I wasn't. I absolutely was not. Not at all. Nope. Not even a little.

Jane smirked at my face. "He is hot . . . in an alpha-male, stern kind of way." Charlie visibly deflated until she said, "Not my type. Seemed like yours, though."

I gave her the most withering look in my arsenal.

He wasn't hot. Okay, maybe he was, up close. Like when his face was so close to mine that our noses touched. Maybe then, he was *slightly* attractive. Maybe. Just because I agreed with a generic comment of Jane's didn't mean I was into him. I could impartially say that Jamarcus was hot. Charlie was good-looking in an artsy way. So, yes, I could objectively admit Calvin was good-looking, and that was why I sometimes thought about his face so close to mine. Because I was appreciating his appearance. But I wasn't attracted to him.

Right?

"So, who are you waiting for?" Jane asked. "Oh, no. Don't tell me. You're waiting around for *Roy Stamos*?"

I shrugged. I didn't want to talk to her about Roy now that she'd accused me of liking Calvin. It was like drinking Ale-8 after 7Up. It ruined the flavor. I cast around for a segue.

"Jane, do you like anyone?"

She shifted away from Charlie before answering. "Not really."

He watched her with sad eyes.

"That's really good." I nodded to the cooler, hoping to distract him. "Is it a turkey?"

"Nah." He stood, picked up the cooler, and looped the plastic handle over a low-hanging palm branch. "Partridge in a palm tree."

I smiled. "Nice."

He blushed, looking pleased, but his gaze flickered to Jane. If she noticed, she didn't let on. Poor Charlie.

I checked my phone again. No texts. Why wasn't he answering?

The beach filled with people as the sky darkened. Maya Johnson and Laeticia Marshall and a bunch of people from church waded out into the water a ways and set up their chairs, far from the little kids. Some middle schoolers were on floats out in the deepest part of the water, waving sparklers while they waited for the show to begin.

This really was a great place to watch the fireworks because the sky was wide open over the fields and pool at the park. I'd only ever seen the show from the courthouse steps. I pictured Dad, smiling his big white smile from the top of the stairs, at his podium, all alone. He would give a short speech before they started—probably Marianne had written something cheesy and forced—and then step away from the podium as the music started. The Christmas Community Choir would sing patriotic songs during the show.

I'd been so eager to get to my friends, to Roy, but suddenly, I felt too far away. I could have worked out a compromise if I'd tried a little harder. A sadness flowed over me. I'd had the best day ever with Jane and everyone, but I missed spending the day with Dad. Sure, it was usually a day of smiling for photos and shaking hands, but he always made it fun somehow.

I glanced at Calvin. He was with his family today, and he looked relaxed in a way he never looked at work. It was funny, the things you knew about people even though you didn't really know them. I knew his sister wanted to be a designer when she grew up and that his brother was obsessed with basketball, all because Calvin had told me back when we were friends. As I watched now, I could see how much he cared about his family. When his brother started splashing and made their little sister cry, Calvin scooped her up and carried her to their dad, who clapped him on the back and swung the girl high onto his shoulders away from the water.

Calvin turned my way, and our eyes locked. Somehow, even though he was twenty feet away and there were dozens of people between us, it felt as close and personal as when we had been in his truck. He smiled and moved toward me, but I quickly looked away. I was just looking around, not looking at him.

I was taking in the scene, that was all: the sparklers . . . the guy waving the huge American flag . . . Jamarcus doing a somersault into the water and soaking everyone . . . Roy walking through the crowd . . .

Roy?

Was I seeing things, imagining him here?

I blinked.

Bright-red fireworks burst across the sky, and the crowd was suddenly lit up with the red glow reflected off the surface of the water.

It was him!

"Roy!" I called.

It was so, so perfect. The fireworks starting as soon as I saw him, the way he walked closer, still not seeing me. I wanted to run to him and throw my arms around him.

Well, why not? I'd told him I would be here, and here he was, walking through the crowd as the sky lit up green and gold and—

He wrapped his arm around a girl with short blond hair and pulled her in. A purple firework bloomed across the sky as he kissed her. She was laughing as their lips met, and I could see the gleam of her teeth.

But who was she?

No. Wait.

There had to be—

Why was he kissing someone else?

They finally stopped kissing, and she turned in the circle of his arms to lean against him and watch the fireworks. He nuzzled her cheek. They looked perfect in the glow of the fireworks, like the love scene in a movie.

I felt like I'd eaten a huge tub of stale theater popcorn and was slowly being poisoned from the inside. I turned away. I was going to 6-2-4.

I tried to focus on something so the world would stop seesawing. Jane and Charlie were watching the show; Hannah was laughing while Jamarcus tickled her neck; Riya and Glenda were taking selfies.

I couldn't be here. I needed to lie down. Besides, the tears were coming on fast, and I didn't want anyone to see me cry, especially not Roy. He still hadn't spotted me, and if I hurried, I could get out of here and avoid him altogether.

I grabbed my beach bag and flip-flops and slowly backed away, my feet slipping in the imported sand.

I ran into someone.

"Sorry," I choked out, keeping my head down as I stepped around him.

Firm hands grasped my upper arms. "Whoa, you okay?"

It was Calvin.

I did not need this right now. I wrenched free of him. "I'm fine."

"What a moron."

"I'm not a moron," I snapped.

"I meant Roy, not you."

"He's not a moron," I said weakly.

"Why are you defending him?"

"I'm not defending him, I'm just saying, he's not a—"

"He is. He picked that girl over you. That's about the definition of moron."

It felt like a compliment. But he said it with so much spite, it couldn't have been. Why did he care who Roy kissed? And why did he have an opinion?

Why did I care?

I shook my head. "You're incorrigible."

He laughed. "Only you use words like that."

"Don't laugh at me!" I stamped my foot.

He put his hand over his mouth to hide his smile and looked me over. "You know something? You're kind of cute when you're mad."

I stomped off. I couldn't deal with his mood swings right now. My heart was breaking into a million pieces, and it was all I could do to stare at the horizon and put one foot in front of the other until I was far, far away from Roy and the girl in his arms.

I didn't want to go home to an empty house, though. I really wanted to talk to Dad, but he was probably still busy. I didn't know where to go and I ended up just sitting on the steps behind the courthouse, away from the crowd in the square. The fireworks were over, and people were all headed home or to their hotels or B&Bs or the Third Inn for the night, but I didn't want to risk meeting anyone on the street who I knew. My mascara was running down my face. I didn't even have any tissues in my bag, just my lip gloss and a sandy towel, so I wiped the makeup away with my fingers. Then I held my head in my hands and cried.

How could Roy do this to me? We had only gotten started, and he had already moved on? But . . . but we'd been texting. We'd even talked a couple of times. I thought it was going great.

". . . saving you for when he gets back and doesn't have any other options."

Calvin's words stung like hornets in my heart. Was he right? Was Roy just putting me on hold until he got back here? Should I have expected this?

I was so stupid.

I cried myself dry. It wasn't just Roy, even though he'd given me plenty to cry about. It was the courthouse, it was the exhaustion of doing physical work all summer, it was the way Dad had smiled at Marianne when she fixed his tie, it was the way Calvin's face popped into my head and his words played in my ears.

Most of all, it was the fear that he was right about me that made me cry. Was I really "the Globe girl," always in a bubble, never letting anyone get close? Was Roy kissing another girl right now because of something I'd done wrong?

A burst of laughter drifted around the corner of the building, and then a few moments later they appeared. Her head was thrown back, laughing, her hand on his arm. He was drinking in the sight of her.

It was Dad and Marianne.

When she saw me, she stopped laughing, and the smile slid off her face. She let go of his arm and took a step to the side. It took Dad a second to catch up. To cover his embarrassment, he hitched a campaign smile into place.

"Darby! What are you doing here?"

Marianne peered at me. "What's wrong? You look like you've been—"

My glare shut her up.

I grabbed my bag and pushed past them, giving her a dark look as I went.

No. No way.

I wasn't going to let this happen.

Thirteen

THE NEXT DAY TURNED OUT TO BE SOUPY AND overcast, the kind of day that made it hard to get up and go to work, especially after the night I'd had. I was supposed to pull a double since I'd gotten yesterday off for the parade, but I waited until I was sure Dad had left for the courthouse before I stepped into some shorts, grabbed my work bag, and went downstairs.

He had knocked on my closed bedroom door when he'd come in right after me last night, but I'd told him I wasn't feeling well. I could hear him stalling in the kitchen this morning, probably hoping I'd come down and eat cereal with him, but I couldn't bring myself to do it. I wanted to talk to him, but at the same time, I didn't want to listen to whatever he had to say.

I shuffled down Kringle, scuffing my tennis shoes on the sidewalk. Truthfully, I was feeling sick. About Roy and that girl. About Marianne and my dad.

He liked her. Her! Marianne Walker, the Frankfort gem. She was at least twenty years younger than he was, which made her as close to my age as to his. Gross. I didn't mind that he liked someone. There were times growing up when I'd hoped he would fall in love and get married. But I always imagined she was soft looking, with her hair in a bun. Kind of like Mrs. Goodwin. But Marianne? She was so . . . so . . . bony. And tall. And *blond.*

Blond. Like the girl with Roy. She wasn't so tall. But she had a perfect body, curvy but somehow incredibly thin and toned, like she was a walking airbrushed image.

Roy hadn't even told me about her. Who was she? Why had he asked me to wait for him if he wasn't waiting for me? I had liked rereading every text between us since he'd left, thinking they were romantic. But last night as I'd read them again, I'd noticed I'd always texted him first. He'd never said much back. And as the weeks went on, he'd said less and less. We hadn't spoken on an actual call since my first day of work.

It took seeing him kissing someone else to get it: Roy was done with me. If he'd ever really been interested at all.

Why hadn't I seen it before?

My mind went around and around. Marianne. Dad. Roy. Marianne. Dad. Roy.

The trolley driver sighed when she saw me boarding the bus with a couple of tourists.

"Don't you ever get a day off?"

"Don't you?" I mumbled as I swiped my card.

I put my earbuds in and flipped through my music, wanting to get lost in my thoughts, but my phone died in my hands. Mushmelon.

I'd been so upset last night, I hadn't charged it. I sighed and stared out the window as we drove down the highway.

By the time everyone unloaded at Santa's Stables, it was just me and the driver. She glanced at me in her huge rearview mirror and raised an eyebrow.

"What's the matter with you?"

"Nothing," I lied.

"You look like someone ran over your dog."

"I don't have a dog."

"Your cat, then." She pulled the lever, and the door whooshed closed. "I'm a dog person myself. Got two."

No wonder we couldn't seem to get along.

We didn't say anything else until she dropped me at the park's trolley stop. "Chin up, girlie."

"It's Darby."

"Darby." She tapped the name on the pocket of her shirt. "Pauline."

As I trudged down the steps, she said, "Tell Nick I say hello."

"You know him?" I asked.

"Everyone knows Nick." She waved me away. "You tell him, will you?"

"I will," I said as the doors shut. She took off without another glance.

Rain threatened overhead as I crossed the parking lot. The blanket of gray clouds was as suffocating as a quilt over my head. I pulled my hair into a ponytail as I headed past the ticket booth. Already, the back of my neck was damp with sweat.

I kept my head down in the locker room as I changed into my

coveralls, not in the mood to talk to anyone. Maybe because of the gray sky, the crowd at the park was extra light. I only had a handful of 6-2-4s radioed in before noon, and bathroom duty was a breeze. I even polished the faucets in the women's rooms. There was something oddly satisfying about scraping the gunk from around the edges of the spouts.

As I exited the bathroom onto the midway, I realized how brown the bushes were around the building. I wondered if the night crew had forgotten to water them. I wheeled my cart back into the bathroom, filled one of my mop buckets with clean water, and went back out. It took three bucketfuls to water them all. Maybe it was just wishful thinking, but they seemed perkier as I pushed my cart away. After that, I checked the other plants around the park. Most of them were okay—shabby and shapeless, but okay.

Then, as I emptied the trash cans at the end of Santa Claus Lane, I noticed the signpost was peeling and faded. I'd seen some paint cans in the maintenance closet, so once I finished my afternoon rounds, I headed that way to grab some supplies. I spent the rest of the day touching up the signs in bright red, holly green, and white. I finished painting and took my time cleaning up. The park would be closing soon, but the thought of going home and facing Dad kept me dawdling. I decided to head for the bunker to change and then wait around for Jane or someone to get off work.

The bunker was vacant. I changed back into my cutoffs and went to the break room, and still, nobody was around.

I went and listened at Nick's office door; it was slightly ajar, and I didn't hear any snoring. I knocked softly, and the door creaked open. Khaki metal desk and filing cabinets, a mess of pictures on the wall, and a chair with wooden arms. No Nick. Maybe he was riding around the field in his red cart.

I was about to go when the picture of Mrs. Patterson on his desk caught my eye. I stepped into the office and picked it up. She was so pretty with her dark hair and deep eyes. Her smile had a magnetism to it that drew me in, even through decades and ink and photo paper.

"Hello, honey."

Nick hobbled into the office.

I quickly put the frame back next to the Santa mug full of markers. "I didn't mean to pry, I was just—"

"That's my wife," he said. He looked at me over his star sunglasses. "Course, you know that."

I nodded. "She's been gone a year now?"

"Nine months, twenty days. Cancer. She fought her battle with honor."

"I'm sure she did."

He smiled at the picture of her on his desk. "Sweetheart."

The look on his face—like he would give anything to talk to her—I understood how that felt. But he knew what her voice sounded like. He knew what made her laugh and what she would say if he asked her a question. I wondered if that made it worse.

He looked up from the photo and snapped into Sergeant Nick mode. "Something you needed, soldier?"

"No, sir," I said quickly.

"What are you still doing here? Weren't you scheduled until seven?"

"Yes, sir. I was just going to wait around for some friends."

Nick studied me as he settled behind his desk. "Made friends, have you?"

I nodded.

"Knew they'd come around. All of 'em have caused a disaster or two of their own. Least yours can be fixed. Your father has set the Globe unveiling for the twelfth."

"He has?"

"Mm-hmm. Says the new bubble will be here by Friday. Gives us the weekend to move the scene in."

"Anything I can do?" I asked.

"Affirmative. Keep cleaning the field and stay alert for the enemy."

The enemy again? I stepped back, about to leave, when I remembered. "Pauline the trolley driver says hello."

Nick smiled as he shuffled some papers. "Good girl, that Pauline. Worked concessions back in, oh, eighty-seven, eighty-eight. Never called in sick, never was late."

I raised my eyebrows. He remembered that? I was about to ask if she was surly back then, too, when he pushed some papers to the side, and I got a shock. There, in the pile of papers, was a navy-blue folder with gold trim. Just like the one I'd seen at the tourist board meeting.

Suddenly, the obvious answer to the obvious question I'd asked at the meeting came to me.

"Oh, no!"

"What's the matter?" Nick asked.

"The Whitman Group is interested in building a mall in town."

"Is that right?"

"Yes, sir." I hesitated. "They've pledged to the town council and board of tourism that the location will be far enough away from the square not to interfere with local businesses."

"Not a big town. Doesn't leave many options," he said, poker-faced.

"But they also promised to be near the highway."

"That narrows it down by eighty percent."

He'd probably learned to stare blankly in the military. I couldn't get a read on him at all. I thought about waiting him out; sometimes people will start talking if you're quiet long enough. But not Nick. I counted to twenty; his gaze didn't waver, and his mouth stayed clamped shut.

"Are they trying to buy Holly Jolly Land?" I blurted out.

"Might be."

My heart sank. "You're selling, aren't you?"

"Brass tacks, just like your old man." He considered me. "I might as well tell you, since you seem to know everything, anyway. Shut the door. Not everyone here is privy to classified information."

As I closed the office door, he picked up the navy Whitman Group folder from his desk and waved it at me. "Lady came to see me a few weeks ago, about the time you broke my Snow Globe. Gave me this offer."

"And you took the deal." I pinched the bridge of my nose.

"No, I didn't."

I looked up at him. "You . . . didn't?"

"You don't wave the white flag as soon as the enemy reaches

the gates. No, I didn't take the deal. Yet. Still considering. Have to study all the possible maneuvers."

So, there was still hope. I just had to convince him. "Sir, if you sell to them, it will destroy the town."

Nick laughed his insane laugh and pointed his cane to the photographs on the wall. "That's what they told me when I broke ground in 1979. The town is still here, and it'll still be here even if they build a mall."

"This is different. Holly Jolly Land has become a local landmark since then. Now that we're getting better known, these people just want to come in and make money and cash out."

"That's for the town council to figure out, not me."

"But what about us?" I cried.

"You?"

"The Misfi— Your employees."

Nick waved this away. "You'd all be fine. Lots of work for soldiers who salute."

I couldn't believe he was so coldhearted. I gestured at the photo on his desk. "What about all the work you and your wife put into this place? You can't seriously be thinking about throwing away all the memories—"

"Now, hold on there, private," Nick said.

"What would she want you to do?" I asked.

"That's enough," he whispered.

"But—"

"I said that's enough, Darby. I won't tolerate insubordination. Why don't you wait for your friends outside." He pointed at the door, and I left.

I ended up at the dreidels, watching Jane unload the last of the night's visitors. When she came over to switch off the power and lock up her booth, she spotted me. "What's wrong?"

"What makes you think something's wrong?" I asked.

She raised an eyebrow. "You look like you drank a blue slushy."

"Definitely not." I'd seen too many of them reappear as 6-2-4s.

I followed her into a dreidel and sank onto the seat. She turned it around so we were facing away from the midway lights. I laid my head back. There were no stars. Just indigo and gray clouds.

I wondered if Roy was back at camp yet. I wondered if he and that girl were lying in the grass looking up at the sky. Maybe she went to his camp and they had snuck off to some secluded spot, and maybe she was leaning against him like she had been last night.

Marianne was too tall to lean against Dad. There were so many reasons they didn't belong together.

"So? What's wrong, dude?"

I sighed. "I think my dad is dating someone. I saw them together last night."

"Gross. Were they naked?"

"No! He was looking at her. Like, *looking* at her."

"Oh."

"And the guy I was waiting for yesterday—"

"I saw Roy sucking face with that girl."

I swallowed hard. "Yeah, well, anyway."

"You're too good for him. Moving on." She spun the dreidel slowly. "These are not reasons to be blue."

I looked out at the midway. The lights over the games were mostly burned out, but the ones that worked cast pretty pink and yellow light over everything. "He broke my heart."

"Which one?"

Both of them, I thought.

She spun the dreidel faster and faster. I grabbed the wheel and helped her spin. Soon, we were spinning so fast my bangs were blown off my face and everything was a blur. Jane shrieked and laughed.

I let go and fell into the seat. I closed my eyes and lost all sense of direction. Roy. Dad. Marianne. Roy. Dad. Marianne.

The Whitman Group.

"That's not all," I said, opening my eyes again. We were coming out of the spin, and the world was slowly slipping from stripes of light to blobby shapes. "Nick is thinking of selling Holly Jolly Land to some developers who want to build a mall."

"WHAT?"

She wrenched the wheel to a stop.

Everything tumbled back into place, and my stomach flipped over.

Jane stared at me. "What did you say?"

"Some developers want to build a Christmas-themed mall."

"What about Nick?"

"They want to buy the park. So they can tear it down and build a fancy shopping mall here. He's thinking about it."

"No. That's not true."

"It is. I talked to him tonight."

She jumped to her feet. "Why didn't you tell me?"

"I just found out," I explained.

"I can't believe he would sell."

"Maybe he won't. But if he does, you can get another job. It's not like this is such a great place to work, anyway."

"What do you know about it?" she snapped. "What do you know about anything? This isn't your home. You're only here because you broke the Snow Globe."

"It's not home to you, either," I said. "It's just a job."

"It's not just a job!" She pointed at herself. "Misfit, remember? This is my island!"

"I know. I get it."

"No, you don't. I thought you did, but maybe you don't."

"I do," I insisted. "I know how it feels to have your entire world turned upside down, believe me. This isn't my island, okay, but the courthouse was until this woman from Frankfort came along and kicked me out. I know. Believe me, dude. I know."

She took a deep breath and sank back down to the seat. "So, what do we do? We can't let him sell."

"Let who sell?"

Charlie was out of his box, looming over us.

Jane filled him in. "Nick might sell Holly Jolly Land."

"Why?"

"It doesn't matter why!" Jane cried. "He can't sell the park. It would be the worst thing ever."

"So, we stop him," Charlie said. He stepped over the wall of our dreidel and sat next to Jane, oh-so-casually resting his long arm on the edge behind her. "We need a plan."

"What?" Jane challenged.

"Oh." He shrugged. "Dar-Dar?"

"Don't look at me. You two know him better than I do."

"Protest rally?" Charlie said. "Sit-in?"

Jane snorted. "Yeah, I'm sure an old war vet would appreciate a peaceful protest."

"You never know," Charlie said slowly. "A lot of people reminding him how much they love the park might do it."

"Yes!" I said. "But not protesting. What if he had a really good day of sales? Then he'd see the benefit of staying open and making money."

"He doesn't care about the money," Jane said.

"Yeah, well, the investors are probably offering enough that he might care a little bit about the money."

"We're focused on the wrong thing," Charlie said. "We can't build a dam, maybe we dry up the source."

"What?" Jane said.

"We need to stop the investors."

"That's genius!" Jane said, and he grew two or three inches.

We tossed around ideas, most of them ridiculous. Charlie suggested infiltrating and taking them down from the inside. Jane wanted to blackmail them. We went around and around as the sky grew black, but we didn't come up with a way to get to the source.

"They're not going to stop," I said.

"Fine." Jane sighed. "Then what about your father?"

"My dad?"

"He's mayor. Make him stop the sale."

"Yes!" Charlie said. "First Dar-Dar you are. Stop him you must."

Hmm. Could I convince Dad to block the sale somehow? I

wasn't sure. Maybe I *could* have if Marianne hadn't come to town and bulldozed my life. But now?

What would Dad do in my shoes? He had a way of getting people on board, of making them believe in things. Usually, he rolled up his sleeves and showed them what they were missing.

"Oh!" I sat up.

"What?"

"I need to show him! If I can get him out here, I bet my dad would look around and realize what a mistake it would be to approve the Whitman Group's proposal for a mall! He's just distracted by the bright and shiny right now, but if I can get him away from town . . . I can make him remember what Christmas is all about."

Jane and Charlie looked at each other. Jane bit her lip to keep from laughing.

"What?"

"You. You're all . . . the magic of Christmas."

"Yeah, well, my dad believes it, too. At least, he used to. If I can get him to remember, there's no way he'll let this happen."

"It's worth a shot if you think it will work," Jane said. "Get him out here tomorrow to see what these developers want to destroy."

"Tomorrow?"

"Nick could sign the papers any minute!" she reminded me. "It's got to be tomorrow."

"Hey!"

Calvin. Funny how I knew his voice even without looking. I guess after a month of someone yelling at you, you know their voice better than your own. I sighed as Jane spun us around to face him.

"What?" she yelled back.

"Quitting time!"

"So why are you here?" Jane shouted back.

"I'm trying to lock up. Come on, y'all, it's nearly ten."

We climbed out of the dreidel. Charlie-in-the-Box loped up to Calvin and clasped his shoulder. "We have a plan, Cal. We're going to save the park."

Calvin looked at him like he was crazy. "Can it wait until tomorrow? It's closing time."

Charlie-in-the-Box pressed his hands together and bowed. "Closing time. But not the end of all things old or the opening of all things new. We will save the park, or we will die trying. Just like you're trying to do. Your chariot, my lady," he said to Jane.

She jumped on his back, and they took off toward the bunker.

I started to follow, but Calvin touched my arm. "Can I talk to you?"

"Um, yeah."

Jane looked back and raised an eyebrow at me.

I waved her away. It wasn't like that.

"What's up?" I said.

"What's he talking about?" Calvin watched Charlie and Jane disappear into the dark. "Save the park?"

"Oh, it's . . ." For some reason, I didn't want to tell him about the Whitman Group's offer. Maybe it was the way Jane had reacted when I'd first told her, but I had the feeling Calvin would take it hard, too. I didn't want to disappoint anyone else, especially if our plan worked and Dad shut down the investors. "Nothing. Charlie being Charlie."

Calvin shook his head. "He's a strange guy. But a good guy. I hope your friend doesn't break his heart."

"Who? Jane?"

"Yeah."

"She's not the kind of person to do that."

"What kind of person would?"

"I don't— What?"

"What kind of person would string someone along and then break his heart in the end?"

I glared at him. "I don't want to talk about Roy."

He shook his head. "Who said we were?"

"I get it. I know what you're trying to say. I was stupid to fall for—"

"You're not stupid, and I wasn't trying to talk about that moron. I was talking about—"

"He's *not* a moron."

"There you go defending him again when you should be mad as hell. But like I said, I wasn't talking about him."

He watched me with soft eyes that caught the light from the midway, and somehow the gold in them sparkled. It was a shame he didn't wear contacts; his eyes were kind of spectacular.

"Then who are you talking about?"

He looked away, suddenly shy.

Did he mean— No, he couldn't. Calvin didn't like me. There was no way. He'd totally ditched me on our just-friends date, and then he hadn't spoken to me for months. So why was he acting differently now?

"What are you thinking?" he asked.

"I was wondering why you're being nice to me. You're usually so mean."

"Just because I make people work hard *at work* doesn't make me mean."

"That's not what I'm— You were mean to me way before I came here. Every time I saw you at school, you were staring at me and frowning."

"That's just the way I look."

"No, it's not!" I argued. "I see you smiling all the time. You're always nice to Penny in the cafeteria. And you smile at Vanessa Marshall when she talks to you at your locker."

"Sounds like you're the one staring at me."

"No!" The smug smile on his face was infuriating. "I'm just saying, that's not your normal face. You look at me like—like—I ran over your cat. And I don't even drive."

He shook his head, but he didn't answer me.

"I'd like to know," I insisted as we headed up the midway. "If I did something to you, I promise I don't know what—"

"Can you help me with a repair before you go?" he asked suddenly.

Sliced apples turned brown slower than his moods changed. "What?"

"It will only take a few minutes."

"Um, sure?"

"Good. Let's go."

Boys.

Fourteen

SANTA'S WORKSHOP WAS AN IT'S A SMALL WORLD knockoff, right down to the slow-moving boat floating through dimly lit animatronic scenes. The wooden elves sang "Santa Claus Is Coming to Town" while they hammered toys, wrapped presents, danced around the workshop, and loaded the sleigh. The last scene showed them waving as Santa flew away into the night.

Three-year-olds and their exhausted grandparents loved the ride. No one else did.

"So, what are we doing here?" I asked as we headed up the exit ramp.

"Decapitated elf." Calvin smiled at my expression. "You'd be surprised how often it happens."

At the loading dock, we went around the control booth to a door that blended into the North Pole mural on the wall.

He held it open for me. "Watch your step."

Beyond the door was a narrow walkway, a wall on one side,

the water on the other, no railing. It was pitch-dark. I turned back to him. "Do you have a light?"

He took the small flashlight from his tool belt and flicked it on. He shone it on my feet so I could see where I was going.

I pressed my left side firmly against the wall and tried to walk, one foot in front of the other. Everything was painted black so as not to distract from the scenes across the little river. We edged around a corner, where the water turned to the left.

"It's this one. We need to cross," Calvin told me.

He lowered a plank over the river and walked across. He turned and shone the light on the plank so I could see.

"Um, how deep is the water?"

"About three feet. It's fine."

I walked across with my arms outstretched. He offered me his hand as I reached him, and I took it.

"Thanks," I said, letting go as soon as I was on solid ground.

He panned the scene with his flashlight, and I nearly screamed.

Unholy mother of evil elves.

The little robot beings were frozen in their tasks in the dark. Some wrapped boxes, some held gleaming scissors to cut long strings of ribbon, and some stuffed colored tissue into gift bags. All of them had smiles painted onto their faces, but caught in the weak beam of his flashlight, they looked like demonic versions of themselves.

The headless elf was easy to spot; she was right up front, in the middle of several elves, making a red-and-white bow. A white pole stuck up from her shoulders like a headless spine. The elves around her weren't the least bit bothered; they smiled up at her, their tiny black eyes flat and their smiles all teeth.

I was careful not to bump into anything. I had a feeling the elves were waiting to come to life, or worse, devour me, if I touched them. Calvin moved the light quickly across the floor of the scene, casting random parts of elves into view.

I was in a horror movie.

"There," he said. He aimed his light at a pile of papier-mâché wrapping paper, where an elf face smiled up at the ceiling. He retrieved it and shoved it back on the elf's shoulders. It fell right off again and rolled into a web of ribbons and string.

"It needs superglue," I said.

He took a small tube from a pocket of his belt and handed it to me. I squirted some on the white PVC spine, and he stuck the head on. "Is it straight?"

"Lemme look." I stepped back to get a better view and almost fell into the river.

"Watch out!" he cried, reaching for me.

I snatched the front of his coveralls to keep from toppling into the water. As he grabbed hold of my arm with one hand and the elf's head with the other, his flashlight fell to the ground and rolled away.

The light illuminated the spindly legs and metal gears of the elves, but it was weakened as it reached our feet. I was holding onto Calvin Sherman in the dark.

His hand was wrapped around my arm, and I still had a handful of the front of his coveralls. I wanted to break away, but I couldn't risk letting him go, unsure if he had his balance.

I could feel his breath on my hair. His feet shuffled back, farther from the edge of the river. And then. His hand moved up my arm and rested on my shoulder. His thumb brushed my neck, and I gasped. The electric shock was so strong it was like it lit us up for a second. His eyes were on mine, and my skin was on fire, and his breath was warm, and—

"You can, um, let go," he said.

I stepped back, straight into the headless elf, and shrieked.

Calvin found his flashlight and shone it on me. "You okay? You didn't break anything, did you?"

I turned away from him, humiliated. "No, I did not break anything."

He found the elf head again and waited while I put more superglue on it. I shoved it onto its pole and said, "That's straight enough."

We awkwardly retreated through the scene and headed back across the plank. We went out the way we'd come in, me in front, him shining the light just ahead of my feet.

I headed straight for the exit. I couldn't catch my breath; the air was damp in there or something.

What had just happened?

He caught up to me at the entrance. "You all right?"

I put my hands on my head and tried to catch my breath. "I'm fine."

"You look a little spooked," he said with a grin. "Elves get to you?"

I glared at him. "No."

"Then what? Is it—"

I started down the path past the Holly Bally Pit.

"It's nothing."

"Oh, it's definitely something," he said.

"Just leave me alone, okay?" I said, walking faster.

He burst out laughing. "That right there? That face you make when you're frustrated? I like that."

"I didn't make any face."

"You did." His eyes were still full of humor, but he frowned. "You made it on your first day of work, when I gave you the M-O-P. And that day when you said talking to me was like doing a puzzle."

"Because it is!"

"Mm-hmm. It is. Because you make things complicated that don't need to be."

"What things? What am I complic—"

"This, Darby. You and me." He paused. "Nothing to say about that?"

"Oh, plenty," I shot back. "But you have a really bad habit of interrupting me! Like whatever I'm saying isn't important because I'm just Darby and you're . . . you're . . ."

"I'm what?"

"You," I said, poking him in the chest, "are a self-righteous know-it-all, and you know it."

He considered me for a minute and then donned. "What I know is that there's no one else I'd rather argue with."

"Why?" I said, annoyed. "Because you think you'll always win?"

He threaded his thumb through the belt loop on my shorts and pulled me closer. "Because win or lose, I win. No one gets under my skin like you do."

A thousand turtledoves took flight in my stomach, and it tickled. I nearly laughed.

"There's the smile," he said.

"The smile?"

"I told you before, I like that face you make when you're mad."

He brushed my bangs out of my eyes. "But you're a knockout when you smile."

No one had ever called me a knockout before. Dad called me beautiful, but he was Dad and he was kind of required by the law to do so. People in town called me lovely because that was the best they could muster. I was pleasant plus polite plus put together, and that equaled lovely. But knockout? No, not me.

Did Calvin really see me that way? He wasn't the type to say things he didn't mean.

"I—" His lower lip was as soft looking as it had been in his truck that night.

He smirked. "You want me to kiss you, don't you?"

"Says who?" I stammered.

He leaned his head to the side. "Says me. I think you want me to."

My mouth went dry and I had to swallow. "Well, I think you should wait until I ask before you try."

He nodded.

We were so close our noses touched.

"Ask me to, then."

I drew in a breath. "What?"

"Ask me," he repeated. "If you want."

His breath was warm and smelled like peppermints. Part of me wanted to kiss him. But then I remembered Roy and my broken heart, and something didn't feel right. I shook my head. "No, I—"

He let go of me and took a step back. "All right, then."

"So that's it?" I said.

"I guess so," he said. "See you later." I got a sinking feeling in my stomach as he walked away from me. I didn't want him to kiss me, so why did I care if he left me here by the entrance to Babes in Toyland? Oh. Right.

"Wait," I called.

"What?" He sounded hopeful and turned toward me.

"I want you to give me something, but it's not what you think."

He frowned for a minute, and then his expression smoothed as he figured it out. "You need a ride home."

"Yeah?"

I could see him smiling. "Come on, then."

When he dropped me off in front of my house, I was a little disappointed when the truck door opened on the first try.

For some reason, I didn't expect Dad to be waiting up for me when I got home, even though it was nearly midnight. When I walked into the cool kitchen and found him sitting at the table, I was surprised.

He sat in the pool of light from the pendants over the table, the only light in the dark kitchen shining on his floppy blond hair. There was a half-eaten Piggly Wiggly apple pie on the table, and plates, one covered in crumbs, one waiting for me, and forks and coffee mugs, his usual green one and my favorite *It's a Wonderful Life* mug with George lifting Mary off her feet.

Dad sniffed and crossed his arms when I approached. I knew this moment, but it felt off.

"Hi," I said lamely.

"Have some pie." Dad nodded at the empty chair on his left. I went around the table and sat down, feeling like a stranger in my own house. Like I'd walked into someone else's kitchen, found someone else's father having a late-night snack.

I squirmed in my seat. The soft glow of the overhead light suddenly felt like an interrogation tactic. This wasn't the table where Dad carved the turkey every Thanksgiving when our cousins from Cincinnati came to town. It wasn't where he'd taught me to write my name with red and green crayons. It was a place for good cop/bad cop questioning, for deals and leaning in and maneuvering.

Well, I had some leaning in to do, too.

Maureen O'Hara meowed and padded into the kitchen. She wound between my feet and rubbed her face on my leg. I cut a piece of pie and dropped a tiny bit of apple filling on the floor for her. Dad watched me as I slid the rest onto my plate. In the quiet, every clink of fork on plate was as loud as the clicking of Rudolph's Wild Ride as the chains pulled it up the first hill.

"So?" Dad asked as I took a bite. "Where have you been? The park has been closed for nearly two hours."

I swallowed the crust. It was dry. "I stayed to hang out with my friends."

"Who?"

"Jane and Charlie."

"Are they the ones who were hollering at you during the parade yesterday?"

I smiled; I'd almost forgotten the way they'd jumped up and down and screamed at me. So much had happened since. "Yeah."

"I don't think I know them. Who are their parents?"

"I have no idea." When he raised his eyebrows, I explained.

"They go to Liberty. I don't think they live in town. But they're really nice, you'd like them."

He didn't seem convinced.

"Really, Dad, all the kids out there are nice. In fact," I said, using this to my advantage, "why don't you come see for yourself? You've never even seen where I work all day."

"I'll see what I can do."

That's what he said when Mr. Oates asked for a traffic light on the corner by Big O's Tires. It's what he said to Mrs. Jenkins when she asked for a copy of the minutes of a private town council meeting. It's what he said when he meant no. I knew because me and Dad, we were a team.

Something was different between us this summer, though, something I couldn't explain but I could feel. I wished I could get us back to the way we were, but I didn't know how.

"There's something else we need to talk about," he said, resting his elbows on the table. He stared at my pie instead of meeting my eye. "Last night, you might have gotten the wrong idea about Mari—"

Nope. I couldn't talk about that. I cut him off.

"Why didn't you tell me the Whitman Group was making an offer on Holly Jolly Land?"

He blinked. "How did you find out?"

"I kind of figured it out." I pushed my plate away. "How long have you known?"

"Only a couple of weeks." He sighed. "I didn't tell you because I could see you were getting attached to the place, and I didn't want to take that away, too."

"Too?"

"You were pretty upset about not working at the courthouse. But lately, you've seemed okay with it—I thought because you were enjoying yourself at the park. So I wasn't going to tell you until it was official."

"I didn't think you noticed," I said softly. "That I was sad about not working at the courthouse."

"Of course I noticed," he said. "I've missed you this summer. It's been too quiet around the office."

Yeah, right, I wanted to say, thinking of Marianne's hand on his arm last night. If she hadn't kicked me out of the courthouse, none of this would be happening. Dad would never have agreed to a meeting with the Whitman Group, and he would never have given them the green light with the board of tourism or the zoning commission or Nick or anyone.

"You can't let them buy the park," I said. "They'll ruin everything."

He scrubbed his face and sighed. "I believe Marianne is right—if I don't get on board and help maneuver this thing, they could ruin the entire town."

"How? If you vote against the zone change, they can't build, even if Nick Patterson did sell."

"It's not that simple," Dad said. "Nick Patterson came back from the Vietnam War a pretty big hero, you know. Some of our boys didn't make it home. So when he and Mrs. Patterson wanted to open the park, the town gave them a great deal on the land. It was the least they could do for a war hero and his new bride, and at the time, no one expected Christmas to need that land."

"So what?" I grumbled. "Now that he's old and alone, let the Whitman Group steal the war hero's land out from under him?"

"I understand they're making him a very generous offer for his business," Dad said sharply. "They're not stealing anything."

"But it's his life's work! His memories with his wife! You can't let them do this!"

"It's not only my call," he said. "Mr. Patterson can decide for himself. If he wants to sell, he'll sell. But I hope he does."

"Why?"

"You were the one who told me how run-down the place has gotten." Dad raised an eyebrow. "What was it you said? It was kind of sad and dirty?"

"No, not at all. Maybe it needs some sprucing up, but nothing major." I leaned forward. "Why don't you come see for yourself? I mean, when was the last time you were there? Please."

Dad stared across the kitchen, drumming his fingers. "Maybe this weekend."

"I wish you would visit," I said quietly. I rose from my seat. I was tired, and all I wanted was to crawl into bed with Maureen O'Hara and Netflix.

"I'll try," he said.

That meant maybe, which was better than seeing what he could do. I'd take what I could get. I gave him a hug and kissed the top of his head. "Thank you! You won't be sorry."

He patted my arm. "There's something else—"

"Can it wait?" I pulled away. "I'm beat."

He nodded. "Sure. Sleep well."

Fifteen

I STOPPED BY THE TICKET BOOTH TO SAY HELLO to Charlie on my way into the park the next afternoon. He looked halfway to dreamland as he doodled on the toe of his Chuck Taylors with a Sharpie. He was using a bandana as a headband to keep his hair off his face, but the industrial fan in the booth with him was blowing it every which way.

"Hey, Char-Char."

He looked me over, nodding to a slow beat I couldn't hear. "You know, maintenance used to be my gig before I got promoted to sales."

I couldn't imagine Charlie being promoted to anything other than a longer nap. I wondered if Nick had switched him to a job that required less exertion since he moved like he was constantly doing tai chi.

"The uniform definitely looks better on you."

"You wore this?"

He shrugged. "It rode up a lot."

I tried not to think about what that meant. "Right. I better go, my shift starts at four."

"It's already four?" He shook his head, amazed. "Where does the time go? When it passes by, I mean. Maybe it reincarnates itself into, you know, déjà vu or something."

"Yeah, maybe?"

He scratched his armpit as he nodded at some thought off in the distance. "Maybe every second that passes unused dies a miserable death because it was destined to be the second we figured it out, y'know? But we're all clueless, so we miss it. And then those seconds, full of, like, *knowing*, cling together until they're long enough to make an 'aha' moment that the universe cannot miss. Like a volcano. Y'know?"

"Yeah?"

He smiled at me the way parents smile at their children, like I was cute but clueless.

"So, bye." I turned to go, but he called me back.

"Hey, Dar-Dar? Do you think anyone has noticed my subliminal messages?"

"If by anyone you mean Jane," I said, sneaking a look at him, "I don't know. She hasn't said anything to me."

His shoulders slumped even more than usual. I hadn't noticed before; he was drawing her profile on his shoes, tangles of hair trailing down the side of his shoe, the one eye showing faceted like a diamond. It looked nothing like her, really, but it *felt* like her. My heart hurt for him in that moment. He was more than hung up on Jane; he was literally head over heels.

Poor Charlie. He had broadcasted a new message to her over

the sound system every day that I'd been at work. Most of them were riffs on "Charlie is adorable," but my favorites were the ones where he overenunciated words within phrases, like:

"Thank YOU for visiting Holly Jolly Land! SHOULD you need help just ASK for assistance. Visit CHARLIE-IN-THE-BOX at the ticket booth for season passes because there are no rain checks FOR A later DATE! Thank you, and have a Holly Jolly day!"

The truth was, I didn't know if Jane hadn't heard the messages or if she had but was ignoring them. She had a poker face, and she hadn't confided in me. If she liked anyone, let alone Charlie, I didn't know it.

"Don't give up," I encouraged him. "You never know when the messages will start to work."

"You think?" he asked as hopefully as a kid hoping Santa is real.

"I hear them, don't I? She might, too, eventually. Give it time, for the volcano to erupt or whatever."

"Touché, First Misfit. Touché."

I left him and headed through the rusty gates of the park.

I jumped right into my routine. The park was busy, which kept me busy cleaning up after the patrons. Truthfully, I was glad the place was a bit trashed. It was soothing to clean up messes that had nothing to do with me. I pushed every thought out of my head and focused only on what was right in front of me.

Besides, if there was even the slightest chance Dad would show up, I wanted the park to look its best. I was glad I'd taken the time to paint the directional sign yesterday. It gleamed in the sunshine. And when I checked on the plants by the bathrooms, well, okay, they were still brown, but they didn't look quite as crunchy. I dove into my work, determined to do my best.

A clogged toilet in the women's room? Wonderful! I had become a plunger pro this summer.

Neon-blue 6-2-4 by the gate for the Carol-sel? Bring it on. Nothing me and my trusty M-O-P couldn't handle.

Tipped trash can by Santa's Scrambler? Easy as pie! Swept and bagged in a jiffy. There was no sign of Calvin all afternoon. I was glad about that. No sign of Dad, either, though.

And so it went all the way into the evening. I was sweaty and dirty and exhausted, and felt better than I had in days. As the sun was going down I took a break. I bought a couple of Cokes from the candy store and went to see Jane.

She drank hers in one gulp. "What's the deal with your dad?"

I told her about our conversation last night.

She didn't seem convinced. "Parents, dude. Never do what they say they're going to."

I frowned. That wasn't true, at least of my dad. I watched Jane out of the corner of my eye as I drank my soda. I'd never heard her talk about her family. I wondered what they were like.

"He'll be here," I said. "Maybe even tonight."

"When he shows, bring him over to the midway—it looks better in the dark."

"I'll try."

"And make sure Jamarcus doesn't do the whiplash trick to him if he rides Rudolph."

"I doubt my dad will want to ride a roller coaster."

"Yeah, well. And make sure—"

"It'll be fine," I assured her. "Once he sees the place and how much everyone loves it, he'll withdraw his support for building the mall here. Don't worry, I know my dad."

"Yeah? Then how come he approved it in the first place?"

Because of Marianne, I thought. But I didn't say that.

My radio crackled, and Calvin's voice broke across the rock version of "White Christmas" playing over the speakers. "Santa's Helper Darby, you're needed at Rudolph's Wild Ride, over."

My stomach flipped as I radioed back. "I'm on a break. Can it wait? Over."

"No, I need your assistance on a repair. Over."

"Peachy," I muttered. I capped my bottle and clipped my walkie-talkie back to my belt. I'd had a plan to avoid him today at all costs, and now I had to go work with him on a repair?

Jane was watching me. "What happened with you two last night?"

I blushed. "Nothing."

"I was right, wasn't I?" She smiled so big her eyes went squinty. "You're warm for his form!"

"No, not exactly. Not at all," I corrected. "I have to go."

She got on the microphone and sang, "Make his wish come true, all he wants for Christmas is you!"

I glared at her, and she cracked up. "Go get 'em, Darby!" she cried.

I wasn't going to get anyone. I was working.

Rudolph's Wild Ride was the biggest—well, the only—roller coaster in the park; on a clear day like today, you could see the red tracks all the way from Babes in Toyland. I'd gotten used to the roar of the train as it zoomed past when I was down on the ground, but as I walked through the midway that day, it was as loud as thunder in my ears. The turtledoves flew higher into my rib cage as I climbed the steps to the loading platform and came up on the exit-ramp side of the train.

Calvin was on the platform, watching people load and unload while he waited for me, a gray toolbox at his feet. From a completely objective standpoint, I had to admit he looked gorgeous in those grease-stained coveralls. I tried not to stare, but it was like my eyes were locked onto him. He had a dimple low in his cheek, something I'd forgotten about, since he so rarely smiled. He was smiling now, at a little girl with a pink bow in her braids riding on her mom's shoulders, and that dimple was sinkhole deep. His braids were coppery in the sun, and his eyes shone bright gold behind his glasses. I liked the way his entire body lifted up when he smiled, like even his shoulders were turned up at the edges.

Our eyes met, and his smile softened to something private.

I looked away until the turtledoves in my stomach stopped flapping their wings. The coaster blasted out of the station, blowing my hair off my face. I could feel the burn on my cheeks as he walked up to me.

"What took you so long?" he said.

"I came as fast as—"

"Right." The lead in his voice matched the weight that dropped in my stomach.

"I did! I—"

"What's the matter?"

"Nothing, I—"

"You're making a weird face."

"No, I'm no—"

"Yeah, you are."

I glared at him. "Don't start interrupting me again just because I wouldn't let you manhandle me last night!"

"Manhandle you?" he said. "I didn't— You know what?"

"What?"

His nostrils flared as he took a deep breath. "Nothing. We've got work to do."

He stomped out onto a metal grate walkway that ran alongside the track, out past the loading and unloading station. I forced myself to watch where I was stepping as I followed. The last thing I needed was to slip and fall. The walkway forked; a metal staircase climbed to the top of the first big hill of the ride on the left and curved to an extra stretch of track to the right, where the brown train sat, out of order. We went right, and Calvin climbed into the first cart. He carefully set his toolbox on the seat. Everything inside was neat, ordered by type and then biggest to smallest. He chose a medium-sized wrench thing.

"You really think I can fix this thing?" I asked.

"No. I think you can assist me while *I* fix this thing." He took a smaller wrench from its place and handed it to me. "Hold this."

"You think *you* can fix this thing?"

"I think it's my job to try."

He tightened a bolt on the side of the cart that was holding the safety bar in place. The more he tightened, the higher the bar rose, until it was back in position. He held out his hand for the wrench I was holding. I gave it to him, but he didn't use it. He put both wrenches back in the toolbox and snapped the lid shut.

“That’s it?” I asked.

“For now. Nick will have to check my work before I send it out. I don’t want anyone getting hurt.”

It was sweet, sort of, how concerned he was for other people, not that I was about to say so. I had other issues. I reached up and shoved him on the arm. “Did you really call me all the way over here to hold a wrench?”

He grinned. “I might have.”

“Why?”

“I wanted to see you.”

The way he put it out there like that was unnerving. “Why?”

He shook his head. “I told you, girl. I like that face you make when I annoy you. Now, how am I going to see it if I only bother you by radio?”

I was so frazzled by all of this, I had no words. I gaped for a minute, realized I probably looked like a fish, got mad and almost stomped my foot, then got mad because I knew he would enjoy that and I didn’t want to give him the satisfaction, and then blurted out, “You drive me BANANAS!”

“I know.” He smiled so triumphantly I wanted to scream. I didn’t want to play this game. I also kind of wanted to play this game.

Ugh.

“Calvin, I—”

“Wait. There’s something else I need you for.”

“If you want me to hold your wrench again—”

“Nah, that’s not it.” He looked right into my eyes. “Are you in love with that loser?”

“WHAT!” I gasped. “Who?” But I knew who he meant.

He cocked his head to the side and waited me out.

"You saw him with that—that girl, so I don't know why you're even asking."

"I know he's not into you," he said, and it hit me like a sucker punch.

"Well, there you go," I choked out.

"That's not what I asked, though," he said. "You can be into someone who doesn't feel the same way. So, do you have feelings for him, or not?"

"Why do you even care?"

"Because I like you, Darby!" he bellowed. "And I know you like me. But I have to know if you're into him because if you are, then maybe I don't want to get into it with you. I'm not setting myself up for that kind of hurt again."

"Who said I liked you?" I cried. "I never said—"

"You know you do."

"What I know is that every time you interrupt me, I want to smack that smug look off your face," I snapped.

He smiled. "So, you like to hate me. Same thing."

"It is not!" I argued, but I couldn't help thinking of what Charlie had said.

It's a love/hate thing.

Was he right? Did I love to hate Calvin? It was kind of fun to argue with him, and as much as he drove me bananas, I liked the way he smiled at me. I liked the way I felt when we were arguing. I liked the way he pushed my buttons.

Mother of kiwis, I liked Calvin Sherman.

Some of this must have been playing out on my face, because his expression softened. "See? You like me."

"Yeah, well, I also kind of hate you."

"Thin line, Globe Girl."

"DON'T CALL ME THAT!" I shouted. "Leave me alone!"

I turned to stomp away, but he took my hand with such tenderness that it stopped me in my tracks.

"See, that's the thing. I can't," he said. He stepped closer, still holding my hand. He rubbed his thumb over my fingers. "Is it him? Or me?"

I didn't know how to answer that. I knew that Roy and I could never be together, not after what he did. So what did it matter if I still had feelings for him or not?

Kissing Roy had been like lightning. Were all kisses as electric as his?

I stepped up to Calvin, so close that the fronts of our coveralls were touching; he raised an eyebrow.

I tilted my face up to his, closed my eyes, and parted my lips.

A second passed. Then—

Our radios burst with static. "Away in a Manger Shepherd Riya to all Misfits, mayday, mayday, three-oh-three in progress! Repeat, three-oh-three, Frank *incensed*!"

Calvin ripped his walkie-talkie from his belt and pressed Talk. "Which way did he go?"

Riya cut back. "Headed to Babes in Toyland. All Misfits, be on alert."

Calvin and I broke into a run back down the grated walkway. We pushed through the crowd getting off Rudolph and sprinted down the exit ramp.

"You head toward the Scrambler," he said. "I'll take the Holly Bally Pit."

We split at the path and took off.

I pushed through the stroller parking lot, knocking over unlocked strollers as I went. If Frank was mad, someone could get hurt.

I skidded around the corner of the bathroom building to the Scrambler path, and there was—

"Dad!"

"Hi, Moonpie." He frowned at me as I searched the area for signs of the goat. "Everything okay?"

"Sure," I lied, checking behind the bushes to the left of the bathrooms. "Just, you know, hoping to run into you."

"Who are you looking for?" he asked, stepping into my sight line.

Frank wasn't nearby. I forced myself to breathe and looked him in the eyes. "No one. I'm so glad you came!"

He cleared his throat, just before I saw Marianne coming out of the bathrooms. She was wearing a sundress and sandals that laced up her calves. Her hair was softer than I'd ever seen it, like she'd run her fingers through it a few times. She wasn't wearing her chunky glasses.

Were they on a *date*?

"Hi, Darby," she said shyly.

"What's going on?" I asked.

Dad's smiled slipped a little when he turned back to me. "Marianne has never seen the park, so I thought this would be a good time to show her around before . . ."

I glared at them. "Before she helps the Whitman Group tear it down. Yeah. Great idea."

"Darby—" she said.

My walkie-talkie screeched, and Riya's voice came through. "Three-oh-three is headed to the Holly Bally Pit. Repeat, three-oh-three, Holly Bally Pit!"

I quickly turned the volume down to zero.

"What was that?" Dad asked.

"Oh, it's, um, just a code," I said. "It means the Holly Bally Pit is full, I think."

Dad looked at me for a long second, but Marianne broke his attention away from me. "Maybe we should let Darby get back to work—"

"No!" I snapped. "I'm going to show you around."

"Oh," Dad said.

"Are you sure you can take so much time off?" Marianne asked. "I didn't know you were going to be with us."

Angry tears pricked the backs of my eyes. She might have taken the courthouse away from me, but she was *not* taking this away. It might be the only chance I got to convince Dad the town needed the park. "No, it's fine."

Dad pushed a smile onto his face. "Well, then, show us the sights."

He offered Marianne one elbow and me the other. Marianne glanced at me before gingerly taking Dad's arm.

"This way," I said, walking a step ahead of them.

For the next half hour I gave them the grand tour, all the while on the lookout for Frankincense. Dad was doing his best to keep everyone happy. He kept up a steady stream of questions for both of us, something he did at fundraising events when he had more than one donor vying for his undivided attention.

When I took them on the Santa's Workshop ride, I made sure to sit between them. I turned toward Dad so that Marianne was crammed against the edge of the boat and talked only to him. At the wrapping scene, I pointed out the elf I'd helped Calvin repair.

"You did?" Dad laughed. "I didn't know you knew anything about robotics."

"We-e-ll, we just kind of . . . stuck the head back on," I admitted.

He seemed impressed all the same.

Misfits said hello as we strolled by. I went out of my way to introduce Dad to everyone. I wanted him to see all the people who would be out of a job if the park closed.

Jamarcus caught up to us on the bridge to Winter Wonderland. "Hey, Darby! Oh, hi, Mayor."

"Hello, Jamarcus," Dad said.

"Sorry to interrupt, but, Darby, do you know if the brown Rudolph car is fixed yet?" Jamarcus asked me.

"Sure, Calvin and I fixed it this afternoon. It was just a loose . . . screw thing."

"Sweet," he breathed. "I'm working Rudolph tonight, and I did not want to deal with long lines."

"You should be good to go," I said with a smile.

He left us at the fork, and when I turned to reengage Dad in conversation, I caught him and Marianne sharing a look.

Gross.

I tried not to let Marianne's presence distract me from my task, but I couldn't help wondering if she was making a mental inventory of everything wrong with the park while I tried to sell Dad on everything that was right. As I reminisced with Dad about the first time I braved the Ferris wheel, was she noticing that it got stuck every third time around? As we laughed about the time I named all the horses on the Carol-sel, was she only humoring Dad by laughing, too?

At least they'd come at night. The lights from the Reindeer Games Midway sparkled, and the dark shadows hid most of the broken, worn-down edges of things. I wound them through the crowds quickly before Dad overheard what some of the guys were shouting to the girls as they passed by. But he insisted on stopping for latkes when Marianne said she'd never had one.

"You don't want to miss this," Dad said. "I'll get them."

"Get her a Sugar-Plum Slushy, too!" I called after him as he headed for the food cart. Maybe she'd 6-2-4 all over her dress.

Marianne looked like she wanted to say something, so I stepped away and turned up the volume on my radio. "Santa's Helper to Dreidel, Dreidel, Dreidel, any sign of Frank? Over."

Jane came back. "Avoided capture at Frosty's Freezefall. Still on the loose. Any sign of your dad? Over."

"Present and accounted for."

Jane whooped. "Bring him by the dreidels!"

Hmm. Latkes, Sugar-Plum Slushies, and a spin in a dreidel was exactly what Marianne needed. "Will do."

As I turned my walkie-talkie back to low, Marianne snuck up on me.

"I didn't realize you had planned to spend so much time with your dad tonight. I wouldn't have come along if I'd—"

"It's fine."

"This is a nice park."

I glared at her. She didn't have to be so mean. "It's a landmark. People in town are going to miss it. It's not bright and shiny like a new mall, but it's part of us."

"I see that. A lot of history. Some of these rides are probably antique, like the Carol-sel."

"Yeah, well, out with the old, right?" I snapped.

She started to say something, but Dad came back with latkes and slushies for all of us. I pretended to sip mine. This slushy mix was probably antique, too.

"Want to ride the Ferris wheel?" Dad asked Marianne.

"No, let me show you a better ride. It's perfect with your latkes. The Dreidel, Dreidel, Dreidel is just over here."

I led them up the footbridge that ran to the exits for several of the midway rides, over the shallow edge of Christmas Lake. In the darkness, I hoped they couldn't see how the algae congealed on the surface of it. I hoped they didn't see the way the wooden railing leaned way over where I'd nearly broken it on my first day working here, either. We took the path to the right, to the exit gate of the dreidels.

"Shouldn't we wait in line?" Dad asked. "People might get upset if we cut."

"No, it's fine," I said. "No one would want to slow down the mayor and his girl's special night out."

It was a low blow, but I was suddenly so angry at my father. I'd invited him out here so he'd see how hard I was working and how fun the park was, and he'd invited her along.

Jane stepped over the booth wall. "Hello, Mayor. Thanks for coming."

Her eyes grew round when she saw the slushies in our hands. "Are you sure you want to ride right after—"

"I already told them it was okay to cut the line," I interrupted. "We've got a lot more to see."

Jane loaded them into a dreidel, then let in the rest of the people in line. "Now, explain?"

"I hope she pukes all over him."

"Dude! We're trying to save the park! How is that going to help?"

"He brought her here on a date!" I hissed. "How could he do that?"

"So what? It means he thinks this is a good place for a date—that's great! If they fall in love here, all the better. She's definitely the sappy type, look." Jane nodded at the two of them as they passed.

Marianne was smiling at Dad as he turned the wheel. He laughed like a kid as she squealed.

"See? Maybe they'll keep it open so they can bring their kids here one day," Jane said.

"I'm his kid," I muttered. "Besides, she's all wrong for him."

Jane raised her eyebrows but didn't argue. She looked around at the line waiting for the next turn and pushed the button to bring the ride to a stop. "I'm not letting them stay on any longer. If she pukes, the park is done for."

"Fine." I sighed. Dad hopped out as soon as the dreidels stopped and held his hand out for Marianne.

"At least he's seeing how busy it is," Jane said, like it was a consolation prize. "There are a ton of peop— Oh, crap! FRANK!"

I whipped around.

The goat was on the bridge leading from the Dreidel, Dreidel, Dreidel's exit gate over the lake to Babes in Toyland. He wasn't quietly munching on trash tonight, like that day in the woods, or happily nuzzled in the ball pit. He was raging mad, his head shaking back and forth so fast all I could see was a blur of horns. Several people stood back, watching, their children high in their arms.

Jane and I jumped the booth wall and ran toward him.

"Everyone, get back!" Jane yelled to the people nearest.

I caught sight of Riya on the path on the other side of Frank. She held her arms out, keeping the crowd coming from Babes in Toyland from getting closer to Frank.

I radioed her. "Riya, it's Darby. Jane and I are going to try to herd him toward you."

"Okay, hurry!"

"On my mark," I called to Jane. "One, two—"

But before I could yell three, Dad opened the gate for Marianne, and they stepped onto the bridge. They were so busy laughing and talking, they didn't even notice Frank shaking his mad head.

"Neh-h-h-h-h-h!" The miniature maniac charged at them, his head down, horns out.

Frank butted Dad in the legs, and he fell into Marianne.

She fell against the wobbly wooden rail of the bridge, and it started to give way beneath the force of her fall. For a split second, she clung to Dad, and he clung to the railing, but then the rail broke completely away, and they splashed into Christmas Lake.

Sixteen

JAMARCUS FISHED DAD AND MARIANNE OUT OF the water while Jane and Riya corralled Frank back to the petting zoo. I stood on the bridge and watched Dad help Marianne through the water. He asked her twenty billion times if she was all right, like she'd been tossed into a raging sea instead of waist-high muddy water.

Kyle and Ava pressed everyone on the bridge away from the broken railing, Kyle on the side of the hole in the railing nearest me, Ava on the other.

"You'll have to go around by the North Pole," Kyle told the crowd. "This way is closed until further notice."

I pushed through the crowd being redirected by Kyle, anxious to make sure Dad was all right.

Nick pulled up to me in his red golf cart as I half jogged past the line for the swings. Calvin was riding shotgun.

"Did you find Frank?" Calvin asked.

"It's my dad," I panted. "Frank butted him into the lake."

"That damn goat!" Nick roared. "Hop in and navigate, soldier."

I got in the back seat. There weren't any seatbelts. "Behind the Holly Bally Pit."

Nick zoomed through the crowd. He shouted at people who didn't get out of his way fast enough. "Make way! The enemy has landed!"

A family stared as we passed. Nick shouted, "There will be no civilian casualties! Soldiers, man your posts!"

"Why is your dad here?" Calvin asked as we sped toward Babes in Toyland.

"I, um, invited him," I said.

Calvin frowned at me. "Why?"

"No time for that now," Nick said as we pulled up to the ball pit. "Call the troops. Tell them there's a squadron meeting at twenty-one hundred hours at headquarters."

Dad and Marianne were standing near the ball pit, dripping wet but looking no worse for wear otherwise.

"Dad!" I jumped out of the cart as soon as it slowed, ran over to him, and threw my arms around his neck. "Are you okay?"

"I'm fine, which I keep telling Jamarcus here," he said. "Marianne, you're sure you're okay?" She nodded, but she was hugging herself. Her dress was ruined.

"Bad luck," Nick said as he hobbled toward us. "I'm glad you're all right, Bobby. Ma'am."

"Thank you," Dad said. "Mr. Patterson—"

"Nick."

"Nick," Dad said, and then sighed. "I came out tonight because Darby asked me to take a look around the park. She wanted me to see it for myself before I vote at the zoning meeting."

Nick laughed his Sergeant Santa laugh. "Inevitability at this point. All that's left is the paperwork."

"For now, let's just call it a night," Dad said.

No! This wasn't how tonight was supposed to end. "But—" I sputtered, not sure how to begin to protest.

Nick's lower jaw jutted out, but he offered Dad his hand. "I know when I'm licked. Also know you're doing what's best for the town. Holly Jolly Land will close in September. No hard feelings."

Dad seemed taken aback but shook Nick's hand.

"Still . . . sure would like to reveal the Globe next Monday," Nick said as they shook. "My battalion's been working on it for weeks, wouldn't want to let them down."

"Of course, I've been looking forward to it," Dad said. "We'll do the unveiling on the twelfth as planned. We can talk more after that."

Nick nodded, satisfied.

Dad donned at Marianne. "Why don't I take you home?"

Before she followed Dad, she touched my arm. "We'll figure this out."

I yanked away from her.

When they were out of earshot, Nick sighed and turned to me. "Well, honey, you did your best. Didn't think you'd last a day, let alone half the summer. Guess this means you're discharged. With honor." He turned, supported by his cane, and patted Calvin on the shoulder as he limped off. "Let's go."

Calvin nodded and helped him into the golf cart without a word. He glared at me until I met his eyes, and then he shook his head at me. No one had ever looked at me with so much disappointment.

I stood frozen, not sure who to go after. Calvin, to explain that I had invited Dad so he would want to save the park, not close it; Nick, to apologize for all of it; or Dad, to convince him to change his mind.

Dad. I caught up to him and Marianne as they turned onto Santa Claus Lane.

"You can't close the park!"

"Not now, Darby. It's been a long night."

I took a breath and forced myself to stay calm. "Can't I do anythi—"

"You've done plenty," Dad said wearily. "This isn't the time to have a conversation. In fact, I don't think you need to be involved in this at all anymore. It's courthouse business, not yours."

"What?" I whispered. "But—Dad."

"I've got to get Marianne back to town. I'll see you at home."

As they walked away, Charlie-in-the-Box's closing announcement broke across the sky. It was the glummest I'd ever heard: "The park is now closed. Everybody out."

Nick had told Calvin to call in the troops. Every Misfit at the park showed up at the bunker for the meeting.

Nick explained about the offer he'd received from the investors.

"It's been a hell of a war," Nick said from his office door. "But I've waved the white flag. Time to pack it up and move it out. If the deal goes through, I'll be shutting the gates on Holly Jolly Land for good come fall."

Guess who they blamed? The whispers swept past, along with harsh looks and the occasional outburst of "Way to go." After all, they thought, it was my father and his "girlfriend" who got butted into the lake, and he wouldn't have even been at the park if it weren't for me.

I didn't see Jane in the locker room after the meeting. I hadn't seen her since we'd tried to herd Frank. Needing someone to talk this whole thing out with, I went to the dreidels to find her. She had her back to me, her long hair hanging over the edge of a dreidel. I climbed over the wall and into the ride.

"Where have you been?" I said. "Nick had a meeting and—"

"I heard."

She had her eyes closed, but tears were leaking down her face.

"Are you okay?"

She sniffed and wiped her arm over her eyes. "You never should have come here, you know. You don't belong here. You're not a Misfit. You're just . . . a politician."

"What?"

She opened her eyes and looked at me. "You don't care about Holly Jolly Land. You never wanted to save the park. You wanted to get your way and get that chick out of here."

"That's not true, I tried—"

"Whatever, dude."

"Dude, I know you're upset, but—"

"Dude," she mimicked. *"Dude.* The only reason you say *dude* is because I say it. Like I said, politician. You're who you think you need to be for different people, say what they want to hear, play the part to get what you want from them."

"So you think I'm fake?" I said dully. "Thanks."

"You're not fake, you're just trying so freaking hard to, like, fit the mold of the people around you, you don't get to know them."

"I do not!" I said. "Not all the time. Not with my friends."

"You think we're friends?" She laughed.

I curled into myself. "Yes."

"Really, because friends know each other. What do you know about me, huh? When's my birthday? Or, I don't know, even more basic than that . . . where do I live?"

I glared at her. "I know who you lead around like a hound dog, does that count?"

"What?"

"Charlie is in love with you!" I said. "You have to know that."

She sat back and studied the ends of her hair. "Whatever. He's just messing around."

"No. He's not. Have you seen his shoes?" I asked. "He has pictures of you on them. He's so in love with you, he draws your face on his SHOES."

Jane turned beet red. "That's not me."

I shook my head in disbelief. "The subliminal messages? The way he looks at you like you're another life-form? It's so obvious."

Jane's kaleidoscope eyes went flat and lifeless. "Holly Jolly rule number three: mind your own business."

She climbed out of the dreidel and headed for the exit.

There wasn't an *Andy Griffith* episode for this one. I didn't know how to fix it. There was no Aunt Bea to make me dinner, no Andy to talk to on the porch.

I sat on the bench and cried while I waited for the last trolley to come by.

"Why didn't you tell me?"

I didn't jump this time. Maybe I knew Calvin would show up here to check on me. Or maybe I hoped. The trolley pulled into the lot and bumped over the potholes as it made its way over to us.

"I don't need a ride," I told him without turning around. "And I definitely don't need a lecture, so . . ."

"Someone needs to give you one!" He came around the bench and stood in front of me. The trolley's headlights cast a glow around him but blacked out his face. It was probably for the best; I didn't want to see that disappointed look again.

"I don't need anything from you." I grabbed my bag and jumped up as the trolley hissed to a stop. I didn't need this right now.

"Yeah, right. Always have that wall up, don't you? I don't know why I thought I could get through to you."

I thought about what Jane had said to me tonight. Then I thought about what Calvin had said to me the first night he gave me a ride home.

"I don't know why you thought so, either," I choked out. "I'm the Globe girl, remember? I keep everyone at a distance."

I stepped onto the trolley without looking back. Pauline glanced at me with curious eyes as I took the seat right behind hers, but she didn't ask me any questions. I wouldn't let myself cry until we were out on the dark highway. After a few minutes, she passed back a pack of tissues.

Seventeen

I DIDN'T HEAR FROM JANE.

Or Calvin.

I didn't have a job at Holly Jolly Land anymore, and Dad didn't want me at the courthouse. *I* didn't want to be home.

This was why Misfits needed an island. They didn't belong anywhere else. I was adrift in my own hometown. I wandered around, no destination in mind but too restless not to move. Wasn't there anything I could do?

"Oh, darlin', you've done enough," Mrs. Goodwin said when I went to the bakery to confide in her. She put me to work as I talked, and soon I was elbow deep in flour and butter. She gave me a little ball of lemon crinkle dough to dunk in powdered sugar and place on the massive cookie sheet. "If Nick Patterson wants to sell, he'll sell. And if your father has made up his mind . . ." She frowned and pushed a wisp of hair out of her eyes. "You're sure he's going to back the mall?"

"Definitely."

"Hmm."

I glanced at her as I dunked another cookie ball. " 'Hmm'?"

"Well, I probably shouldn't be telling you this, but the zoning committee had a preliminary meeting with the Whitman Group this morning. They've already changed some of the covenants of their offer. They want us to loosen the zoning restrictions even more than they originally requested so they have, and I quote, 'options for buyout possibilities' in case the mall goes belly-up."

I frowned at the flour-coated counter top. "What does that mean?"

"It means they're strong-arming us."

"And my dad is letting them?"

"I didn't say that. Bobby held his own in there. In fact, he didn't seem too happy about the way those lawyers were trying to change things on the sly."

"What can we do about it?" I asked.

She shrugged. "If all that really happened last night, sounds like there's not much left we *can* do."

I sighed. "You're probably right."

She *tsk*ed. "It's really such a shame. That park has been open nearly forty years. You know, Mr. Goodwin took me there when he was calling on me, back when it wasn't any more than a strip of carnival rides." She smiled down at the dough in her hands. "He used to tip the Ferris wheel operator to stop us at the top."

"Why?"

"Why do you think?" She winked, and I laughed.

I helped her finish the lemon crinkles, and then I headed over to Holiday Beach.

The place was packed with families and middle-school kids. I found a patch of beach under a palm tree, far from the water's edge, and sat down on the hot, white sand. I watched some little kids playing in the water, filling and emptying buckets, squealing with delight. I saw Maya Johnson and some other seniors down at the other end of the beach, but I didn't feel like joining them. I didn't like sitting all alone in the crowd, either; I felt so lonely.

My phone dinged. Jane? Calvin?

Roy.

miss u

He missed me? He *missed* me?

Text bubbles appeared across the bottom of my phone, and then:

r u still waiting 4 me? im waiting 4 you ;)

I wanted to scream. I wanted to cry. I wanted to text him back exactly why I knew he was not waiting for me, how I'd seen him kissing that girl on the Fourth of July on this very beach, and oh, by the way, why had he never at least texted me on the Fourth to say he couldn't meet me after all? I wanted to call him a scum-sucking Scrooge. I wanted to tell him how my heart had broken into shards of glass when I'd seen him with that girl, and how the shards had punctured my lungs when I'd seen them kissing.

But as I stared at my phone, I realized I didn't want to tell him anything at all. I'd spent so much time hoping he'd notice me. Then I'd spent so much time trying to say things I thought he wanted to hear. Then I'd reached out over and over and been left hanging. I didn't want to say anything anymore.

And just like that, Roy Stamos became Christmas past.

I deleted the texts—all of them—and I deleted his contact

information. I went through all my social media and unfriended and unfollowed him. I wasn't angry, I wasn't bitter, I was just . . . done. Done believing in people who didn't believe in me, who didn't know me, not really.

I stood and brushed the sand off my shorts. I didn't want to be here, so I followed the walking trail back to town.

I rounded a curve in the path and saw Marianne sitting on a bench, swiping away tears as they fell down her cheeks.

I faltered, not sure whether to turn and run in the other direction or keep walking, but my moment of indecision cost me. She looked up and saw me dancing on the spot.

"Oh." She smoothed her bob and tucked one side behind her ear, sniffling. "Hi."

Why was she everywhere? Now I couldn't even take a walk without running into her? Oh, no. Was she with my dad?

Maybe the horror of the thought was playing on my face, because she seemed to guess what I was thinking. "Your father's about to meet with Ms. Bradley from the Whitman Group. At the courthouse."

"So why aren't *you* there?" I asked.

She hesitated. "I'm headed that way now. I just . . . needed some air."

"Well, enjoy the meeting," I said. I planned to go right by her. What business of mine was it that she was crying? Besides, I was so mad at her for taking my job and dating my father.

"Was there something you wanted to say?" she asked.

I glared at her. "Everything was fine before you got here. If you hadn't come, none of this would be happening. Nick wouldn't be selling, and—"

"And you'd still be First Daughter and all that. I know." She shook her head at me. "But you still would have broken the Snow Globe. The Whitman Group would still be trying to buy land from the town. The only difference is that you would be working at the courthouse instead of me."

I raised an eyebrow. "Why do you care so much if I work there or not?"

"Because you don't belong there."

"He's my dad!"

"Yes," she said softly. "And he's a great one. But at work, he's the mayor. He shouldn't be asking you to help him run this town. You're just a kid."

"It's none of your business!" I said. "The governor sent you here to help, but you didn't have to kick me out!"

"Your presence didn't look good to the developers. It made your father look weak, and he didn't need to bargain from that position."

"He's not weak."

"No, he's not. He's stronger than he knows." Her eyes went starry, and the sharp edges of her voice went fuzzy like the old soft-screen filter they used to make starlets more attractive to the audience in movies.

"I know you like my dad," I blurted out.

She cleared her throat. "It's complicated. I don't want to be a cliché. I have a career to think of." She pulled at a loose thread on her shirt. "If anyone at the governor's office found out . . . He's eighteen years older than me! There's no future there. And then there's you," she said icily.

I glared at her. "That's not nice."

"Exactly. You've never been nice to me. Why would I get involved with someone whose daughter so openly despised me? You'd be trying to sabotage me at every turn."

"Wait. What?" I said. "You think I'd run *you* off?"

She raised an eyebrow behind her black-framed glasses. "Wouldn't you?"

I didn't answer.

"Well, either way, I'll be gone soon, and you won't have to worry about it," she said. She stood, smoothed her suit pants, and headed down the path. I watched her until she was nearly out of sight and then said, "Marianne?"

"Yes?"

"It's just . . . it's always been me and him."

She gave me a small smile. "And that's the way it will stay. I'll be gone as soon as the deal is done."

There's an episode of *The Andy Griffith Show* where Opie gets jealous of one of Andy's girlfriends. He sabotages their relationship until they break up. The guilt eats away at him, though, and he finally confesses.

This wasn't like that. This was different. I didn't feel guilty because I hadn't done anything wrong. I'd eaten too much cookie dough. That's why my stomach hurt.

The walking trail dumped me out at the roundabout on the other end of Main, and the view stopped me in my tracks.

Downtown really was beautiful. From here, I could see all the way to the courthouse at the other end of the street. The diner had a new green-and-white-striped awning that immediately caught my eye. Mr. Johnson's toy shop had the bubble machine going, and huge bubbles drifted down the street to the kids eating ice cream. They reached up to pop them. Even the boring stuff, like the law firms, looked postcard pretty.

How long would Christmas look like this once the Whitman Group got started? Maybe Dad was ready to sell off pieces of the town. Maybe Nick was ready to wave the white flag. But I couldn't stand by and watch without at least giving Holly Jolly Land the send-off it deserved.

I whipped around. I could just make out the green trolley pulling into the depot.

The Snow Globe set was still a, um, work in progress. From what I could make out, the crew was rebuilding the same scene, but they were having problems.

Jane, Jamarcus, Hailey, Hannah, the midway guys, and Glenda and Riya were grouped around the Holly Jolly Land sign, having a heated conversation. Charlie was standing behind Jane, staring at her hair.

I took a deep breath and went up to them.

"Because it looks like crap on crackers!" Jane was saying.

"It does not!" Glenda cried. "Just because you don't have any taste!"

Charlie-in-the-Box slowly extended his arms between the two camps, though his stance was more peaceful than defensive. "Hey, now, let's all chill."

Jamarcus saw me first. "Darby? What are you doing here?"

"I, um . . ." I avoided looking directly at Jane. "I came to see if I could help."

"No," Hailey said at once. "We told you before, Misfits only."

"I am a Misfit," I said.

Glenda's eye roll gave me strength.

"I am. I may not be a veteran of this thing like you guys. And, okay, yeah, maybe I'm a screwup, and maybe all of this is my fault, but—"

"Maybe?" Riya said. "You mean, definitely."

I nodded. "Fine. It's definitely all my fault. But I have a claim here, too, now."

"Let me guess," Glenda said. "You want to be in the Globe for the unveiling?"

"No!" That was the last thing I wanted. "I just want to be a part of this. For Nick. And for Christmas."

Jamarcus put his arm around my shoulder. "I say yes, if you'll be the tiebreaker between these two. Jane says no glitter this time. Riya says more glitter this time. What do you think? Glitter or no?"

I studied the set for a moment. "Both."

Riya threw her hands into the air. "Helps a lot. Thanks."

"I just mean, can't everyone get a say in this? Maybe . . . I don't know, maybe put a bunch of glitter on the Ferris wheel or something, but not all over the entire thing. The main spotlight for Globe unveilings sits on the roof of the theater. If the Ferris wheel is the tallest set piece, it would really catch that light."

"Yeah," Jamarcus said with a grin. "That'd be cool."

"Look, do what you want," I said when Riya huffed. "I don't know anything about building stuff, but I do know what the town wants to see. I know which past Snow Globes have flopped and why, and I know the ones the town loved. It's about the Globe, but it's also about how we present it. Like my dad always says—"

"Oh, please, tell us!" Glenda sneered. "We're all dying to hear what Daddy says about anything."

I bit my lip. Right, I needed to consider my audience here. "I just meant, we can make it great if we bring the spirit of the park to town."

"How?" Jamarcus asked.

"Holly Jolly Land isn't just about the rides. It's us, the Misfits. The way you guys holler at the crowd," I said to Hailey and the other midway games workers. "Or the music Jane plays at the dreidels. It's Hannah's snowflake dance. Or the way Charlie sets the tone with his announcements."

The tips of Charlie's ears turned pink, but he seemed pleased.

"It's all of you. It's . . . the magic." Some of them seemed convinced, but Jane still hadn't looked at me and Riya was glaring. I gave my final, best shot. "Don't you want to make Nick look good one last time before it's all over?"

"Yah," Charlie said. "Love it, Dar-Dar."

Riya and Glenda shared a look. Riya popped her gum and said, "Fine, I'm in."

Hannah elbowed Hailey lightly in the arm, and she nodded. "Okay, yeah. So how do we do that?"

I smiled. "I have an idea."

Jane kept her distance while I talked, but I could tell she was listening by the way her brow furrowed. Riya and Hailey seemed more and more on board as I spoke. Jamarcus, Steve, and the midway guys slow-clapped me when I finished.

"Let's get on it, then," Steve said.

"Okay, we'll need walkie-talkies," I said.

"I'll go get them," Hailey said.

"I don't know how far the range is—"

"They work for miles. They're military grade," Hailey explained. "I was in the office when Nick ordered more. They cost like a thousand bucks apiece."

I thought of the one I'd used all summer. "But they're sparkly."

"Because we bedazzled them," Glenda said. "Duh."

Jamarcus crossed his eyes at me. "Yeah. Duh."

"Okay, great," I said. "We'll use frequency one."

"Boring," said Charlie. "Make it twelve, for the twelve days of Christmas."

I smiled. "Frequency twelve," I said. "Let's split up. We'll meet back here in an hour with everything we need."

Charlie-in-the-Box floated his hand out to the middle of our circle. "Holly Jolly Old St. Nick on three. One—"

We piled our hands on top of his.

"Two—"

"Holly Jolly!"

Riya and Glenda headed for the hardware store with Jamarcus. The midway guys went to round up supplies from their booths. Hailey went to get walkie-talkies, and Hannah asked Charlie for a ride back to town. Jane, however, hadn't moved. She stood with her arms crossed. When everyone was gone but us, I went over to her.

"Jane, I really want us to be frien—"

"I'm sorry I called you a politician," she interrupted.

"You were right, though. I kind of am." I raised my thumb and closed one eye until I'd blocked out the worst parts of the set. There. We could work with that. "But I really do want to help, not just to get something out of it, but to give something, too."

"The Globe was a good start," she offered.

"Thank you." I cleared my throat. "I'm, um, sorry for what I said about Charlie. I know you care about him."

"It's okay."

"Can I just— Jane, he loves you. Like, chocolate-covered-strawberries loves you. If you love him, too, don't be afraid to try."

"He's my best friend. I can't risk it."

"That's like . . . like a big, shiny present all wrapped up in pretty paper with a big bow!" I cried. "What's inside is way better than what's outside, but you'll ruin the wrapping paper if you open it, so you just look at it."

"Dude. That makes no sense."

"Yes, it does."

"Explain it for the cheap seats, then."

I rolled my eyes. "I'm saying, you need to take Charlie out of the box."

Her lips twisted off to the side. "Valid."

I let it be. We'd just made up, after all. Maybe I'd bring it up again tomorrow.

I checked my phone. No messages.

"Have you talked to him?" she asked.

"Who?"

She raised her eyebrows. "Depends. Who popped into your head first?"

I didn't have to think twice. "No, I haven't heard from him."

"Have you tried to call him or anything?"

"No."

"What about Calvin? Have you heard from him?"

I pushed the palms of my hands into my eyeballs. "I was talking about Calvin."

It was quiet so long I peeped out from under my hands.

She was grinning like a goon. "Dude," she said. "I knew it! It's a love/love thing now, isn't it?"

"No." I sighed. "It's a hate/love thing now."

"So, the roles are reversed," Jane said. "So what? He loved you before. He'll love you again."

"Not this time," I said. "It's over."

"Rule number four: it's not over until the Misfits sing."

It occurred to me she was making these rules up as we went along. But I just sighed and said, "According to Nick and my father, it's over on Monday."

"Yeah, well," she said, "if we can pull this off, at least we'll go out with a bang."

Later that night, as I headed out the main gates, I ran into Nick. "Didn't expect to see you again so soon, honey."

I hugged him, and he froze. After a second, he patted me on the back once and stepped away.

"I ruined everything for you this summer."

"Well, now, that's bull-honky," he said. "You showed up for every shift you were assigned. Never complained. Cleaned up six-two-four better than anyone I've ever had on the M-O-P."

I blushed and stared at my hands. I had calluses so thick I could barely make a fist. My nails were chipped and broken, and I had paint on my arms. But my shoulders had never looked stronger. Or tanner.

"Besides, where else could you have gone this summer if I hadn't given you a job?" he asked. "You got cut loose, a soldier without a company. I was glad to have you join the ranks. Us Misfits stick together."

I blinked up at him. "So, you knew, even then, I was a Misfit? Did I stick out that bad?"

His beard twitched. "What none of you ever figure out is we're all Misfits. Every single person on the planet. But Misfit doesn't mean unfit."

"Thank you, Nick."

" 'S all right." His eyes twinkled. "Tell the truth. Had fun this summer, didn't you?"

A hint of happy fluttered from my stomach and pushed up the corners of my mouth. "Maybe a little."

"Then the park served its purpose. Now it'll serve a different purpose." He snapped a salute. "For standing firm in the line of fire. Your commanding officer thanks you."

I offered him a solemn salute, and whispered, "It was an honor to serve."

A blue truck with a rusted bumper drove up to the curb. My heart hammered against my ribs when I saw Calvin in the driver's seat. He kept his gaze fixed straight ahead, and I could see the twitch of his jaw.

One thing at a time. First, I had to send Holly Jolly Land out in style.

Eighteen

THE CROWD FOR THE SNOW GLOBE UNVEILING, take two, was the biggest turnout we'd ever had. Everyone in town wanted to see if the new scene would be as bad as the last one, and tourists had descended in flocks for the event. The line of people to have their photographs taken inside the Globe ran all the way down Main Street; folks still wanted to get their miniature keepsakes with their miniature selves inside, even if they wouldn't be ready by Christmas Eve this year.

July in Christmas brought sticky, heavy humidity, so there wasn't a breeze blowing down the street tonight. It had been an overcast, soupy day, and the sky threatened rain but wouldn't deliver. The crowd fanned themselves and sucked down lukewarm drinks. The ice-cream parlor brought out their soft-serve cart, and children were placated by the free cones.

I was running late; I'd been busy all day with the Misfits,

finishing the set, and I'd barely had time to run home to shower and change. For whatever reason, Dad wanted me with him on the courthouse steps. He'd texted earlier to tell me to arrive by seven sharp. I wasn't thrilled to spend the evening with him, but I was glad to have an excuse to be near the Globe.

As I pushed through the crowd, I did a final check-in.

"Santa's Helper Darby to Misfits, confirm position, over," I whispered into my walkie-talkie.

"Charlie-in-the-Box, ready," squawked Charlie.

"Jamarcus and Kyle, ready," said Kyle.

"Hailey, ready."

"Hannah and crew, ready."

"This is so lame," Riya said on her call-in.

"Can it, Riya!" Jane shot back over the airways. "Confirm position!"

She sighed into her walkie-talkie. "Riya and Glenda, ready."

"Jane, ready."

"All present and accounted for," I said. "Charlie, you're up first. Over."

"Yah. Over."

I turned the volume all the way down on my walkie-talkie and dropped it in my bulging, oversized bag as I headed for the knot of people on the courthouse steps.

A spotlight danced over the red-velvet curtain, building anticipation of the unveiling. The town council stood at the bottom of the steps. Dad was with them, but he was craning his neck to search the crowd. Nick and Marianne stood off to the side of the podium.

My stomach turned over. I wished Nick didn't have to stand

there smiling for the crowd while his park was snatched away from him. I wished Dad had been more sensitive and offered to let him stay in the audience tonight.

Whatever, I thought. We were about to cheer him up. *It's not over until the Misfits sing.* As the Christmas Community Choir started a medley of carols, I brushed my bangs off my face and joined Dad. He smiled, relieved, when he saw me.

"There you are. I was worried you wouldn't come."

"You asked me to." I couldn't meet his eye. I'd done my best to avoid him since the night at the park, which had been easy since I'd been so busy with the Globe set.

"You look nice," he said.

"Thanks."

I'd found the pale-blue sundress at Walmart out on the highway when I was there buying more supplies for the Snow Globe. I thought back to the beginning of summer, when I'd been shocked to see Dad in a blue tie; it wasn't Christmas. But then I realized, maybe it was more about keeping Christmas than dressing for it. Besides, I wasn't in a festive Christmas mood tonight. I was in a Misfit mood.

I scanned the crowd as the choir finished "O Holy Night." Dr. Hoey and her brood of kids were sitting on the edge of the fountain. Mr. and Mrs. Oates had brought lawn chairs. I saw old Mrs. Lowenstein, sitting on a bench by herself, scowling at the little kids playing on the curb. Harris Bradley and the Whitman Group delegation stood just in front of the raised platform where *The Herald* and the TV news out of Bowling Green had set up their cameras. Harris Bradley and her delegates from the Whitman Group looked city slick and out of place in our little town.

I kept looking, but I didn't see the one person I was searching for.

As the last note rang out from the choir, Dad muttered, "Here goes nothing," and approached the podium. He smiled broadly and said into the mic, "Let's give another big round of applause to the choir for those wonderful carols."

Dad stepped back from the podium and clapped off to the side. The entire town applauded and whistled. I joined in, remembering I was playing First Daughter of Christmas tonight and was supposed to be smiling and happy.

"What a beautiful town we live in," he said, and his voice blasted out of all the speakers hidden in the shrubs on the sidewalk and the big square speakers set up around the edges of the crowd. "To all of you visiting for the first time, welcome to Christmas! I am Mayor Bobby Peacher, and I am honored to introduce this year's Snow Globe. Again."

Dad gave a rueful smile and the crowd laughed.

"For those of you who weren't here for the original unveiling, this year's Globe scene was sponsored by Holly Jolly Land amusement park."

This was it.

Dad was still speaking. "Holly Jolly Land has been an important part of the town of Christmas since—"

His lips were still moving, but all the sound was gone. He kept going, not realizing the mic had gone out.

"Can't hear you!" someone cried from the crowd.

Several others called out, too.

Dad got the message and tapped the mic. He leaned in and tried again.

Dad's eyes met mine for a second, but I just shrugged. I hadn't done it. I was on the courthouse steps with him.

Dad held up both hands and shouted to the crowd, "Folks, just a technical difficult—"

Suddenly a guitar was strumming, sleighbells were ringing, and voices were dinging and donging from the speakers.

Then the familiar croon of Burl Ives filled the air, telling us to have a jolly holiday. He assured us that there was no better time of year.

"Darby!" Dad called hoarsely. "What is going on?"

"We just want to show the town what they're giving up," I said. I looked around him to Nick. "We wanted to say thank you."

Nick grinned as Burl sang that he wasn't sure if there would be snow (my guess was probably not, since sweat beads were running down my back), but encouraging us to gulp down a mug-ful of cheer.

"You couldn't have waited until I was finished speaking?" Dad said. "We have some big news to tell the town about the—"

"I know. But can't it wait until tomorrow? Can't tonight just be about Holly Jolly Land?"

He looked at me, completely exasperated. "Darby—"

The curtains opened wide just as Burl Ives returned to the refrain, and the crowd gasped.

We had worked for three days straight to re-create Holly Jolly Land inside the Globe. At the front, we built the gates, and Glenda had strung twinkle lights to make them glow like the gates at the park. To the right, we'd rebuilt the Ferris wheel—the only part of the original Snow Globe that had survived. Jamarcus had fixed it so it really spun. Riya had glittered every spoke of it so that it sparkled as it turned, catching the light from the main spotlight like I'd predicted. Hannah and Hailey had made a miniature Carol-sel.

We'd used forced perspective to make the tiny roller coaster seem life-sized in the background, twisting through the real shrubs Jane bought. Charlie painted old-timey-looking people on plywood cutouts, to scale this time, and we'd stuck them here and there among the set. At the front, he'd painted Nick and his wife, Lanh, waving at the crowd, just like in the photo in Nick's office. The snow machine blew fluffy white flakes around and around, making it truly magical.

It was perfect.

I actually felt a shiver of happiness as I looked at it and my favorite Christmas carol played on, with Burl reminding us about mistletoe kisses.

The Snowflake dancers twirled around the base of the Globe, throwing glitter into the air. The spotlight caught every tiny glimmer, making us glow.

Charlie had mashed a pop version of the song into the original, full of bass and guitars. As it kicked in, Hailey and the midway workers climbed onto the raised news platform, their arms full of stuffed animals from the Reindeer Games, including the huge abominable snowmen. They tossed them into the crowd as they sang along. Little kids ran toward the platform, hands outstretched.

Jane led some of the freshman Misfits down the street, handing out reindeer antlers and HOLLY. JOLLY. GOLLY! T-shirts from the shop in the park to the people waiting in line. I hurried down the steps to join them, pulling more antlers out of my bag. I handed some to Mr. and Mrs. Oates as I passed their lawn chairs, and I made sure to give some to Dr. Hoey's kids and to Mrs. Lowenstein, who smiled and plopped them on her head.

I danced through the crowd with the other Misfits, handing out antlers and singing. I hoped Nick was impressed with what we'd done. I hoped Dad was, too. Most of all, I hoped the town would remember how amazing we were without help from any developers.

The song screeched to an abrupt stop, and the crowd groaned. They thought it was all part of the Snow Globe unveiling, and they were right. This time, with this Globe, it was all part of it. But it wasn't part of Dad's plan; I knew it was just a matter of time before he stopped us.

He tapped the mic, and a thumping sound rang across the square. "Sorry to interrupt, folks, but I have a very important announcement to make."

I doubted anyone but me could hear the note of frustration in his voice. His eyes locked onto mine for a moment. "I had the honor of visiting Holly Jolly Land last week, and I was amazed at the place."

He was?

"As you can see, the kids who work there take a lot of pride in the park. For some of them, it's as much a part of Christmas as Main Street.

"That is why I cannot in good conscience promote any endeavor that would tear down a piece of our past, our present, or our future. Mr. Patterson," Dad said, turning to look at him as he spoke, "as your mayor, I think it best to advise you not to sell your park to the Whitman Group or any other developer. My hope is that Holly Jolly Land will remain a landmark in our community for decades to come."

I may have squealed. I *may* have. Maybe.

The Misfits in the crowd went wild. My gaze went to Harris Bradley; her mouth hung open, and the delegates around her were in a frenzy, demanding an explanation from her and wondering what was happening.

I probably looked as shocked as they did. When had Dad changed his mind?

"Enjoy the festival!" Dad shouted. The crowd cheered.

Jane threw her arms around me, and we hugged and jumped up and down.

"We did it!" she cried. "We did it! How did we do it?"

"No idea." I laughed. "Come on."

I grabbed her hand and pulled her toward the courthouse steps, where people were descending from all sides: Mr. Jenkins was leading Charlie from the soundboard to the steps. The town council swarmed forward from the left as Harris Bradley and the developers rushed forward from the right. Dad and Marianne were helping Nick down the steps.

I ran forward and hugged Dad. "Thank you! What made you change your mind? The Snow Globe?"

"No, it wasn't the Globe."

"The music?" I asked, surprised.

"It was the other night at the park."

"You're kidding!" I said.

Dad and Marianne shared a smile.

What? Marianne had changed his mind? After all the work we did, it was *her*? I swallowed hard as Dad turned to me.

"Well, I hadn't really made up my mind one way or another," Dad said. "I want what's best for our town, and the Whitman proposal was a good one."

"Then why . . . ?"

"Seeing you out there reminded me that Christmas is—has always been—about the people. Holly Jolly Land is an asset to our community, in so many ways, because it gives so much, to the tourists, sure, but also to the employees and the town. Like you."

"Me?"

"Sure. Look how you've grown this summer."

"Awwww," said Jane and Charlie.

"Da-a-ad," I said, embarrassed, but my heart was full. "You're so cheesy."

He nodded. "I'm also very blessed."

"Thank you," I whispered.

"Don't thank me yet," Dad said. "Mr. Patterson still might sell."

"You're not selling, are you, Nick?" Jane asked.

"Well, sure is a lot of upkeep," Nick said. "Now that I'm doing it on my own."

"You're not doing it on your own," Jane said. "You have us."

"All of us," I added.

"Just a minute!" Harris Bradley snapped. "You don't get a say in any of this! None of you do," she said to Jane and Charlie and me. "You're all just children!"

"Yah, but Christmas is for children, yo," Charlie-in-the-Box said.

We all looked at him.

"What? Santa and . . . you know"—he rocked his arms back and forth—"baby Jesus?"

Harris Bradley peered into his eyes. "Are you on drugs?"

"No way!" Charlie said, clearly offended. "Bad for the spirit. And the sperm."

Mrs. Goodwin turned her laugh into a cough, and she nearly choked. Mr. Grant pounded her back until she held up a hand that she was all right.

"Nick," Harris Bradley said, "you yourself said the place was too much for you. You're getting older, and I know you'd like to retire, wouldn't you, Nick?"

"The name's Mr. Patterson to you," Nick barked. "No deal."

"Is it money?" Harris Bradley demanded of Nick. "Because I'm sure we can renegotiate—"

"It's not the money," Nick said. "Looks like you're surrounded, ma'am. Best to move out before we take prisoners."

"Well. If you change your mind, and I sincerely hope you do, give us a call," Harris Bradley said. She waved her delegates away and stomped off.

Jane whooped and kissed Nick on the cheek. "I knew you wouldn't surrender!"

Nick smiled. "But as I say, it's a lot of work to keep that place running, Misfit army or not."

"Actually," Dad said, glancing at Mr. Gomez, who nodded, "Marianne had an idea on that front. She looked over the town's budget with Mr. Gomez, and we found we have quite the surplus. The town council is proposing investing capital in Holly Jolly Land. With your permission, of course, Nick. We'd like to make it a historic landmark."

Nick tilted his head to the side and considered my father. "I think we can work something out."

Jane whooped again and threw her reindeer antlers into the air.

"We'll need some funds for new midway prizes," Nick told the council. "Seems my platoon has run off with the rations."

Mr. Gomez patted his shoulder. "I'll send a check tomorrow. In fact, why don't we talk about what else you need right away?"

Mr. Grant said, "Diner's open. How about a burger? A *ham*-burger."

Nick nodded. "Charlie, round up the troops and give them the news. I'll be in the war room."

Mrs. Goodwin went with Nick and the men. Charlie bowed and backed away. "No rest for the weary. Later, Jane. Dar-Dar. Dar-Dar's dad. Dar-Dar's dad's girlfriend."

Marianne blushed, but Dad shook his head at Charlie as he loped away. "That kid is . . ."

"That's Charlie," I said.

Dad gazed at Marianne with stars in his eyes.

Marianne pretended not to notice. "I better go. I have to be in Frankfort first thing tomorrow morning."

"Stay," Dad said.

"No, really, I should go, I . . ." She smiled at me. "I'm sorry I kicked you out of the courthouse. I hope your summer wasn't too awful."

"It was the best summer of my life."

She squeezed my arm and stepped away. "Good-bye."

Dad watched her go with puppy-dog eyes.

"Dude," Jane whispered. She nudged me and then moved to the other side of the podium to give us some privacy.

I took a deep breath. If Nick and the town could turn down beaucoups of money, I could make a sacrifice of my own. Right?

"Go," I said.

"What?" Dad said.

"Go. Go get her."

He hesitated. "I don't think she's interested."

"She is," I said. "She told me. But she's afraid of hurting her career by being your girlfriend. And she thinks I'll run her off."

Dad raised an eyebrow. "She's probably right."

I sighed. "No, I won't. As long as you keep the PDAs to a minimum. No one wants to see that. Believe me."

Dad knew a good negotiation when he heard one. He kissed the side of my head to seal the deal. "I can do that. If you're really okay with it."

"I want you to be happy," I said. "If you love her, or if you think you could, then you need to see it through. I'll be fine."

He hugged me tight. "You know, Darby, you're really something."

"Go," I said, pushing him away. "Catch up to her before it's too late."

He grinned, and five years melted off his face. "I love you, Moonpie."

"Love you, Dad."

I watched him until he caught up with her on the square. She turned, and Dad started talking a mile a minute. She shook her head, but he stepped closer. She put her hand on his face. They stared at each other for a really, really long time.

He leaned in.

I had to turn away. I was okay with them dating, but I wasn't okay watching the highlight reel. No one wanted to see their father kissing his girlfriend. Gross.

"IS THIS THING ON?"

I whipped around. Jane was standing at the podium, her hand wrapped around the microphone.

"Are you crazy?" I shrieked.

She ignored me. "CHARLIE? CAN YOU HEAR ME? Yeah, so this is Jane? Charlie, you're my best friend in the whole world." She took a deep breath. "And, you know, I love you."

The crowd "Awwed" as one.

"SHUT UP, LOSERS!" Jane shouted. "This is a private conversation! Gah!" She cleared her throat. "Anyway, Charlie, I know this isn't as subtle as all the messages you've been sending me this summer, but I'm not subtle. I love you, Charles Maurice Gordon. So . . . yeah."

She stepped away from the podium, green faced.

"That was awful," she gasped. "Why would anyone ever do that? What if he didn't even hear it? What if he heard it but he doesn't care? What if—"

The crowd split, and there was Charlie running at a full sprint toward the courthouse. I'd never seen anyone run so fast in my entire life. He dashed up the steps and skidded to a stop right in front of her and said, "I love you, too, Jane."

She smiled.

I knew he'd be here.

I stepped off the trolley into the dark lot. His truck was parked just outside the pool of light from one of the streetlamps.

"You sure you want me to leave you out here?" Pauline asked.

"I'm sure. I have a ride home . . . I think."

"With that boy from the other night?"

I nodded.

"All right then, suit yourself." The doors hissed closed behind me as she called, "Good night."

I waved.

I didn't know how long I would have to wait, but I didn't want to risk going inside to look for him and miss him. So I lowered the rusty tailgate and hopped on. I kicked off my flip-flops since they'd fall off, anyway.

I put in my earbuds and stared up at the sky. There weren't stars out; the gray clouds from earlier had darkened to navy blue. The moon pushed through now and then, a half circle in the sky.

I thought about what Dad had said, that he was blessed. I felt the same way as I smiled back at the moon. When I'd first started working out here, I thought my life was ruined. The summer I had planned was destroyed when Roy and I broke the Snow Globe.

Funny how one disaster had led to another and another, but somehow they'd all led me here. For years, I was the girl in the Globe, the First Daughter who knew everyone in town but didn't really *know* anyone or let people in. I was so glad I'd let Roy into the Snow Globe that night, because of all the people I'd let into my life since: Jane, Charlie, Nick, the midway guys, Hailey, Jamarcus, even Riya.

Calvin.

Someone touched my shoulder.

I jumped off the tailgate, spinning around in midair as I went. My arms windmilled as I tried to keep my balance, but I landed on my flip-flops and slipped.

He reached out to help me gain my footing, but as soon as I was steady he let go. "Oh, holy pineapples, you scared me."

"What are you doing here?" he asked flatly. He had on a green shirt that brought out the gold specks in his eyes, and his braids were loose over his broad shoulders.

"I came to tell you."

"Yeah? What?" he said, but he walked around to the driver's side of his truck and dropped his bag in the cab, not once looking my way. "What?" he said again.

"Nick isn't selling the park to the Whitman Group."

He slammed the door. "Really."

"And the town is going to invest in the park. Nick is staying in business."

His face lit up, but he quickly pulled his smile back into a scowl. "So they did the right thing. Good. They probably want a medal or something."

I rolled my eyes. Why was he so impossible?

"Was that it?"

I wanted to scream. Instead, I said, "Yeah. That's it."

"Great."

I started to stomp away, but I turned back around. "No, you know what? That's not it."

I marched up to him and shoved his shoulder. Not hard, but still, he looked at the place where I'd shoved him, raised his eyebrow, and looked at me.

"You. Are. A. Jerk."

"Yeah, you told me that before. Anything else, or can I go now?"

"You act like I'm the only one who won't let anyone in, but

what about you? You act tough just to keep me at arm's length, too. But I see through you, Calvin Sherman. You're just as tenderhearted as anyone else."

"Tenderhearted," he snorted.

"You are! You're a tenderhearted sucker!" I cried. "Giving out free ice cream to kids when you think no one is watching, carrying your little sister out of the water when she was afraid on the Fourth of July, taking care of Nick the way you do. You're a soft touch, and you just hope no one notices. The only person you're mean to is me! What did I ever do to you?"

He glared at me. "You broke my heart on New Year's Eve."

"I— What?"

"You were on a date with me, and I thought we were finally getting somewhere—and then you go and get all starry-eyed over your *boy* when he kissed you. I don't know why I wasted my time."

"You liked me back then?"

"Yes."

"And you like me now?"

He cut his eyes at me. "I thought so. But I told you, I don't want to go through this again. If you're still hung up on your boy—"

"I'm not hung up on him. I'm done with him."

He stepped closer. "That the truth?"

I swallowed. "Yes."

He tilted his head to the side and considered me. I leaned forward, the turtledoves in my stomach flapping and preening.

"All right."

"All right," I echoed.

Why wasn't he taking me in his arms and kissing me? Had he changed his mind? Was he done with me? I leaned back.

"So?" he said. "You ready to do this or what?"

"Oh. Me? Yes. Wait, what?"

He shook his head, but his mouth was turning up at the corners. "Always so wishy-washy."

I narrowed my eyes at him. "Always so arrogant."

He donned. "That's me. So?"

"So what?"

"Do you like me, too?"

I stepped closer. "You know I hate pizza. You know how to make me laugh when I'm crying. You know when I need a ride home. You know I stamp my foot when I'm frustrated."

"This your way of saying I'm a know-it-all?"

I shook my head. "You know me. So, you already know that, yes, I like you, too."

He smiled.

"So." I wrapped my arms around his neck and pulled him down until our noses touched.

He shook his head slowly. "You want me to kiss you, you got to ask—"

Kissing Calvin Sherman was nothing like waking up on Christmas morning and finding everything you'd asked Santa to bring you under the tree. It wasn't a kiss on the cheek at a party, under a handful of mistletoe. It wasn't a stolen kiss in a Snow Globe, either.

My knees didn't get weak. They got stronger.

Kissing Calvin Sherman was a roller coaster. We bumped noses and banged lips, and his hands got tangled in my hair because we were going so fast, trying everything at once. We were upside down and downside up and spinning around.

When we finally broke apart, he pressed his forehead to mine, and we regained our balance and our breath. He pulled me closer, and then—

"Kiss me again?" he asked.

I may have kissed him again. I *may* have. Maybe.

Definitely.